SWITCHBACK

A PATRICK FLINT NOVEL

PAMELA FAGAN HUTCHINS

SKIPJACK PU

FREE PFH EBOOKS

Before you begin reading, you can snag a free Pamela Fagan Hutchins ebook starter library—including an exclusive *Switchback* epilogue called *Spark*—by joining her mailing list at https://www.subscribepage.com/PFHSuperstars.

CHAPTER ONE: FORWARD

Buffalo, Wyoming
September 18, 1976, 2:00 a.m.

Patrick

If there's one thing he'd learned working the emergency room at the Parkland Memorial Hospital in Dallas as a med student, it's that nothing good happens after midnight. Maybe in the sleepy town of Buffalo, Wyoming, he didn't get the prostitutes with fractured jaws, overdosed teenagers, gangbangers with lead between the eyes, or sex adventurers reluctant to explain the gerbils stuffed in their posteriors, but still, when the phone rang at two in the morning, Patrick knew it would be bad.

He rolled over and jostled his wife, who was unseasonably buried under layers of blankets that he'd kicked off himself in the night. "Susanne, I've gotta go in."

"Be careful." Her mumble was on autopilot—the same words she always said—and he was certain she didn't break out of REM sleep.

"Susanne. *Susanne.*"

"What is it?" She jerked to a sitting position, looking wide-eyed, wild-haired, and suspicious in the meager moonlight streaming in the window. But still so damn beautiful. His heart did a somersault. The same woman he'd been in love with since he was a fifteen-year-old honor student at A&M Consolidated High School in College Station, Texas.

He touched her cheek. "Everything's okay. I have to go in to the hospital. Can you make sure everyone finishes packing in case I'm late getting back?"

She slumped back onto her pillow. "Sure."

"Thanks."

He dressed in the near-dark in the clothes he'd left out the night before—he was the doc on call, after all. Before he left, he pressed his lips to Susanne's temple. A contented "hmm" sound interrupted her soft snores.

Then he walked quickly from the upper-level main living area to the lower level—which was built into the side of a hill, and mostly a basement—and out the front door to his car parked on the circle drive. With no garage, it was the same trek he made year-round.

He moved stealthily, using the Indian fox-walking techniques he'd learned as a child in Boy Scouts: crouch low with the hands on the knees, raise the foot high, set the outside of the foot down, roll to the inside, and put the heel down, toe down, and weight down. Repeat. If someone were to see him, he'd feel silly doing it, but he was alone, and it was good practice for his upcoming hunting trip. He was just passing his daughter Trish's room, and he sure didn't want to wake her. *Lord, save me from moody teenagers.* Perry wasn't as bad at only twelve, but his day would come. It would be bad enough when Patrick rousted his family at the crack of nine to herd them into the truck and up the mountain.

He shut the door of his white Porsche 914 as quietly as he could. Last night he'd parked in preparation for a quiet getaway, facing the car downhill and setting the emergency brake. Now, he released the brake and let the sports car gather speed until he was nearly to the bottom of the driveway. As he made the roller-coaster descent, he cranked the windows down. The only sound was wheels on dirt road. Then he popped the clutch, and the Porsche roared to life.

The drive to the hospital usually only took five minutes, but they were always five minutes of white-knuckled terror. Suicidal deer and low-slung roadsters were a deadly combination, and the deer came out in full force at dusk, terrorizing the roads until nearly dawn. Susanne had chewed him out and good for buying the Porsche. There were only two drivers in their family, she reminded him, and they already had two cars: her bronze station wagon and his old truck. It probably wasn't time yet to tell her he had his eye on a Piper Super Cub airplane now that he had his pilot's license. But he loved the Porsche. And dammit, when a man married at nineteen the only girl he'd ever dated, had a child at twenty, and worked multiple jobs while studying medicine just to keep the wolves at bay, well, that man deserved a Porsche as soon as he could afford it. It wasn't that extravagant—he'd bought the cheapest version they made. But it still said PORSCHE on it like the fancier models, and the black hardtop could be removed to make it a convertible. He'd been proud of his frugality until he'd promptly spent the savings on special-order parts and mechanics who only knew American cars and big trucks. As if it were reading his mind, the engine sputtered when he stopped at a traffic light.

"That's it. This turd is going on the market." He mouthed the words to himself.

Glancing sideways, he saw a bleary-eyed fellow driver staring at him from the next lane over. It was a teenage boy in a truck with the windows up.

"What's the matter, buddy, haven't you ever seen anyone talk to himself before?" He nodded. "At least I always know I'll get an intelligent response."

The light turned green. Patrick gunned the engine. The Porsche roared forward, but the truck shot away ahead of it. The little sports car was more bark than bite. Loud, but with about the same acceleration he'd had in his old VW Bug.

Driving along the quaint Western main street with its dim streetlights, Patrick passed under bunting celebrating the bicentennial—Buffalo had taken the event to heart and had been observing it the entire year—and a few minutes later pulled into a spot reserved for the on-call doc outside the ER. Inside, a fluorescent light buzzed and blinked, giving the austere space a *Twilight Zone* feel.

He hustled up to the X-ray tech, the one whose call had woken him. In most places, a duty nurse would have made the call. Most places didn't have Wes. "What've we got, Wes?"

The tech stood a head taller than Patrick and weighed fifty pounds less. His blue scrubs didn't quite make it to his ankles. "Well, Doc, we've got a possible fractured leg."

Wes said it matter-of-factly, but Patrick caught a twinkle in his eyes. What could possibly be funny about a broken leg at two in the morning? "Where's the patient?"

"Out in the parking lot, of course."

Patrick had been walking toward the interior of the ER, but he stopped and turned to face Wes head-on. "Aren't we going to bring him in?"

"Her. And no, I don't think that would be a good idea."

"What's the problem?"

"No problem."

"What am I missing here?" He didn't usually have to drag answers out of Wes. Maybe the X-ray tech was sleepy. Sluggish. Like Patrick.

"I'm not sure, Doc. Want me to come with you to see her?"

Suddenly Patrick was certain Wes was almost laughing. "Damn right I do."

The two men walked out together and came upon a young man in dusty blue jeans, a threadbare Western shirt, and scuffed boots. He was standing at the edge of the parking lot, and he whipped off his hat when he saw them.

"Thank you so much for coming in." The hand that reached for Patrick's was calloused and rough like sandpaper, its squeeze bone-crushing. "I'm Tater Nelson."

"Doctor Flint. I hear we've got a possible leg fracture."

"Yes, sir."

"What's the patient's name?"

"Mildred."

"Mildred. Okay." He followed Tater into the parking lot, where they stopped at a two-horse trailer. Tater swung the rear door open.

"You've got her in here?"

"I didn't want her to spook in the parking lot and hurt herself worse."

Patrick peered into the trailer. A hoof lashed out, short of him by six inches. He jumped back two feet, taking no chances. "Mildred is a horse." He was going to kill the X-ray tech. Wes should have warned him.

Tater nodded enthusiastically. "Yes. She's a helluva saddle bronc. Can you help her?"

Patrick turned to Wes, who held a hand over his mouth like he was covering bad teeth. But it was a smile he was hiding. "I don't know. Wes, can we help her?"

"I sure hope so, Doc, since you're covering for the vet tonight."

Patrick's eyebrows rose, but his voice was flat.

"Covering for the vet." Joe Crumpton, the vet, hadn't arranged for him to cover.

"Yes, sir. Doctor John always covers for him."

"And vice versa?"

"Now, that wouldn't be right. A vet taking care of people? Folks wouldn't stand for it."

"But it's okay for a doctor to take care of animals."

Both men nod. Patrick wasn't so sure. About the closest he'd come to veterinary medicine was reading *All Creatures Great and Small*.

"Tater, give Wes and me a minute. We'll be back to care for Mildred soon."

"All righty."

When they were out of earshot, Patrick said, "Okay, wiseacre, what do I do with a broken-legged bronc?"

"What'd you do with a broken-legged bronc rider?"

"You mean that kid from Kaycee?"

"That kid from Kaycee—Doc, you're killing me. That *kid* is the champion bareback bronc rider of the world. Chris Ledoux."

"He didn't say anything about that when he came in. Just told me he'd be back the next week for another cast, because he'd be taking off the one I put on him for"—Patrick made air quotes—"*work*."

"That's Chris. But before you put the cast on him, what did you do?"

Patrick looked at him blankly. "Is that a trick question?"

"X-rayed it, Doc. So you're going to x-ray Mildred's leg, of course."

Patrick sighed and rubbed the thinning spot in his hair, which he couldn't help doing no matter how many times Susanne told him to stop. "I thought we'd established that Mildred wasn't coming inside."

"The portable X-ray machine. Of course."

"And if it's broken?"

"We'll cast it." Wes left off the "of course" that time, but Patrick heard it anyway.

"We will, huh?"

"Yes, we will."

"I've never cast a horse's leg before." And he doubted medical malpractice covered it.

"Piece of cake for an old Sawbones like you."

Whenever Wes switched from calling Patrick "Doc" to "Sawbones," it meant he was easing up. He'd given Patrick a six-inch pocketknife for his birthday earlier that summer with SAWBONES etched in the handle, plus a card that instructed him to "throw away that Minnie Mouse starter knife and carry something useful." Now Patrick never went anywhere without it. At night, it went on his bed stand by his wallet and watch. Putting the big knife in his pocket was just part of getting dressed in Wyoming.

Patrick patted his pocket and the knife, then snorted. *Piece of cake. Right.* He was feeling dumber and less capable by the second. He'd never been a horseman until moving to Wyoming two years ago. But he'd learned enough to respect a cornered animal with hard hooves, big teeth, and a strong jaw.

Remembering the kick Mildred had levied at him, Patrick asked, "Do we have a twitch?" He always twitched the muzzle of his horse Reno so he couldn't bite the horseshoer. It worked fairly well.

"Nope." Wes broke into a wide grin. "The trick will be to move fast and stay out of the line of fire."

"Great." But now Patrick smiled, too. Having grown up in Texas, he thought he knew the West, but Wyoming out-Wested Texas and then some. A man had to be able to laugh at himself, or life got pretty unfunny real fast.

"Or some folks lift the opposite foot at the same time. Most horses stay pretty still with two feet off the ground."

"You can have the back end, then. I pick the front."

Wes laughed.

Back in the ER, the two men continued their

good-natured gibes as they gathered supplies and equipment. Then Patrick heard a commotion in the reception area. Loud voices, a clattering, and a sound like flesh hitting flesh.

A woman shouted "Stop" in an agitated voice.

Patrick was out the door of the crowded supply room—knocking only one row of pill bottles off a shelf in the process—one step ahead of Wes, who was dragging a wheeled portable X-ray machine. In reception, they rushed up on a man in a Game and Fish uniform with the short, muscular build of a wrestler. He was holding a woman facedown, one arm behind her, his knee against her back. Her hair covered the side of her face but didn't muffle her voice. The woman was cussing like she meant it, expertly and with great variety. The fluorescent light crackled and blinked, strobing over the grayish-white walls and floors and silver-armed chairs. A thin man in overalls and a round woman in a lavender flowered housedress and slippers huddled in the corner. On the opposite side of the lobby, Kim, the duty nurse, was standing between Patrick and a wiry young guy in hiking boots who was clutching his red, pimply face.

Kim was a solid woman who wore her hair in a no-nonsense gray bun. She had her hands up and was speaking to the hiker in a firm voice. "Come with me, sir. I'll get you set up in an exam room."

He wailed to her. “She hit me. The bitch hit me.”

The Game and Fish warden nodded at Kim. “Can we put her as far away from him as possible?” He shook out his cuffs. Patrick hadn’t met him before, but he knew the previous warden, Gill Hendrickson, and assumed this man was Gill’s replacement. In fact, when Gill’s body was brought into the emergency room earlier in the year—shot on the job and DOA—Patrick had been the doctor on call.

Kim pointed. “I’ll put him in number one. You put her in number four.” Number four was farthest from the waiting room.

Patrick glanced at the cowering older couple. *Good call, Kim.*

The warden said, “Sir, do you want to press charges?”

The man was bouncing back and forth on his feet, shaking his head, hand still to his jaw. “What? No. No. Uh-uh.”

The warden hauled the woman to her feet, not *un*gently. Her face was red where it had pressed against the linoleum, but she looked otherwise uninjured. Her T-shirt was pitted out and damp around the neck. Her respiration was high, but she didn’t appear to be hyperventilating.

Her eyes flitted from person to person, settling

on Patrick in his doctor's jacket. "I think I'm having a heart attack." Her hand went to her chest and shoulder.

Unfortunately, Patrick had seen behavior and symptoms like this before, and often, in Dallas. But only once in Buffalo. She didn't look like she was having a heart attack. He was willing to bet she was high on speed. That they both were, her and the male hiker. The sweating, his hyperactivity, her chest pain—they were often side effects of amphetamine-induced anxiety. But why was Game and Fish here?

"I'm Alan Turner," the warden said to him and Wes, without releasing the woman.

Wes introduced himself.

"I'm Doctor Flint. Nice to meet you. Where are these two from?"

"They were driving erratically up on Red Grade near their campsite. I decided they needed a lift here, for obvious reasons." Game and Fish wardens were full law-enforcement officers, with the authority to enforce all the laws of the state of Wyoming when necessary, although the wildlife management laws were their special responsibility.

Kim walked back in from getting her patient situated.

"Kim, can you take vitals while Wes and I tend to a patient outside?" If Patrick was right that speed was all that was wrong with them, it was nothing a couple of Valium wouldn't fix.

Kim bobbed her head toward the female patient. "Alone?"

"I'll stay with her," Alan said.

Kim nodded. "In that case, no problem."

"Don't leave me, Doctor," the woman said. "I'm dying." She clutched her chest.

"You're in good hands. I'll be back."

Patrick hustled outside with Wes.

"I hate seeing drug cases around here," Patrick said to Wes.

"A lot more of it lately. Had a few last weekend when Doctor John was on call."

The contrast between the quiet night and the waiting room drama was stark, save for the clattering wheels of the portable X-ray machine. Patrick stopped just shy of the parking lot.

"I wonder what's going on? Hopefully it will end with tourist season." But tourist season ended with Labor Day, which had been several weeks before. Patrick's mind returned to the horse. "Did you get a look at Mildred's leg before I got here?"

"I did."

"How bad is it?"

"It's not broken through the skin, but Miss Mildred is hurting and unhappy. Pretty near her pastern joint, but I think it's clear of it. You're lucky,

Doc. The prognosis for horses that break into their joint is bad. A fair number of them die of joint sepsis."

Not a compound fracture, not in the joint. No open wound, so no infection. Those were good things. Patrick didn't want another patient to die of blood poisoning on him, even a horse. Especially not after losing a patient to it for the first time the previous week. Bethany Jones. That had been her name. If her family hadn't waited to bring her to the hospital until she was next to death, Patrick might have had a chance to save her. People in Wyoming were nothing if not self-reliant. A little too self-reliant sometimes.

"Good." Patrick resumed walking toward the trailer.

Wes put a hand on his arm, stopping him again. "One of those Jones boys came by this afternoon wanting a copy of his mother's autopsy report."

"Again, huh?" Patrick hadn't met them, but he kept hearing reports of their visits.

"They've always been pushy."

"Hopefully we'll get the report soon, so they won't have any more reason to show up here. I'm pretty anxious to get my hands on it, myself." It was hard not to feel responsible when someone died on him, whether it made sense to or not.

Wes released Patrick's arm, and the two men

rounded the back of the trailer. Mildred was facing out now, and Tater was whispering in her ear. He nodded when he saw them.

"I'm going to give Mildred a painkiller before I examine her and x-ray her leg," Patrick explained.

He got into the trailer with Tater and Mildred. Mildred immediately pinned her ears and started battering the inside of the trailer with her back hooves.

"Shh, Mildred." Patrick stepped closer to her. "It's okay, girl."

"Maybe we oughta take her out of here, Doctor Flint," Tater said.

"Good idea." Patrick wanted room to run.

Tater pulled at the knot in Mildred's lead rope. "Well, hell. She's gone and snugged it up so we can't never get it untied."

Patrick pulled his Sawbones pocketknife out and held it up. "Yes?"

"Sure. I'll hold her, and you move in there quick and slice it off at the knot. We'll still have enough to work with."

Patrick did, then dropped the knife back into his pocket.

Wes said, "That Minnie Mouse knife wouldnta done that, now would it?"

Patrick grinned.

Tater walked Mildred out of the trailer without

further injury, thanks to the first-rate splint someone had put on her leg. Then he tied her lead to a side slat. Patrick approached her again, aiming to give her a shot in her neck. The horse struck quick as a rattler and sunk her teeth into Patrick's chest.

"Aah," he yelled. His shoulder dipped and his knees bent. "Son of a buzzard bait!"

Tater whacked Mildred on her side, but Mildred held on for two excruciating seconds before releasing Patrick. He backed away quickly. She swished her tail.

Wes crossed his arms. "Son of a what?"

Patrick didn't answer. He rubbed his chest. She hadn't broken the skin. He'd have a good raspberry tomorrow, though.

Tater stroked his mare's nose. "Sorry, Doctor Flint. Mildred's a mite short-tempered."

Something he wished Tater had told him before he got in range of her teeth.

"And here I thought everybody loved you, Doc," Wes said.

Patrick shot Wes a look. To Tater, he said, "You ever given a horse a shot?"

"A time or two."

Patrick handed him the syringe. "Knock yourself out, then."

Wes coughed into his hand, but it sounded a lot

like more laughing.

Pounding feet and a breathless voice startled Patrick. "Doctor Flint. We got a call." It was Kim. Kim never ran.

"What is it?" He backed away from Mildred to keep both himself and Kim out of range.

"A deputy. Attacked by a prisoner. They're transporting him here."

Patrick could move to the ends of the earth and not get away from the worst of what man was capable of. His heart plummeted. He knew the local deputies. One lived next door to him and his family. "Johnson County?"

"Big Horn."

He didn't know any of the Big Horn County deputies. That didn't minimize the tragedy, though. "How far out are they?"

"Forty-five minutes."

"And the patients inside?"

"Their vitals are consistent with amphetamines. No other indicators. And the older couple? She's diabetic and forgot to refill her insulin."

Patrick closed his eyes for a long second. "All right, then. Five milligrams of Valium and observation for our speedy customers. Check the glucose level of our diabetic patient. We'll get Mildred squared away, and then I'll be in to check on everyone and sign prescriptions. We should be done before the ambulance arrives. Thanks, Kim, and let me know if anything changes."

"Got it." She nodded and retreated to the hospital.

A heavyset man appeared in her place with a Great Pyrenees in his arms. The dog's head hung on his shoulder, facing away from Patrick. One paw rested on the man's arms. Patrick did a double take. *Make that one paw caught in a bear trap.*

The man said, "Are you the doc covering for the vet?"

Patrick wanted to deny it, but he said, "I am," and thought, *It's going to be a long, long night.*

CHAPTER TWO: STOP

Buffalo, Wyoming
September 18, 1976, 10:00 a.m.

Susanne

Susanne knew she should feel guilty, but she didn't.

Trish was still sawing logs and Perry had parked himself in front of the TV, where he was watching college football. She glanced at her son. Belly-down on the brown shag carpeting, he wore only his Superman underwear. His chin was in his hands, his knees bent, his feet swinging in the air. *A mini Burt Reynolds on his bearskin rug,* she thought, and giggled. Neither kid was ready to leave. Neither of them had packed. Her either, for that matter.

She sipped from a hot mug of what Patrick called her "coffee-colored water." It was ten o'clock, and she was at the kitchen table in a bright red kaftan housedress she'd made herself. A swap-meet local radio show touted puppies, fencing supplies, and workhorse harnesses. It competed with the TV in the other room and the snores of Ferdinand, their Irish wolfhound foundling who ate them out of house and home and perpetually smelled like he'd rolled in dead prairie dog. Through the picture window across the back of the combined living and dining room, she could see the golden fall leaves on the aspens in the backyard shimmering in the breeze and sun. Despite the urging of the ticking clock, she didn't move. She was missing her mother and sister in a paralyzing way. She'd already used up her monthly long-distance budget talking to them in the first two weeks of September. Letters would have to do, but they only wrote her back one to every three she sent to them. She understood. They had each other and their familiar family, friends, and communities. She was the lonely one.

Why had Patrick had to move them so far away from everyone they cared about? Except for each other, of course. It seemed like he was trying to recapture an element—location—of the dream he'd abandoned in favor of medical school: to be a happily impoverished wildlife biologist or forest ranger. Sure, she'd made a few friends in Buffalo, but it wasn't the same as back home. Well, except for Evangeline Sibley. The rancher's pregnant wife was the next best thing to having her own sister here. Patrick was great friends with Vangie's husband, Henry, too. But truth be told, the rest of the native Wyoming women were just too rugged and outdoorsy for Susanne. Most of them had never met a tube of lipstick or compact of rouge. They hunted and fished with—or without—the men. Susanne was *proud* of being a Southern lady. She didn't want to be like the local women, but she still felt somehow . . . insubstantial . . . around them.

As if to confirm her thoughts, the radio announcer said, "Becky Wills has drawn a moose tag over near Jackson and is looking for someone to keep her boys, aged three, five, and seven, for about ten days while she and her husband are out of town for the hunt."

Only in Wyoming would a woman advertise on the radio to find someone to babysit her kids so she could go hunting. Susanne would have never left her kids with strangers. Not in Texas, anyway. She might be in the same boat if she had to leave town in a hurry for an emergency, but it sure wouldn't be to hunt.

How was she supposed to gel with women like Becky Wills? And they were all like her.

Trish walked into the kitchen, rubbing her eyes. Some of her blonde hair made a fuzzy frame around her face and head, having worked its way loose from two long French braids. "What's for breakfast?"

Ferdinand stood. He stretched his skinny, scraggly, pony body into a downward dog. Then, like a greyhound, he bounced and floated over to Trish. She hugged him around the neck and cooed to him.

"Perry, Ferdie, and I ate two hours ago. There's Life cereal in the pantry."

Trish's eyes narrowed and her nose wrinkled, but she grabbed a bowl and spoon, setting them down a little too hard on the thick slab tabletop. Susanne winced. The table was special to her, along with the matching hutch beside it. Rich, polished walnut, brass fittings, glass doors. The first pieces of new furniture she and Patrick had ever purchased. Luckily, the placemat absorbed the impact of the bowl. Trish went back for the cereal and milk.

"Your dad is at the hospital. He's going to want to leave as soon as he gets back."

"Like, goody for him."

"Trish." The tone of her voice said, *Enough of that*. She sighed. "You're not too old to spank." She wasn't proud of it, but Susanne had broken yardsticks, wooden spoons, hairbrushes, and sticks on her kids' behinds. It hadn't slowed them down much.

"If you can catch me."

Susanne pointed at her daughter's hair. "That's what tails are for."

Trish poured cereal and milk into her bowl. She clanked the spoon against her teeth, then slurped the milk out of a big bite. "What time will he get here?"

"Manners, Trish. I expected him already."

"Thanks for waking me up."

Susanne pretended not to notice the sarcasm. "You're welcome."

The phone rang. Hoping it was her mom or sister, Susanne dove for it. She wasn't as fast as her daughter.

"Flint residence, Trish speaking." The teenager rolled her eyes as she said the greeting her parents required of her. She listened for a moment. "He's not here right now. Let me get my mother." Holding the phone out to Susanne, she said, "They want to leave a message, you know."

"Don't say 'you know.' I don't know unless you tell me." Susanne growled but snatched the phone from her daughter. "This is Susanne Flint."

"Hello, Mrs. Flint. This is Hal Greybull, the county coroner."

"Hello, Mr. Greybull. We met at the pancake breakfast for the fire department, I believe?"

"Indeed we did. I just tried Patrick at the hospital and didn't reach him there. Can you have him call me?"

"Sorry. He must be on his way home. Will he know what this is about?"

"I have some final questions for him before I release the Jones autopsy and report." He recited a phone number.

Susanne knew which case that was. Her husband had been out of sorts ever since he hadn't been able to save the elderly woman's life. Patrick was brilliant, and she knew he'd done his best. Sometimes bad things just happen. No reason why. Humans live, humans die, and doctors aren't God, but too few people understand that. "No problem."

"Thanks."

Susanne placed the phone back in the cradle. Her mind drifted to the night Bethany Jones died. Patrick had cried in Susanne's arms. Her eyes burned. She had gotten so lucky in the husband department in many ways. Maybe Wyoming wouldn't be forever.

Trish's spoon clattered to the table, off the placemat. With her mouth full, she said, "Why is Dad making us go elk hunting with him, anyway?"

Good question. One she ignored from her

daughter. Arguments with teenage girls were to be avoided at all costs. "Get your wet spoon off my table."

Trish did it, slowly.

A thought struck Susanne. She understood why Patrick wanted to go. He loved to hunt. She even got how much he wanted to spend time with the kids and share this activity he loved with them. But why did *she* have to go? She was with the kids all the time. In her mind she ticked off points against hunting. She hated, in no particular order, being cold, sleeping on the hard ground, shooting, horses, and dead things. In a flash, she knew why she hadn't made the kids pack or finished getting her own things ready.

She wasn't going.

"Mom, did you hear me? I asked why Dad is making us go?"

The front door opened and shut. Patrick was home. Ferdinand trotted downstairs to greet him. She heard Patrick say hello, then send the dog outside.

"Ask your father."

Perry was so engrossed with the TV that he didn't hear his father come in. If he had, he would have jumped up and turned off the set. Patrick and Susanne usually limited the kids to *The Undersea World of Jacques Cousteau* or *Mutual of Omaha's*

Wild Kingdom, and one cartoon a week. In her funk, Susanne had let Perry's unauthorized add to the watching schedule slide.

Patrick's light-brown head appeared at the top of the stairs, which opened onto the living room, and Perry. "Who's ready for the hunt?" His handsome face looked drawn and his light blue eyes hollowed, but his voice was cheerful.

"Hey, honey," Susanne said. "Long night?"

Trish went back to her cereal. Every milk slurp and teeth clank raised Susanne's ire. She felt on the brink of an ugly mood swing, so she pasted on a smile.

"Unbelievably hard. I'll tell you all about it on the way into the mountains." Patrick frowned as he approached Susanne. He ducked to avoid a light fixture hanging from the low ceiling. He was only six feet tall, but the fixture was oddly placed. "Why is Perry watching football?"

Hearing his name, Perry finally registered his father's presence and jumped to his feet. He backed to the TV and turned it off.

"I just let him turn it on for a second while he ate." Susanne crossed her fingers in her lap and hoped the kids wouldn't rat her out.

Patrick kissed Susanne's cheek, then put his wallet and keys on the kitchen counter. "Are the bags ready to load in the truck?"

Perry wandered over to the table. He ducked his head. "Not yet."

"I thought you were excited to finally be old enough to hunt, bud?"

"I was. I am. I'll be ready fast. But, Dad, how come I can't play football? I'm old enough for that, too."

"Because I don't want you to have a cracked skull. We've already talked about this. You can play when you're in the eighth grade." He looked away from his son and at Trish and Susanne in turn. "Now, get ready. All of you. Daylight's a-wasting, and we're going hunting." He almost sang his last few words and did a few bad steps of the hustle.

"Do I have to?" Trish asked, her voice wheedling.

The dancing stopped. "I'll pretend you didn't just ask that. Get moving."

The kids filed out, Perry on his tiptoes and excited, Trish with hunched shoulders and a scowl on her face.

"What's with her?" Patrick asked. He poured himself a bowl of cereal and a cup of coffee.

"She's a fifteen-year-old girl. She wants to be with her friends. And I think from the way she's jumping every time the phone rings that there may be a boy in the picture."

"She's too young for boys."

"Same age I was when I started seeing you."

"Exactly my point."

Susanne smiled at him. "Maybe she's like me in more ways than one."

"What do you mean?"

There's no way what she was about to tell him would go well, but she had to get it over with. "I hate hunting."

"You don't hate hunting."

She braced herself. "I do. I don't like guns at all. Or horses. Cindy stumbles all the time. It scares me. And I've decided I'm not going on the trip."

Patrick's bowl crashed to the floor, splattering milk and cereal on the linoleum, the cabinets, and all the way over to the carpet. "You've what?" The eyes he turned on her were stormy.

Yeah, it wasn't going well at all.

CHAPTER THREE: SIDEWIND

Buffalo, Wyoming
September 18, 1976, 11:00 a.m.

Trish

Trish picked up the yellow doughnut phone her parents had given her for her fourteenth birthday. She dialed, messed up, and dialed again. As the line was ringing, she sat in her hanging basket chair and swiveled back and forth, admiring the flare of her bell-bottom jeans. Her mom wouldn't let her wear the platform sandals with them that she craved, but they didn't look bad with her imitation Dingo boots.

She heard raised voices upstairs. Planting her

feet in the carpet, she held her breath so she could hear.

"I said I'm not going." Her mother's voice was firm. She didn't stand up to Trish's father too often, but when she did, she did it in a big way.

"You're going to ruin the trip for everyone?" her dad asked.

A woman's voice in her ear interrupted her eavesdropping. "Hello?"

"May I speak to Brandon, please?" Trish asked, using the polite voice she reserved for grown-ups other than her own parents, and speaking softly so her parents wouldn't hear her. Who was she kidding? Her dad had just yelled something back at her mother. When the two of them got all emotional, they were in a world of their own.

"Who's calling?" The woman sounded skeptical.

"Trish Flint."

"Flint?" Mrs. Lewis made a hard *t* sound at the end of the word. It reminded Trish of when a baby grasshopper had flown into her mouth, and she'd spit it out.

"Yes."

Trish could hear the woman breathing while she considered Trish's request. Mrs. Lewis was a nurse, and Trish had overheard her parents talking about her getting fired last month. Something about stealing stuff, and that her dad had been the one to catch her. Mrs. Lewis probably didn't like Trish's dad too much. Would that mean she wouldn't approve of Trish either? Trish didn't have time to try to win her over. If Mrs. Lewis didn't get Brandon soon, Trish wouldn't have a chance to talk to him before her dad force-marched her out the door for the stupid camping trip.

"Hold, please."

A sharp clank told Trish that Mrs. Lewis had dropped the phone on the counter. *Not nice, lady.* Trish started to count. If she reached one hundred and Mrs. Lewis hadn't brought Brandon to the phone, she'd hang up. Her dad would *not* be happy if he came downstairs and found her on the phone instead of packing.

Trish's mother shouted loud enough for the neighbors to hear, something she would not normally do. "I hate hunting. And guns. And camping. And being told what to do. And you knew all of this before you planned the trip."

Right on, Mom! If she won't go, Dad won't make me! Then she remembered all the church activities going on that weekend. If she stayed here, her mom would make her go. She forced Perry and Trish into every single function their church offered. Sunday school, Vacation Bible School—the only thing she liked about VBS was memorizing verses to win prizes, because she always won—church camp, car washes, bake sales, and now youth group. Brandon's family belonged to the same church, but hardly ever showed up. Which was better—missing church or not having to hunt?

Her dad was getting more and more wound up. "I've been looking forward to this trip. I never get to spend time with the kids."

Nothing sounded scarier than her dad's voice when he was mad. Trish shivered, but Susanne wasn't scared of Patrick.

"I do. I could use a break."

Nice, Mom. Love you, too.

Then she heard Brandon. "Like, hello." His voice was smiling.

Heat rushed into Trish's face. She couldn't believe she'd gotten up the nerve to call him. She'd never called a guy before. She forgot all about her arguing parents. "Like, hi, yourself."

"What's crackin'?"

Around Brandon, Trish felt so square. She loved the way he talked. Like he was from California or something, even though he was born and raised in Buffalo. "My dad is taking us bowhunting. For elk, you know."

"Far out."

Trish considered agreeing with him. Brandon was a serious hunk, and a senior, two years ahead of her in school. All the girls liked him. She was pretty sure he liked her, but he'd only called her a few times, and he hadn't asked her to *go* with him or anything. Her friends agreed that it was important to let guys talk about themselves and act as if you liked the same things they did. But Trish wasn't very good at pretending, even if it might mess things up.

"Not far out. He's making us miss school and everything."

"Miss Perfect Grades might get a B?"

She heard a click on the phone line. "Did someone just pick up?"

"I don't think so," Brandon said. "Hello, hello, is anyone there?"

There was no answer.

Trish rotated her chair toward the window and spoke lower. "My mom doesn't want to go either, but she's letting my dad take me. She's, like, aiding and abetting kidnapping. I should just run away."

"Right on. Don't let the man push you around." Trish heard laughter in his voice.

"Are you trying to fake me out?"

"Yeah, a little. Relax. Hunting is far out. You're lucky."

"Like, if you say so." She felt goofy trying to talk like him, and she wasn't even sure she was doing it right.

"Where's he taking you?"

"I don't know. Somewhere near Hunter Corral is what he told my mom."

"You're packing in?"

"Backpacking?"

"No, on horses, goof."

"Oh. Yeah. On horses. And then we're camping."

"Groovy."

"Maybe you should go instead of me."

"Or I could just drive up there and say hey."

"That would be cool." Heat gushed into her cheeks again.

Her father's voice boomed from the bottom of the stairs. "Trish, why isn't your bag by the door? I need you outside right now."

"I've gotta go, Brandon." She paused, almost holding her breath, hoping he would make things official between them. That would be worth a few extra seconds and her dad's wrath.

All he said was, "Keep on truckin'."

Some of the high she'd felt from talking to him leaked out of her. If she came back to find he was going with Charla Newby, she'd never forgive her dad. Charla. Gag. Long, curly black hair and big, dark eyes. First-place barrel racer at the junior rodeo this year. Charla got everything she wanted, and lately Trish had heard she wanted Brandon. "Uh, yeah. Check ya later."

She hung up and faced the glowering parent who was now in her door. He didn't look so tough with blue flowered wallpaper framing him in her doorway, though.

"Were you on the phone?"

"Sorry. I had to talk to a friend about getting my assignments for me. Since I'm missing class."

"Get. Moving. Now."

She screwed up her courage and blurted, "Dad, if Mom's not going, I'm not either."

"Oh yes you are, young lady."

"But I don't like to hunt."

It was true. She didn't mind shooting targets. Her dad thought shooting was a necessary life skill, and he had taught her to shoot when she was eleven. Perry had been even younger. "Everything starts with safety, and safety starts with knowledge," he'd said. He made her load and operate a rifle, a revolver, and a shotgun, all on her own. Her mom had insisted that if he was going to teach them to shoot, he should teach them to defend themselves in other ways as well. He'd run self-defense like a class, with a mat on the living room floor and his three students, if you counted her mom, facing him. He'd lecture them. "Whatever a bad guy is going to do to you somewhere else is always worse than what he is going to do to you right here. So fight, fight, fight." Then he'd drill them on self-defense moves. Eye stabbing. Head-butts to the nose. Groin kicks.

Honestly, her dad was kind of intense. And super geeky.

In the end, she didn't like fighting. But shooting was fun, and she was good at it. She liked the revolver best. It didn't kick her shoulder. Lately his new compound bow had been her dad's obsession, and she and Perry had been practicing with him.

But then he'd made her go antelope hunting with him last year. She hadn't wanted to shoot it alone, so he'd reached around her and held the rifle with her. He'd even put his finger over hers on the trigger. Their first tandem shot had hit the animal, but probably thanks to her, hadn't killed it. Her dad had quickly taken a solo shot to put it out of its misery. The thought that she'd hurt an animal and that it had suffered, even for a second, because of her? It was horrible. She'd cried and cried. After she calmed down, they'd had to field dress it. Her dad had made her watch the whole thing. Gross. Gross and sad. And it took forever. Then they had to haul it into the truck and home. *Yuck.* And all they ate was antelope for weeks. She liked antelope, but she got really sick of it, and she remembered the awful hunt every single meal.

Her dad was still talking. "You don't have to like to hunt. You're still going."

"I don't want to."

"I didn't ask if you wanted to." His voice changed from dark to light. "But it's going to be fun. You'll see."

She changed her tone from defiant to sad. "My friends are all going to be at a birthday party."

"Too bad they don't have cool dads to take them on elk hunts."

Since sad didn't work, she rolled her eyes. "I'm missing a week of school."

"Not a whole week. I told your mother we'd only stay out four days."

Trish's heart leapt. "Only four days?" She did a fist pump. "Yes."

"Don't act so excited." He turned halfway from the door, looking at her over his shoulder. "I'm going to hook up the trailer. Meet me down at the gate to help me load the horses. And bring your bag and your brother."

She jumped to her feet and stood at attention. "Yes, sir, Sergeant, sir."

"Very funny. And change your clothes into something you can wear in the mountains," he said, and left.

Seconds later, the front door slammed shut behind him.

Grumbling, Trish pulled clothes haphazardly from her drawers and stuffed them in a bag. Then she hopped on one leg and tore off her boots. She tossed her cute outfit onto the almost-Dingos, making a crumpled pile in the middle of the floor. When she was dressed in a T-shirt, jeans, and cowboy boots, she made one last change, removing the black rubber bands from her braids and replacing them with the smiley-face ball fasteners she still loved but couldn't wear in public anymore. Then she hefted her bag over her shoulder. Maybe she wouldn't need all this stuff. But she didn't care. Sometimes it got colder than a deuce in September in the mountains. Being cold sucked.

She hustled out of her room, sighing, and nearly ran into her mother in the hallway. It was dark, since the whole back of the downstairs was underground and didn't have windows, although the front did. It was kind of like a giant dugout, which she only knew because her dad had made her play baseball two summers ago. On the boys' team, because there was no girls' team. It had been mortifying.

Trish expected to see a laundry basket in her mother's arms. The only room on the hallway besides her own was the laundry room, and since her mom claimed to be happier not seeing the mess in Trish's room, she never went in it if she could help it. But she wasn't carrying laundry. In the other direction was the central staircase and beyond it a big open room their parents called the playroom. Trish listened to records in it. Perry did whatever it was Perry did while she was ignoring him. But her mom wasn't heading to the playroom either. She was coming for Trish.

"I didn't hear the phone ring," Susanne said, blocking Trish's path. Her long brown hair was pulled into a low ponytail at the nape of her neck. She was pretty and curvy and vivacious. So much so that half the boys at Trish's school had a crush on her. Trish hoped Brandon didn't. How embarrassing would that be?

"Like, it didn't."

"But I heard you talking to Brandon Lewis."

"Were you on the phone?" Trish's voice rose. She remembered the click.

Susanne didn't answer her question. "Nice girls don't call boys. Especially older boys."

"Maybe, back in the Stone Age, but it's 1976 in Wyoming, and girls can call boys."

"He'll never call you if you do it for him."

Was her mom seriously saying she wasn't a nice girl and that Brandon would never call her? "Thanks for the tip, Mom. I've got to go. Dad is making me help him load. Where's the brat?"

"Don't talk about your brother like that."

Trish stepped around her mom. When she got

to the bottom of the stairs, she hollered, "Perry, we've gotta go. Come on."

Perry appeared, dragging an army-green canvas duffel down one step at a time behind him and carrying his tackle box and fishing pole in the other hand. "I'm coming."

"Like, if you move any slower, I'll be as old as Mom by the time you get here."

Her mother sighed from right behind her. "Trish."

"It's true."

"Listen, tell your dad the coroner wants him to call."

"Why don't you tell him yourself?"

"Ooh, smart mouth, you're going to get it," Perry crowed. He bounced on his toes, and his face was gleeful.

"I'm too mad at your father to speak to him."

Trish tossed the tail of her braid over her shoulder. "You can't be too mad. I didn't hear you break anything."

"I don't break things."

"You did that time you threw a coffee cup at Dad," Perry said.

"And another time when you threw a plate at him," Trish added.

"I have no idea what you're talking about." She sniffed and kissed each of them on the cheek.

Trish and Perry looked at each other with raised eyebrows. Their mom always acted like she couldn't remember whatever she didn't want to talk about.

Her mom climbed the stairs to the landing. "Mind your father. And be careful. I'll see you in four days."

Trish groaned. "If we survive that long."

Perry bunched his fists and twisted them in the corners of his eyes like he was crying. "Wah, Trish has to go hunting. Wah, wah."

She threw open the door, letting in bright fall sunlight. Ferdinand stood just outside, wagging his long, curved tail. "Come on, dork. Let's get this over with."

CHAPTER FOUR: CHARGE

Interstate 90, North of Buffalo, Wyoming
September 18, 1976, Noon

Patrick

At the intersection of Main and Airport Road, Patrick stopped the truck, even though there was no traffic in either direction. The Ford engine was purring like a kitten after its tune-up earlier that week.

He breathed in the air through the open windows. Freedom. Four whole days with his kids, not being on call, with no phones. No kicking horses, drugged-up hikers, snapping dogs, or worst of all, murdered law enforcement officers. Because the deputy that had been rushed into the ER early that morning had been dead. Violently, senselessly dead. People could be so depraved. As a doctor, he hated that sometimes good wasn't enough to best evil. As a parent, he just worried about how to protect his kids from it. This had happened *here.* Not in a big city. Not in a foreign country. But right here in northern Wyoming, too close to his home, and because of his job, he was thrown into the thick of it. He enjoyed practicing medicine, but he wasn't going to miss the hospital while he was gone. He needed a break.

The only thing he'd miss while he was on this trip would be his wife. He felt a pang at the thought, deep in his chest, melancholy mixed with annoyance. Maybe he'd been too hard on Susanne, but he shouldn't have had to be. She should have wanted to be with him. Still, the last thing he wanted was to be harsh with everyone around him, like his own dad had been. He and Susanne had a great relationship, and it shouldn't matter that she didn't like some of the things he did. She was fun and adventurous and his partner. But if he didn't get her out enjoying what made Wyoming wonderful, she'd never fall in love with it. Then it would only be a matter of time before he'd be driving a U-Haul back to Texas.

Trish looked up from her book. He knew she

was reading Judy Blume's *Forever*, again, even though she was hiding the cover. He and Susanne had decided to just let it go, even though the novel dealt with teen sexuality. Every teen tackled these issues. Hell, that's why he and Susanne had married so young—because the teenage sex drive would not be denied. He smiled.

"Like, why are we stopped? And you're talking to yourself. Again."

Patrick hadn't even realized his lips were moving. He gave her his best impression of a cool cat and mimicked her speech pattern. "Like, because I'm deciding which way to go, you know." But suddenly he'd made up his mind. He turned left.

Trish groaned. "You can be such a geek."

But she didn't say "like" or "you know." He'd shut her slang down. Mission accomplished.

She frowned. "Dad, Hunter Corral is to the right."

"I was only taking us there because your mother likes campsites with bathrooms."

"So do I."

"It will be too crowded on the weekend. We're going to Walker Prairie instead." Patrick was excited. There were more elk up there. Fewer people. And new places to explore.

From the back seat, Perry snored. Patrick glanced at his son in the rearview mirror. He was pretty darn cute with his blond crew cut, freckled face, and drool pooling on his chin. Five minutes into the trip, and his boy was sleeping. He smiled. That was par for the course.

Trish slammed her book shut and turned to face him, her voice suddenly loud and shrill. "But you said Hunter Corral."

Perry sat up. "Huh? What?"

Patrick put on his blinker. Left. Toward the northern Bighorns. "What's the big deal?"

Trish re-opened her book, muttering something about him messing up her plans with her friends. He knew from past experience that discretion was the better part of valor and didn't ask her to repeat herself. Instead, he turned on the radio. "Joy to the World" by Three Dog Night was playing. He turned the volume up as loud as it would go without static. Pounding the steering wheel, he sang along. Perry joined in.

"Would you guys stop? Someone could see you," Trish said.

There was nothing and no one but them on Interstate 90, five miles north of Buffalo and thirty miles south of Sheridan. Perry leaned toward her ear and sang louder. She swatted at him, and he ducked. It wasn't long ago that she would have sung along, bouncing in the seat. *Where has my little girl gone, and when did this sulky creature replace her?*

Her attitude took some of the wind out of his sails, but he didn't let her see it. No way was he going to let her ruin this trip for Perry. Or for him.

They passed Lake Desmet. "Look, guys." He pointed to a herd of antelope. Big, because it was rutting season. Fifty or more of them, enjoying the last offerings of the season from some poor farmer's fields. It was an everyday scene this time of year. What he wanted most to see, and hadn't yet, was a herd of bighorn sheep in the wild up in the Bighorns. He'd seen them at Yellowstone, of course. Anyone could see them at Yellowstone. They were practically domesticated there. What he craved to see was the rapidly vanishing creatures wild in their "home" mountains, where they were once so numerous that Indians had named the Bighorn River for them and later Lewis and Clark had adopted the name for the entire mountain range. "That male must be quite a stud to have such a big group of ladies. Did you know that the pronghorns communicate danger to each other by raising their white rump hairs?"

"Really?" Perry said.

"That's kind of gross," Trish said.

"They have exceptionally good vision, and they're—"

"The second-fastest land animal in the world," the kids recited together.

"We know, Dad," Trish said.

Patrick smiled and stared into the herd and beyond. The early fall grassland colors looked monotone to some people, but he saw a whole palette of tans, browns, grays, and blacks. The life cycle of the prairie never ceased to amaze him. As he contemplated nature, the truck wandered to the shoulder.

"Da-a-ad." Trish's voice made the word into three syllables. "Watch where you're going. Like, I don't want to die today."

"Whoops." He corrected course.

"Bad, Bad Leroy Brown" came on. Jim Croce was Patrick's favorite. He and Perry shouted the words over the music. Trish's foot started tapping. By the last chorus, her lips were moving, too.

"Bald eagle," Perry shouted in his ear. His son pointed to a power line.

One of the majestic birds was perched there, head swiveling as it scanned for prey. "Good eyes, kid." He snuck a glance at Trish. "Who wants to stop in Sheridan for McDonald's?" he asked.

Trish knocked her book to the floorboard, with enthusiasm. "Last real food for days—are you kidding me? Fat Freds, yes!"

Patrick steered off the interstate and parked the truck and trailer on a side street, feeling only a little bit like a sellout for buying his kids' affection with fast food. When Trish and Perry were little, he and Susanne couldn't say "french fries" in the car without a riot. They'd started discussing potential McDonald's stops in code, calling french fries "fat Freds." They thought they were clever, but four-year-old Trish had been on to them from the first utterance and ratted them out to her little brother. And french fries became fat Freds henceforth and forevermore in their family lore.

As they parked and got out, a loud crash sounded from the trailer.

Trish said, "There she goes again."

It was Cindy, Susanne's horse. She had a terrible habit of kicking the inside of the trailer. She could do it for hours. The sides of their trailer bore hoof-shaped dents as witness. He hoped she didn't get her little undersized feet stuck in there someday. Although it might cure her of the kicking.

They filed inside the restaurant. His friend Henry Sibley was depositing wrappers from a tray into the trash.

Patrick walked up behind the lanky rancher and clapped him on the shoulder. Dust puffed up from his shirt. "Hey, Sib."

Henry whirled, then grinned. "Doc. Kids. What are you guys up to?"

"Elk hunting," Perry said, his voice excited.

"Oh man, you lucky dogs. I wish I could go hunting this weekend."

"What do you have going on?" Patrick asked.

"Hay delivery."

"Too bad. We'll invite you and Vangie over for elk steak sometime soon, then. I'm using my new compound bow."

"What'd you get?"

"A Darton."

"Nice. Which one?"

"The Trailmaster Forty-five K."

"Let me know how it performs in the field." Henry frowned. "Hey, can I talk to you for a second?"

Patrick pulled a twenty out of his wallet and handed it to Trish. "Get me a Big Mac, small fries, and a Coke."

"Yes, sir." She and Perry raced each other to the line, throwing a few elbows as they jockeyed for position. So much for his daughter worrying about what people would think of their behavior.

As soon as the kids were out of earshot, Patrick said, "What's up?"

"I was just talking to Harry Bethel."

Patrick had to think for a second until he remembered who Bethel was. "He's a Sheridan County deputy, isn't he?"

"Yep. He told me a prisoner killed a deputy and

escaped custody last night during transport from county to state facilities. Billy Kemecke, the one that killed that Gill Hendrickson with Game and Fish."

"Yep. I was on call. They brought the deputy into the ER. A young guy named Robert Hayes. He was gone by the time he arrived. Nothing we could do. Left behind a wife and a baby. Very sad."

"How did Kemecke get him?"

"Strangled him with a wire, then snapped his neck for good measure."

"That's bad. Really bad." Henry wiped his hand down from his forehead to his chin, leaving a weary expression behind. "Did you hear anything else when they brought him in?"

"They said it happened on the west side of the mountains near Ten Sleep when they were driving him down to the state penitentiary. But that's about all I know."

"You don't want to run into Kemecke. Not a nice fella."

Patrick nodded.

"Where were you planning to hunt?"

"Walker Prairie." Patrick hadn't really thought about it, but Walker Prairie was all the way across Cloud Peak Wilderness from Ten Sleep. That was a plus.

Henry said, "Good." Then he gave Patrick directions to his favorite spot to camp, close to what he considered the best hunting areas. He'd grown up hunting the area, so he knew what he was talking about.

Perry trotted up, dangling a paper McDonald's bag and grinning. "Dad, we got your food."

Patrick rubbed the boy's stubbly hair. The kid hadn't had a growth spurt yet. He was pretty much a runt with a high-pitched voice and a soft middle. Had Patrick been like that as a kid? He seemed to recall growing late. He'd turned out normal-sized, and Perry would, too, he hoped. But damn if the boy wasn't all heart. His smile washed away a little of his lingering disquiet from the hard night before and from his row with Susanne.

He couldn't help smiling back at him. "On my way, son." Then he noticed Trish wasn't with him. "Where's your sister?"

"Pay phone." Perry gave him a conspiratorial eye-roll and sigh.

"Huh." Who in the world did she already have to talk to? She'd only hung up from her last phone call an hour before. Oh well. He'd just have to accept that when it came to teenage girls, he might never completely understand.

Henry nodded at him. "Watch your six."

Patrick saluted with two fingers to his forehead. "Always."

CHAPTER FIVE: PAUSE

Buffalo, Wyoming
September 18, 1976, 12:30 p.m.

Susanne

Through the storefront windows, Susanne could see locals and a few late-season tourists crowding the Busy Bee Café. The place was a local institution. Sandwiched between Clear Creek and the Occidental Hotel, it shared some of the latter's Old West charm. Wooden siding. An old wood-burning stove in the dining area. An ornate countertop and bar back. The tourists were easily identifiable by their bulky cameras and relaxed demeanors. Labor Day was the end of the summer season, but the area did get some early autumn visitors to admire the fall leaves and enjoy the crisp weather in relative solitude. Hunters, too, were starting to show up—in too-much camo and in need of a bathtub—but she didn't see any in the restaurant.

As she reached for the door, Susanne heard her name called from behind her. She turned to see Hal Greybull, the county coroner. He was crossing the street and waving, his figure a cutout against the red brick facades of the downtown buildings. *Darn.* She hadn't told Patrick that the coroner had called. Leaving it to Trish had been petulant of her, and she regretted it. This was Patrick's job, their livelihood. She pasted on a smile and waved back.

"Mrs. Flint. Nice to see you so soon after speaking to you." Greybull's ruddy cheeks and white beard reminded her of Santa Claus, but one in need of a few good meals. His belt was fighting a losing battle against gravity with no hips or butt to hold his pants up.

After they shook, she shielded her eyes from the midday sun with one hand. "You, too."

"Were you able to get my message to Doctor Flint? We're under a fair bit of pressure from the family to close out the Jones case."

"Did he not call you?" It wasn't a lie, but still she almost touched her nose to see if it was growing.

"I'm so sorry. It was a hectic morning. He left to go elk hunting with the kids for a few days, but he'll be back Wednesday."

Hal tugged at his beard, his face somber, but then he smiled. "'Tis the season."

"Yes, it is. They're camping at Hunter Corral, if it's an emergency."

"I'll just take my phone off the hook, and then it won't be."

She laughed. "Is everything okay on the case?"

"I'm not at liberty to say much, other than Doctor Flint did all he could. I wouldn't be surprised if the family files suit anyway." He lowered his voice and looked over both shoulders before stepping closer to her. "You didn't hear this from me, but it wouldn't be the first time they've sued someone when things didn't go their way."

"Oh no."

"So we're needing to make sure we dot all the i's and cross all the t's. But again, don't worry. Your husband wasn't at fault."

"I'll be sure he calls you first thing when he gets in."

"Hopefully they'll have caught that fugitive long before then."

"What fugitive?"

"You haven't heard? It's all over the radio. A prisoner killed a Big Horn deputy and escaped in his vehicle over near Ten Sleep. The same guy that murdered the game warden."

"Oh my goodness!" Ten Sleep was on the other side of the mountains, but she was spending the night alone, and she lived in the country. She'd have to keep Patrick's shotgun by the bed.

"They've got every state, federal, and local law enforcement officer in the northern half of the state looking for him. He's a local guy, too—grew up in Buffalo. The radio promised updates on the hour."

"I'll be sure to tune in."

"Take care, Mrs. Flint."

"You, too, Mr. Greybull."

He tipped an imaginary hat to her, then walked back across the street, pants sagging dangerously, whistling "Blueberry Hill."

Susanne hustled into the restaurant and stood at the door looking for Vangie. A group seated under the huge bison head looked familiar, but she couldn't remember their names. She kept scanning. In addition to the packed tables, every round-seated stool at the bar was full. Some of the waitstaff were clustered near the coffee station, staying out of the way as patrons stood in line for the sole bathroom. Cutlery clanked pottery, cutting through the din of conversations. The place was a zoo.

Susanne heard "Over here." Vangie waved from a table overlooking Clear Creek. Her friend was dressed in jeans and a yellow T-shirt, her black hair in a no-nonsense bob, like the native Wyomingites, but her thick Tennessee accent gave away her Southern roots.

Susanne knew her own Texas accent betrayed her as well. Maybe that's why she'd been so drawn to Vangie in the first place. Two fish out of their native waters. But Vangie was swimming, whereas Susanne felt like she was sinking. Vangie sat with her back to the creek, which Susanne still pronounced with a long *e* sound instead of as "crick" like the locals. Another way in which she didn't blend. She smoothed the neckline bow of her polka-dotted blouse. And another.

"I ordered you a sweet tea." Vangie had set the glass on Susanne's placemat, a laminated menu. "I do that just to mess with them. It always comes out unsweet with sugar packets and a spoon."

Susanne shuddered. "Not the same thing." Actually, she drank her tea unsweet, so she was glad for it, but she understood Vangie's point.

"I mean, I boil my hummingbird feed, for heaven's sake. Sugar doesn't dissolve in cold water. Any real cook knows that." Vangie arched a brow toward the kitchen, as if to suggest that possibly there was no real cook back there.

The two women ordered chef salads and caught up on each other's lives.

"How's the baby?" Susanne asked. Vangie's pregnancy was a secret except to close friends. She'd had several miscarriages, and she wasn't yet through her first trimester with this baby.

Vangie looked out at the creek. It was low. Mostly rock instead of water. "I'm spottin'."

"Oh no. But maybe it's nothing. What does your doctor say?"

Vangie had started seeing an obstetrician in Billings, Montana. "I haven't told him yet. I'm afraid to talk to him."

"You've got to call."

"I know. I will if it gets worse."

Susanne reached for Vangie's hand and squeezed it. "Can I do anything?"

"Your prayers and friendship are all I need." She wiped a tear, then her face changed. She smiled, which accentuated her high, round cheekbones. "I was surprised when you asked me to lunch. I thought you were going elk huntin'."

"I was."

"And?"

Vangie may be her closest Wyoming friend, but Susanne doesn't talk out of school about Patrick. Not to anyone. "Patrick needed some bonding time with the kids."

"What a good dad."

The waitress placed their salads in front of

them. "Anything else?" Her mouth had the dry, wrinkled appearance of a lifelong smoker.

Vangie winked at Susanne. "More sweet tea, please."

The waitress sighed and headed back to the kitchen.

Susanne dug into her salad. Forget sweet tea. What she missed was good ranch dressing. Homemade with real buttermilk. All she could find in town was the kind made from regular milk and one of those new seasoning packets with fake buttermilk flavor in it.

"How are the kids?" Vangie asked.

"Perry is great. Boys are so sweet."

Vangie smiled. "And that means Trish is . . ."

"Less likeable all the time. Am I a bad mother for saying that?"

"You're a great mother. And it's a stage. She'll grow out of it. Besides, I saw her in town last week and she was nice to me. It's probably just a girls-and-mothers thing."

In town. Susanne wondered how she got there. Trish rode the bus to school. "Who was she with?"

"A group of kids."

"Walking?"

"They were getting out of an old truck."

"One of them wasn't Brandon Lewis, was it?"

Vangie nodded. She taught at Buffalo Elementary and thus knew all the kids in town. "I believe he may have been the one driving. Why?"

"I overheard her calling him today. He's too old for her."

"Ooh. Yes. He's a very mature boy. Quite the Casanova with the teen set, if the rumors are true."

Great. Just what I wanted to hear.

A woman's voice interrupted their conversation. "Ladies. How are you?"

Susanne looked up. The newcomer with the coronet of blonde braids and light blue eyes smiled down at them from her considerable height. Ronnie Harcourt. If Susanne had to identify a woman who embodied every trait that made Wyoming women so different from her, Ronnie would be the one. And she just happened to live on the neighboring property to the Flints. *S-h-i-t,* Susanne spelled in her head. Ronnie was a deputy in training for the Johnson County sheriff's office. She roped and branded and yes, hunted. She also had a habit of showing up every time Susanne revealed herself as a hopeless flatlander greenhorn. Like putting the wrong foot in the stirrup to mount a horse. Getting the truck stuck in a snowdrift. Or accidentally pointing a loaded gun in the wrong direction, sending everyone around her to their bellies.

"Hi, Ronnie. Care to join us?" Vangie asked.

Susanne groaned on the inside. She would be

nice, sociable, even, because that was how she was raised. But it didn't mean she'd like it.

Ronnie declined. "I'm picking up a to-go order and heading back to work. But I'm hiking up at Circle Park this afternoon when I get off shift. Anyone care to join me? The leaves should be fantastic."

Vangie looked legitimately disappointed. "I wish I could."

Circle Park—that was near Hunter Corral, where Susanne's hunters would be. Out of nowhere, anxiety rolled through her. The faces of her family clicked one by one like 35mm slides in the carousel projector of her mind. It felt like a premonition, but vague and unspecific. She didn't believe in premonitions. Patrick did. He encouraged her to listen to her gut, waxing rhapsodically on its connection to the mind and all it could tell her. About the only message she got from hers was when it was time to eat. It was surprising that someone so scientific and rational harbored this mysticism. Maybe it was related to his obsession with what he deemed the supernatural connection of Indians to nature.

Susanne shook her head. "I can't, but thanks so much for the invite."

The look in Ronnie's eyes said she wasn't fooled. "Next time, then. See you later."

Susanne said, "Have a nice day."

"Bye, now," Vangie called after her. Then she leaned over to Susanne. "She's not that bad, you know."

"I'm sure."

"Do you really have plans? Because if you don't, you can come with me to Billings to shop." Vangie made frequent trips to Montana to buy things for the Sibleys' ranch, Piney Bottoms. Montana didn't charge sales tax, so it saved a little money to shop there if you were buying big-ticket items or in bulk.

"My plan is to get in a bathtub with that new book everyone's talking about—*Where Are The Children?*—a bottle of white zinfandel, and candles. The house is quiet, and it's all mine." Notwithstanding her weird sense of unease, she felt a little guilty for how excited she was to have a few days to herself. And for admitting it to Vangie, who was having so much trouble starting a family of her own. But it was a luxury, and a rare one. "Rain check?"

"Rain check. For sure."

"But be careful. I'm worried about you." About the baby, of course, but she also worried about Vangie driving alone on the interstate. "Don't stop for hitchhikers. There's a murderer loose. He killed a Big Horn deputy."

Vangie's rosebud mouth flew open. "Really?"

"That's what the coroner told me just before lunch."

Vangie speared at her salad and waved a bite on the tines of her fork. "Best for me to be out doing something, so I don't curl up in the fetal position worrying about this baby. Don't worry. I'm armed and dangerous, and I won't stop for anything."

CHAPTER SIX: EVADE

BIG HORN, WYOMING
SEPTEMBER 18, 1976, 1:00 P.M.

Trish

Trish walked from McDonald's to the horse trailer. Cindy was kicking rhythmically. The horse had a future as a drummer, even though her dad liked to say she was destined for the glue factory if she didn't stop beating up their trailer. Trish petted Goldie's muzzle through an open window in the side of the trailer. The palomino horse had a nose like the Velveteen Rabbit. Trish had wanted a Black Beauty, but she'd fallen in love with her blonde partner. And she liked that their hair matched.

Her horse nickered and nudged her, looking for a cookie. Trish didn't have one.

"Sorry, girl."

Trish got back in the dented white truck. Her dad already had it started and in gear. She was still a little flustered by the call she'd made from the pay phone. She'd had Mrs. Lewis take a message about the change of plans from Hunter Corral to Walker Prairie, after the grumpy woman had told her Brandon wasn't there and started to hang up. Trish hoped he wasn't already on his way to Hunter Corral to see her. And that Mrs. Lewis delivered her message.

Perry and her dad were talking about the Dallas Cowboys' chances for the Super Bowl that season. They loved the Cowboys. It was like if you grew up in Texas, you had to root for them, unless maybe you were an Oilers fan in Houston. Here, people cheered for the Denver Broncos. Trish had decided that since she was a Wyoming girl now, they were her team.

Her dad turned out of the parking lot toward the mountains. Away from the interstate. Again, he was going the opposite direction from what she expected.

"Dad, what are you doing?"

Perry was still droning on. "Roger Staubach is a shoo-in for the Hall of Fame."

Her dad smiled at her. "We're taking a shortcut." He pointed. "See that dirt road up the face of the mountain?"

She squinted. She saw one. Barely. "Yeah."

"That will shave an hour off our drive."

She remembered a heaping handful of times her dad's shortcuts had ended badly. Getting stuck. Dead ends. Broken-down vehicles. Getting lost. "Great."

Patrick went back to the football conversation with Perry. A stodgy voice replaced the music on the radio station with an update on a search for some fugitive. Trish rotated the tuning dial, scrolling through the few stations—all staticky—available in northern Wyoming.

They passed a city limit sign for the town of Big Horn. Trish had never heard of it. Since they were through it in less than a minute, she understood why. It was even smaller than Buffalo. She was convinced there were fewer people in the whole state of Wyoming than in Irving, the town in the Dallas-Fort Worth metroplex where they'd lived before moving to the real Cowboy State.

Slowly the scenery drew Trish in, and she left the radio on a gospel station without realizing it. Deer, antelope, and turkeys roamed everywhere.

The road took them next to a meandering creek, its banks thick with aspens and cottonwoods. She rolled the windows down. A hint of the sweet scent of Russian olive trees still lingered in the air, when she sniffed hard. The last trace of summer. In the distance, the mountains rose steeply, their sides crowded with tall pine trees, save for the enormous rock formations in a variety of hues. Pink, red, black, white, gray. The warm wind whipped through her hair, but she felt a crispness running through it that announced autumn. Snow would be coming soon. Her mom always said Trish was just like her dad. Trish didn't see it. Her dad was a hard-ass and wanted everything his way. But she did love the mountains like he did, so there was that. And horses. She really, really loved horses.

"Beautiful, isn't it?" her dad said.

She kept her gaze out the window. "Uh-huh."

A memory surfaced. Her mom had asked Trish to pass along a message for her dad to call the coroner. She'd tell him about it later. She wasn't through punishing him for bringing her on this dumb hunting trip. He needed to believe in her misery. But she didn't stop admiring the scenery, and when she glanced at her dad, she saw that he was smiling at her, not fooled at all.

The tires bounced from pavement to a dirt road.

The incline pitched upward. The frame vibrated, the engine whined, and the cab noise grew louder.

"Have you ever been on this road?" Trish asked. "Is it even safe?"

Her dad's lips started moving with no sound coming out. That gave her the answer. No.

The truck crested a hill, then a tire hit a rock. There was a pop, then the entire truck lurched to the right, which was the uphill side, luckily. A *buh-bud-uh buh-bud-uh buh-bud-uh* noise started.

Patrick's eyes cut to his side-view mirror, and he pulled over on a flattish section. "Shit." Then, "Don't tell your mom I said that."

"What is it?" Trish asked.

"Flat tire on the trailer. I think the horses may be kind of heavy for this rough road." He put the truck in park and turned off the engine. "Okay, kids. This is where things get exciting."

Perry leaned over the back seat eagerly. "What is it?"

Trish crossed her arms.

"I've heard this road gets pretty steep, and it's not going to get any smoother. I want you guys to saddle up your horses and ride to the top, ponying the other two. That'll take the weight off the truck and the tires. I don't have another spare."

"So it's *not* safe. Are you serious?" Trish asked.

Her mom would not be happy when she heard about this.

"As a heart attack."

"Cool," Perry said. He was already clambering out the door.

Trish followed him, shaking her head. Another story to add to her dad's shortcuts legend. When they had the horses out of the trailer, she said, "How far is it to the top?"

"Not far. A few miles."

That wasn't *too* bad.

She saddled Goldie. Patrick helped Perry with Duke, his paint horse. Duke was tall and a notorious belly-bloater. He sucked in gut-enlarging gulps of air every time someone came at him with a stomach cinch, which made it hard to get the strap tight enough. Trish was mounted and had Reno, her dad's giant black Percheron cross, and Cindy, a short, stocky sorrel, ready before Perry was in the saddle. In addition to being short, he bounced from one task to another like a rubber ball, so it took him forever to do anything. Finally, he was on board.

Patrick said, "I'll just change the tire. You guys go ahead."

"Okay," Trish responded.

Perry took Cindy's lead from her and clucked to Duke. Trish patted Goldie's neck, then shifted forward, tightening her legs slightly around her horse. The six of them—Trish, Perry, and the four horses—ambled off. Not twenty minutes later, their father waved as he pulled the truck and trailer around them and started creeping up the mountain, faster than the horses, but still quite slow. He disappeared through an S curve, and then she and Perry were alone.

Trish drank in the view. Every time there was a break in the trees on their downhill side, she could see across the foothills and deep into the buttes, the color of red bricks. For a few minutes, Perry didn't say a word. Birdsong and the screams of eagles were the only sounds besides the clatter of hooves on the roadbed. But it didn't last.

Perry trotted Duke and Cindy to pull even with her. "Who did you call at McDonald's?"

"Zip it."

"Was it a boy?"

Trish didn't answer.

"Was it Brandon Lewis?"

"What?" Trish whirled on him. "None of your beeswax."

"You like him."

"You're a brat." She increased her leg pressure on Goldie. The horse responded with a slow trot. Reno resisted. The line grew taut. Trish shook her head. Reno was a stubborn beast. Goldie leaned into it, and Reno gave up, although the line never went slack.

Perry shouted, "Wait."

Behind them, a roar of engines approached. Trish moved her horses all the way to the right side of the road, against the mountain face. She didn't look behind her, knowing that would create a chain reaction with Goldie and Reno, and that they'd veer back into the road.

"Scoot over, Perry."

If he answered, she couldn't hear him. A minute or so later, two motorcycles pulled up beside her. The bikes were big and black with silver chrome. They had banana-shaped seats that made the riders lean back. The men wore jeans with leather chaps, leather vests, and bandannas around their foreheads. Both of them had long, wispy beards and mustaches. One had a ponytail. The other had a weird flattop like Perry's. The ponytailed guy, who was shirtless under his vest, whooped when he saw her. Trish tried to unsee his armpit hair. *Gross.* He braked in front of her and turned his motorcycle crossways across the road. The other man did the same.

The horses stopped short.

"Yo, pretty little thing. Who's this ya got with ya?" The ponytailed man thumbed toward Perry.

Shocked, Trish stared straight ahead and guided

Goldie around the bikes. His accent wasn't local. Which made sense, because no one from Wyoming would act that way. But she couldn't place it. Not Texan. Northern. Southern. Or East Coast, like Boston or New York.

"Don't be stuck-up just because you're good-looking."

Perry's voice, when he spoke, was so high-pitched he sounded like one of the Chipmunks. "Leave my sister alone."

The men looked at each other and busted out laughing.

The man with the flattop said, "Her hero. That's a good one."

"What are ya going to do if we don't, runt?" The ponytailer slitted his eyes at Perry.

"Come on, Perry," Trish said. "Ignore them."

"Where ya headed, sugar? Maybe we'll see ya later."

Again, she didn't answer them. Perry was having trouble getting Duke past the motorcycles.

"Smack him on the butt. He needs to know you're the boss," she told her brother.

Perry did as she suggested, and Duke snorted and trotted forward with Cindy, past Trish, Goldie, and Reno.

"I like her attitude," the flattopped man said.

The men started their engines, revving them as

they pulled around Trish, Perry, and the horses, but not stopping. The muffler backfired on one of the bikes. Duke shied hard to the left. Perry grabbed his saddle horn. Some people were naturals with horses. He wasn't. His body lurched and tilted, but he hung on. Goldie tossed her head, snorting.

The motorcycles disappeared into the distance.

Trish heaved a sigh of relief.

CHAPTER SEVEN: CHURN

Bighorn National Forest, Wyoming
September 18, 1976, 2:00 p.m.

Perry

Riding up the steep road, with a major drop-off to his left and a nearly straight-up hill to his right, Perry's heartbeat wouldn't slow down. He wasn't usually scared of heights, but he felt like a giant magnet was pulling him toward the edge. Duke and Cindy weren't making it any easier. He couldn't get them to stay away from it. Duke had nearly jumped over the side when the men on the motorcycles drove off revving their engines and one backfiring.

Those men had looked at his sister in a bad way. He was so mad. Mad like he'd been the time Judd, a bully at his school, had called him a weaselly little girl. Perry had windmilled his fists at him, and Judd had laughed in his face, catching Perry's wrists and not even bothering to punch him. Judd's face was replaced now by the tobacco-stained teeth of Ponytail and the beady eyes of Flattop, his laugh by their voices. They hadn't taken him seriously, either. There had been nothing Perry could do to protect Trish. He couldn't even get his dumb horse to make a getaway without her help.

Why does everyone treat me like a baby?

Tears burned his eyes, and he was glad he was behind his sister. He didn't wipe them away, just let them dry in the Wyoming wind. He wanted to be bigger and stronger—*yesterday*.

The quiet was heavy, broken only by the hoof clomping, heavy breathing, and occasional lip-sputtering sighs of the horses. His mouth felt like it was stuffed with marshmallows. He couldn't even say to Trish what he wanted to. That he was sorry he had been no help. Sorry and scared. Did she feel the same way? Was that why she wasn't saying anything to him either?

He just hoped the two men wouldn't come back.

A top-heavy truck wobbled its way down the

road toward them. Duke's ears pricked forward and his head went up. As it drew closer, Perry could see that it had a wooden deck on top of the cab with a vertical rail fence around it. The tiny paws, pointed nose, and gently flopping ears of a wiener dog peeked over the front of the deck fence, beside a Saint Bernard so enormous it seemed impossible he wouldn't capsize the truck.

A driver with bushy black facial hair lifted two fingers in greeting as he passed. Perry gaped at the vehicle. The top deck matched a larger deck on the truck's flatbed, although the fence around it was a more traditional split rail. Behind the truck was an ancient horse trailer with no roof. A horse spotted like a Dalmatian whinnied at Duke.

Duke snorted.

Trish put a hand on the back of her saddle and turned all the way around to watch the truck. "Only in Wyoming."

Perry nodded. The funny truck made him feel a little better. People in Wyoming were definitely different than back in Texas. Finally he saw his dad's truck and trailer up ahead. When he and Trish reached it, they found their dad reading maps spread out across the hood.

"Took you long enough." Patrick smiled and started folding the maps. "Ready to load up?"

Trish said, "Did you see the motorcycles?"

"I did. Harleys. You don't see many of those up in the mountains."

Perry squeaked, "Those guys were assholes. They were bothering Trish."

Patrick froze as he was stuffing the maps into his waistband. "What?"

"They were all talk." Trish dismounted.

Patrick took Duke's reins.

Perry hopped to the ground. "They scared Duke." He didn't mention how much they'd scared him.

"Did you talk to them?" Patrick's eyes bored into Perry's, knowing well which of his kids was more likely to cough up information.

"No. But they wanted to know where we were going."

"Did you tell them?"

"No."

"Okay."

They walked to the back of the trailer. The three of them were silent as they put up the tack and saddles and loaded the horses. Perry's fear started to shrink. Just being around his dad helped. He looked around. He hadn't seen the mountains from this side before. The view of this peak, close-in, made him feel hollow. From the Buffalo side, Cloud Peak was the biggest. From this angle, an angry-looking black-toothed peak seemed like it was.

They got in the truck, and Patrick started driving slowly along Red Grade Road.

Trish said, "This reminds me of the Swiss Alps in *Heidi*."

"Huh?" Perry said.

"You know, the book, *Heidi*?"

Perry looked out the window. Trish loved to read. He hated it. The conversation stopped, but he didn't mind. For half an hour, his mind floated from thoughts of football to fishing and elk hunting and then to nothing at all as they passed bogs, moose grazing on water plants, streams, wide-open parks with brown grass, and the occasional cabin.

Perry must have fallen asleep, because he woke up when Patrick turned right onto a forest road across from a creek.

"We'll park near here and pack in to camp." Patrick cranked the window down on his side.

Trish left hers up, but Perry rolled both down in the back seat. They drove by a truck and travel trailer with Harley motorcycles parked outside. The trailer windows and doors were blacked out with something taped from the inside.

"Those are the same motorcycles." Perry wrinkled his nose. "Something smells funny."

Patrick tilted his nose toward his open window. "Like ammonia."

Trish shuddered. "They're in there. Let's camp far away from them."

Patrick nodded. "The place Henry recommended is a long way off."

A mile later, Patrick parked the truck and trailer. Cindy, as always, was kicking the trailer.

Patrick banged on the side. "Stop that or you're dog food."

"Dad, she can't help it. She's nervous." Perry reached in and stroked Cindy's neck.

"More like she's impatient." He smiled at his son.

"You won't really sell her for dog food, will you?"

"Probably not."

"Dad! Promise."

Patrick scrubbed Perry's crew cut. "I promise. Even though she's annoying, I won't sell her for dog food."

Cindy kept kicking until the back doors were open. Getting the horses ready took longer than it had on Red Grade. Cindy wore a packsaddle with the archery equipment attached to it, plus she and the other horses carried saddlebags stuffed full of gear, grub, and garments. But not all the garments. Patrick made Trish leave half of hers in the back floorboard of the truck.

Perry watched as his dad checked his .357

Magnum and sheath knife, then loaded them in their holster and scabbard on his hip. "If we're bowhunting, how come you're bringing all the other weapons?"

"The revolver is for self-defense. But the sheath knife isn't to use as a weapon. It's for field dressing our elk." Patrick withdrew his Sawbones pocketknife from his pocket. "And this is my utility knife."

Perry reached for the pocketknife and examined it while his dad loaded the ammo into one of Cindy's saddlebags. The .38 Special ammo, because it was cheaper than .357 caliber. His dad liked things cheap. "Can I carry it?"

Patrick rubbed Perry's head. "This one's man-sized. Maybe Santa will bring you one for Christmas."

"There is no Santa, Dad."

"I wouldn't say that out loud. He might hear you." Patrick winked. He walked over and locked the truck, then reached up to zip the keys into an outer pocket on one of Reno's bags.

Reno looked mean, but he was really nice. His dad loved that horse. His friend Henry gave him grief about riding a draft horse in fast-footed cow pony country, so his dad had taken Reno in for cutting lessons. Now he bragged that he had the slowest cutting horse in the West.

"Everyone ready?" Patrick said, sounding jolly.

"To go home," Trish said. "So's Goldie. You put too much on her." But Trish mounted up.

"Not nearly as much as she'd be carrying if I'd let you bring all that junk in your bag."

Perry said, "I'm ready, Dad."

Patrick stood beside Duke and put a hand out. Perry used it as a step to get on Duke. Then Patrick hefted himself onto Reno's back and took Cindy's line. He led the way. Perry followed, and Trish brought up the rear. They passed other trucks and trailers parked along the road and even some people camped in tents. People were loading and unloading, stringing bows, and cooking out. Everyone waved.

The horses waddled more than walked with their bulky loads. It was nearly an hour before Patrick told Perry to start scouting for the perfect campsite. Perry was sick of riding, but he took his time.

After rejecting a few spots—too rocky, too small, no fire ring—he stopped Duke by a generous clearing in the trees, set back from the trail, with good grass and a well-established fire ring. "How about this one, Dad?"

Trish rode Goldie to the fire ring. "It's still smoldering. Looks like someone was burning trash."

Patrick shook his head. His face was grim and

disgusted. "Good way to start a forest fire, and this is exactly the wrong time of year for that. The whole mountain is dry as kindling."

"There's good grass left. And a highline to tie the horses."

Perry saw tips of branches littering the edges of the clearing. "Why are all the tree pieces on the ground?"

Patrick said, "Most likely squirrels. They bite off the new growth then feed off the buds from the comfort of the forest floor." He swung his leg high to clear the saddlebags. He kicked one anyway. Reno sidestepped. Patrick levered himself off and to the ground. "This is our spot, then. Good pick, Perry."

Perry sighed. He slithered off Duke, suddenly tired, like he'd just played forward both halves of a soccer game.

"Look alive, kids. Daylight's wasting and there's a camp to be set up."

Perry sighed again, this time louder.

"I'll take care of the horses." Trish was already unsaddling Goldie. The mare looked back at her, and Trish stroked her muzzle.

"It's you and me on the tent, then." Patrick ruffled Perry's hair.

Perry ducked out from under his hand. He wished his dad would stop doing that.

Trish smirked. "Sucks to be you, squirt."

He gave Trish the middle finger behind his dad's back, and she puckered her lips and smacked her hand on her butt.

Half an hour later, the horses were watered from a nearby stream and turned out in hobbles to graze. The tent was secure and sleeping bags unrolled inside, on a patch of mostly flat ground without too many rocks. The mountains were blocking most of the sun, even though it was still high in the sky.

Patrick hoisted the saddlebags holding the food high into a tree on the far edge of the campsite. "If we eat a late dinner, we have time to get the lay of the land for our hunt tomorrow."

His dad's words electrified Perry. Tiredness was just a memory. His first year to be old enough to hunt legally. He'd shot plenty of varmints with his pellet gun, and his dad had lined up and let him pull the rifle trigger on deer hunts, but this was different. He'd be choosing his own animals and shots, operating the compound bow by himself, and claiming his own trophy—if he got an elk, that is. He'd been practicing with the bow all summer and had gotten to be a really good shot, but his dad always reminded him that a moving animal was different than a target.

His thoughts were cut short by a bullwhip voice from the trail.

"This is our camp." The voice belonged to a tall, burly man with sunken cheeks above a wispy beard. His hair was sort of black and sort of grayish-white. He was dressed in camo overalls with a black T-shirt under them, the same color as his horse.

Perry hadn't even heard him ride up, and he felt sorry for the horse, having to carry someone that heavy. Belatedly, Goldie, Duke, Cindy, and Reno started whinnying and snorting. Perry guessed that was why there was no such thing as a watch horse. He wished they'd brought Ferdinand. He barked at everything, but that's exactly why his dad had said no dogs on a hunting trip.

But this was his campsite. He'd picked it out.

He puffed out his chest. "It's ours."

Patrick held a hand toward Perry, pushing his palm down, telling him to be quiet. "Good afternoon. Is there a problem?"

Perry and Trish shared a look. Her eyes said, "What the heck?" and he knew his did, too.

Two more horses and riders came around the bend in the trail. These riders were enough like the first guy to be family. Swarthy. Tall. One old like him but thin and with completely white hair, another one who looked young enough to be in high school. The old guy picked his teeth and grinned.

The young guy had his face down and turned away from the campsite.

The first guy repeated himself. "This is our camp. Always has been. All season long."

Patrick shook his head. "There was nothing here when we found it. Did you reserve it?"

The two older riders guffawed. The young one didn't react.

First Guy said, "That's funny. A reservation for backcountry dispersed camping. You're a comedian?"

"No, I'm a doctor."

The teenage boy shifted in his saddle.

"Maybe he could look at Blue's leg." The guy with the white hair was on a blue roan with a big cut gaping on its back leg.

Patrick smiled. "Well, I did see a horse with a broken leg last night at the hospital, but I warn you, I'm no vet."

"No." The bullwhip voice of First Guy again. He stared at Patrick, the look in his eyes weird.

Perry didn't know what to make of that look. Most people act pretty impressed that his dad is a doctor. They line up to talk to him at church, holding out disgusting, rashy arms and bare feet with ingrown nails. This guy didn't seem impressed at all.

First Guy said, “All we need from you is our campsite.”

“Are you serious?” Patrick asked. This time, his voice rose.

Perry and Trish moved closer to their dad. Reno started tossing his head and pawing the ground.

“I am.”

“There’s a really good spot just up the trail,” Trish said. “Better than this one. I saw it when we were watering the horses. Nearer the stream. Bigger.”

The man grunted. “Then, you can take it.”

Perry saw his dad glance at the tent. The bow was propped against a tree beside it, and his revolver was in its holster belt, hanging over a limb on the tree.

“We won’t be moving,” Patrick said quietly. “Best you move along.”

His tone raised the hair on Perry’s arms. His dad always gets quieter when he’s mad. The men shifted in their saddles and White Hair watched their leader, First Guy, who spit a stream of brown tobacco juice. It splattered where it hit the hard-packed ground on the trail.

Motorbike engines tore into the uncomfortable silence as the machines careened around the bend in the trail. Not the roaring street bikes, like the Harleys

Perry had seen earlier, but dirt bikes. Cool bikes—one red, one yellow—that looked pretty new. Two men with shaved heads rode up, their faces almost covered by goggles. They didn't have on helmets—like the Harley guys, Perry realized. His dad said this had something to do with the law of natural selection and Darwin somebody-or-other. The dirt-bike riders let off their throttles as they passed the horses.

They must have realized something wasn't right, because the one in front stopped and cut his engine. The other rode past him and stopped, too. "Hey, man, is everything good?"

First Guy said, "Peachy."

Perry's stomach hurt all of a sudden, and he moved another step closer to his dad.

The dirt-bike guys nodded. They started their bikes, kicking down with their right legs, and took off.

"I hope this campsite is worth it," First Guy said to his dad.

"Worth what?" Patrick put his hands on his hips.

First Guy clucked to his horse, and the glossy animal tossed its head, then swayed forward under the heavy load. The other two fell in behind them and trotted to keep up.

Perry didn't know what First Guy meant, but he was pretty sure it wasn't good.

CHAPTER EIGHT: FLOAT

Buffalo, Wyoming
September 18, 1976, 5:00 p.m.

Susanne

Susanne laid her head back in the scented bubbles. Magnolia. It reminded her of home, and she breathed it in. The water in the tub was perfect—near-scalding. Patrick had adjusted the hot water heater when they moved in. He had to turn the faucets halfway to cold when he showered, just to be able to stand the temperature, but he said he didn't mind.

That was the way it was with everything between them. She liked spicy Mexican food; he wanted his salsa mild and couldn't tolerate jalapenos. Steaming baths were one of her favorite things; he took cool showers. She loved hot, humid Texas summers; he preferred the brisk Wyoming fall. Opposites attract, and in their case, opposites thrived. Because they had. Thrived. She was a blessed woman, she knew.

She reached for her glass on the lip of the mustard-colored tub and took a tiny sip of her white zinfandel. The water sloshed, jostling the white crests of foam. "Crocodile Rock" came on the radio and she smiled. Just last week Patrick had danced her around the living room to this song. It was a happy memory. Even Trish had laughed and danced with her little brother. How could Susanne have ever dreamed that the boy she'd had a crush on as little more than a girl would turn out to be kind, strong, and loyal? A good father. A wonderful provider. Her life the envy of other women. When they eloped to Mexico while she was still in high school, they'd kept their marriage secret until she'd gotten pregnant. So much for condoms—they should put pictures of babies on the packaging, as reliable as it had been at preventing pregnancy.

Her parents had feared the worst. Patrick's wild streak back then, his temper. Alcohol. His smart mouth. Fighting. They'd wanted better for her, but in the end, he'd won them all over with the man he'd become. If she could change only one thing, it would be his yearning for the mountains. If she could change a second, it would be that he always had to have things his way.

But she'd settle for changing one.

"Crocodile Rock" ended on the radio, and the weather report came on. The DJ—she couldn't remember his name, but his son was in Perry's class at the elementary school—did all the announcements. She listened, her head lolled back, her eyes vacantly on the popcorn ceiling.

"At lower elevations, we're still enjoying the warm, clear days and cool nights of the fall season. Tomorrow's high is expected to be ninety-one in Buffalo, eighty-nine in Story, and ninety-two in Sheridan. However, above seven thousand feet, the weather is changing. Thunderstorms and even some hail are expected starting tonight and for the next few days. Hunters, take cover." His voice was deep and gravelly, as if Wolfman Jack was doing their local radio. "In other news, law enforcement officers continue their search for Billy Kemecke, who escaped in a Big Horn County vehicle while being transported to the state penitentiary in Rawlins, killing deputy Robert Hayes in the process. Deputy

Hayes is survived by his wife and son. Kemecke was convicted earlier this year of murdering Game and Fish warden Gill Hendrickson. Kemecke is considered armed and dangerous. Kemecke is a white man, forty-two years of age, five feet ten inches tall, one hundred sixty-five pounds, with black hair going gray and dark eyes. He was last seen wearing orange prison coveralls and is believed to be driving a white truck that says BIG HORN COUNTY SHERIFF on the side. Kemecke has family in the Buffalo area. If you see Kemecke, contact law enforcement immediately. He is considered armed and dangerous."

Seconds later, "Spiders and Snakes" came on. Susanne twisted the dial to OFF. They hadn't found the fugitive. She wondered who his family was in the area. The unease she'd felt earlier returned in full force. She'd locked the doors before she got in the tub, but she hadn't checked the locks on the windows. Her wineglass had a few sips left in it, so she tipped it back and drained it. The water was still hot and the bubbles still high in the tub, but she pulled the stopper out anyway. Her velour robe was hanging on a hook on the back of the door. She snatched it and wrapped it around her tight and fast, then made the rounds of all the windows.

She did the ground level last. Everything was

secure until she tried the window in Trish's room. It opened silently and easily when she tested it. When that girl got home, she was in big trouble. Maybe she'd only left it that way after opening it to let in cool air. Their house didn't have air-conditioning. Or maybe she was sneaking out at night. Either way, leaving her window unlocked was not acceptable.

She went upstairs and opened the back door. "Ferdie?" The huge silver dog liked the higher elevation of their backyard and usually could be found there, nose to the wind, unless Trish was home. Then he curled up outside her window. It took a few seconds, but Susanne spotted him, his shaggy ears flapping as he ran toward her, his long tail curled up and behind him like the string to an invisible kite. "Good boy."

Ferdinand woofed as he slid to a stop at the back door. Burs clung to his wiry hair as did the distinctive odor of horse manure to his breath.

"Yuck." She pushed him away as he tried to lick her foot. "How about a snack, Ferdie?"

She held the door for him, and the dog shot her a questioning look, as if to say, "Don't you always tell me that big, dirty dogs aren't allowed in the house?" She usually tied him up outside and took a brush to his hair several times a day. *She* did. Not

Patrick or the kids. He was "their dog," yet somehow she was the one who fed him, brushed him, and cleaned up after him.

"It's okay, boy, come on in." Rules are made to be broken, especially when killers are on the loose.

Ferdie stepped tentatively over the threshold, testing her offer, then when she opened the refrigerator and came back unwrapping a bowl of stew, he threw caution to the wind. He lifted his nose, sniffing as he trotted over. Susanne put the bowl on the floor, and Ferdie skidded to it and dove in. She locked the back door.

Out the picture window, she saw storms gathering over the mountains. It wasn't a great night for cooking over a roaring campfire. Had she made sure Patrick had enough ready-to-eat food packed? Honestly, she'd been too wrapped up in her own need to not ride, hike, camp, and hunt. Well, they weren't that far away. She could be at their Hunter Corral campsite in half an hour, house door to tent flap. A tingling started deep inside her, the kind she got when she was happy.

She'd told Patrick she wouldn't go on the trip, but she hadn't said she wouldn't visit.

Moving quickly, she packed up. Summer sausage. Cheese. Crackers. Apples. The rest of her bottle of white zinfandel and some plastic glasses. The kids had conned her into buying Halloween candy already, so she added a bag of Hershey's Kisses. She donned the clothes she'd shed onto the bathroom floor and grabbed a rain slicker along with her brown paper bag of picnic items.

Ferdinand followed her to the front door downstairs.

"No. You stay here." She wanted to know she was alone when she came back in the house, except for this big dog.

She flicked on the outside lights. During the short walk from her bronze station wagon to the house door, she pictured herself returning after dark, exposed to the night and anyone who might be out there as she unlocked it. But that was silly. The house was on the high prairie. There was nowhere to hide except one meager Russian olive tree thirty feet away, unless you counted the sagebrush that started growing twenty feet from the side of the house. Not exactly great cover for a bad guy. And if she left Ferdinand out and a deer or a fox ran by, the fickle dog would go off hunting and the house would be left unguarded, inside and out.

Yes, keeping him in was the way to go.

Susanne drove through town and west on Highway 16. The city of Buffalo touted the road on billboards to tourists as the safest route to Yellowstone National Park from the northeast. It followed the path of Clear Creek up into the mountains, climbing gradually instead of making an aggressive ascent up the face like the other roads into the Bighorn National Forest from the north. Still, 16 was nothing to trifle with, and there were runaway truck ramps at strategic locations all along the descent. During his first year at the hospital in Buffalo, Patrick had been called out when an eighteen-wheeler plunged from the road into the creek bed hundreds of feet below. The impact had driven the nails from the driver's boots all the way to his knees. That introduction to the mountains had made an impact on Susanne. She drove carefully, probably more carefully than she needed to, barely paying attention to the immense ancient rock formations that drew geologists from around the world.

Less than ten miles from town, she turned off 16 heading north onto a dirt road toward Paradise Ranch and Hunter Corral. The location was popular with locals and tourists alike because of its access to Cloud Peak Wilderness, and the fact that it was so near Buffalo. The established corrals, campsites with fire pits and picnic tables, trailer parking, pumped water, and Forest Service bathrooms were a plus. She drove through a grove of aspens near the creek. After she emerged from it, a prairie ridge towered to the right, fronted by dramatic rock outcroppings. On her left, the high prairie gave way to forests, creeks, lakes, and the towering peaks of the range. Cloud Peak with its superior height lorded it over the others from the center. All told, when she arrived at Hunter Corral, it had been less than an hour since she'd gotten out of the bathtub, despite the dramatic change in elevation and scenery.

The parking area was jam-packed. She drove slowly around the road that looped through the sites, checking each one as she scanned for their white truck and red trailer. Every now and then, she would flit her eyes back to the center of the loop where the water and the restrooms were. Camping with horses meant a lot of shoveling poop, carrying hay, and hauling tubs of water. But after making one complete circuit, she still hadn't spotted Patrick and the kids.

The anxiety that had started at the Busy Bee Café and never quite left her intensified.

She retraced her path with her windows down. Campfire smoke and the surprisingly sweet scent of horse manure filled the cab. This time around she noticed a white placard that said FLINT on one of the numbered campsite markers. This was both strange, and *not*. She'd made their reservation here, so she'd expected to see it. But what she hadn't expected was that the vehicle parked at the site wouldn't be theirs. She idled behind the unfamiliar blue Ram truck. Then she remembered that each campground area had a host at the edge of the grounds. She drove onward until she reached the last spot, where a trailer with a semipermanent feel was set up. Sure enough, there was a small placard on the site marker identifying it as the location of the host.

She parked and walked to the trailer. Softly at first, then harder, she knocked on the metal edge of the screen door. It rattled against the frame. "Excuse me."

A plump woman in a pink gingham appliqued apron appeared, wiping her hands on the skirt. "Can I help you?"

"Hello. I hope so. I'm looking for my husband and kids. His name is Patrick Flint. We had a reservation, but there seems to be someone in our spot."

The woman's brows furrowed. "Randy, we've got someone here asking about site thirty-six."

The trailer rocked as Randy walked its length. Where the woman was plump, he was positively round. He was holding a chicken leg between a thumb and forefinger, and barbecue sauce dotted his chin. "Sorry. Are you Mrs. Flint?"

"Yes. Susanne Flint."

He nodded, then wiped his bare forearm across his mouth, smearing the sauce on his chin. "We let the site go when no one showed up by check-in time. There's a long list of folks wanting to use it this weekend. I'm afraid we're all filled up."

Susanne rocked back on her heels. How could that be? "My husband and kids should have gotten here hours ago. Around noon."

He cocked his head. "Did you check all the sites real good for them? Sometimes people use the wrong spot by accident."

"I did. They're not here."

He looked off over her shoulder to the right. "Well, ma'am, I don't know what to tell you. They probably found someplace else where they'd rather camp. But if you're worried about them, let the Johnson County sheriff know. And report it at the Forest Service offices in Buffalo."

Susanne stared at him.

His gaze shifted to her, then softened. "I'm sure they're fine. It's a big wilderness. Lots of places to camp."

A big wilderness. Indeed. Exactly what she worried about. She nodded. "Thank you for your assistance."

But as she walked back to the station wagon, she pressed her fist against her mouth. It was one thing simply to be apart for a long weekend, but another altogether to have no idea where her family was in the midst of over one million inhospitable, remote acres.

She drove back to the house in a fog of worry. The outside lights weren't on. *Did I forget them?*

Did a bulb burn out? Her stomach clenched like a fist. With Ferdinand inside, she had nothing to keep visitors away from the house, the four-footed or two-footed kind. She parked as close as she could get to the front door, sweeping the headlights of the station wagon as best she could to spotlight the area. She didn't see anything. Or anyone.

She opened the car door. The wind had been picking up, although it wasn't storming, and it was like a damper on the night sounds. Hair blew into her mouth, and she spit it back out. Drawing in a deep breath, she caught a whiff of something unfamiliar. A foul odor. Bear? *No. Don't be ridiculous. It's nothing. Probably just Ronnie's trash.* For a moment, she thought about driving to her neighbor's and asking for an escort into her house, but only for a moment. She wouldn't humiliate herself forever by providing further evidence that she's not cut out for Wyoming. She stuck her keys point out between her fingers like she'd learned to do in Patrick's self-defense lessons, then tucked her purse under her left arm and jumped out. She hip-bumped the car door closed and ran for the house.

With no lights and clouds covering the moon, she fumbled for the lock she couldn't see. She pushed her hair out of her face and dropped her purse.

"Shit." The stench from earlier grew stronger.

"Don't move," a man's voice said behind her as an arm slid around her throat like a boa constrictor.

Inside the house, she heard Ferdinand growling and clawing at the wood between them. Her keys joined her purse on the ground as she screamed.

CHAPTER NINE: PUSH

Southwest of Walker Prairie, Bighorn National Forest, Wyoming
September 19, 3:00 a.m.

Patrick

Patrick jolted awake. "Susanne. Are you okay?"

He reached out, ready to jostle her, but also eager just to make contact. He had a feeling of dread, connected to his wife. Was he dreaming? But if it was a dream, he couldn't remember any of it. That's when he heard loud snoring. His hand thumped something hard and spikey. That wasn't Susanne. Where was she? For someone as pretty and petite as her, the decibel level of her allergy-induced snoring was occasionally impressive.

And then the day came back to him. Susanne staying behind, the camp he'd set up with the kids, their sleeping bags in a row in the big canvas tent. It was Perry's spikey-haired head next to him. A deep, aching loneliness rippled through him. He didn't like being apart from his wife, even for a hunt with the kids. He wished she had come. Not only that, but he was worried about her on her own. He shouldn't be. She was a grown, capable woman. But he couldn't help it. He had a deep, inextinguishable need to protect her, and he couldn't do it from here.

He'd be annoyed she wasn't here in the morning, he was sure, but right now, he was sorry he hadn't just taken everyone to Disneyland for vacation again, like he had last year. Then, he'd been Husband and Dad of the Year. Now, he was persona non grata with his wife and daughter.

The snoring continued, louder.

"Perry, wake up. You're snoring." He pushed on the boy's shoulder.

"Huh?" Perry's head rose. "I have to go to the bathroom."

Patrick could just barely see a glint from Perry's eyes, thanks to the ambient light of the full moon peeking in the window panel. Full moon. The clouds must have cleared. It had been raining when they fell asleep. Patrick and the kids had taken refuge in the tent with some MREs—Meals Ready to Eat—then fallen asleep early. He listened. The rain had stopped, but the wind hadn't. But even now that Perry was awake, the snoring continued.

"Sorry, I thought you were snoring. Is it your sister?"

Perry rubbed his eyes and leaned over her. "No. What is it?" His voice sounded a little nervous.

Patrick stilled and listened harder. It must be coming from outside, which meant it was *really* loud if he could hear it so distinctly over the wind. Was it a some*one* or a some*thing*? A bear would be unlikely. Even if it had somehow gotten to their stash of food hoisted high over a tree limb, it would eat and retreat, not necessarily in that order. The animals were very shy. For a moment, he imagined a black bear with a full belly curled up near the dwindling warmth of the ashes from their fire. It hadn't been a great fire, not once the sky had started falling.

The noise changed, the rumble broken up by louder sounds. Snapping. Yapping.

It wasn't snoring at all. It was growling, and now it was animals fighting.

Patrick patted his hand around on the tent floor until he found the revolver he'd hidden under his coat. He palmed it and crawled on all fours to the door. "Wait here."

Trish rolled over. "What's going on?" Her voice was thick with sleep.

"Something's out there," Perry said.

"What is it?"

"Dad's going to find out."

Trish got out of her sleeping bag and knelt beside her brother. "It's cold."

Patrick raised the zipper as slowly and as quietly as he could, just a foot. Inside the tent, the sound of the zipper teeth was like revving up a Weed Eater. But with the growling and the wind, he doubted the animals outside heard it. The overflap was still tied in place, and he unfastened the lowest tie. The growling sounded close, and he didn't want to create a big open door for a predator, straight into the tent, right to his kids. He lowered his head and turned it so he could see out the spyhole he'd created.

It took several seconds for his eyes to adjust. It was lighter outside, thanks to the clearing skies and moon, but still nighttime in a forest clearing with no artificial light for many miles. He could hear the sounds distinctly now. Definitely multiple animals. And something else, too. The snorting and huffing of distressed horses. He strained to see them, but couldn't get a fix on their silhouettes. Whatever was out there had them spooked, although with horses, it didn't take much to trigger their prey-animal instincts. He had to scare the visitors off before the horses found a way to hurt themselves, if they hadn't already. Even tied to a highline, horses could still do self-damage. It was the essential nature of horses. Crashing into each other or the trees, lashing out with front hooves, kicking with back hooves. They could even tangle each other's lines if they got too frantic.

"What is it?" Perry said.

"Are the horses okay?" Trish asked.

Patrick held up a hand. The fire ring had come into focus, and he didn't like what he saw. Coyotes. At least three of them, maybe more. Big ones. From their movements, they were eating something. Ripping, tearing, and fighting over a feast. What in the world could they have gotten into? No way coyotes could have raided the hanging food stores. And the horses were far too big for the coyotes to mess with, especially with four horses to work together to repel them. Even with them secured to the highline, that was a lot of hooves.

At least he hoped it was coyotes. It could be wolves. They'd mostly been hunted out of the Bighorns. So it was probably coyotes.

Probably.

He turned to the kids. "It's a pack of coyotes. I think the horses are fine."

Patrick checked the ammunition in his gun. He had six shots. There was more ammo in his backpack, so he crawled to it and dug out the box of .38 Special bullets. It held ten more. If that wasn't enough, he wasn't sure what he could do. He wasn't a good enough shot to pick off running coyotes in the dark with a bow and arrows.

"Wait here."

"Where are you going?" Trish asked.

"To scare them off."

"Can I come?" Perry asked.

"No."

"But I have to pee."

"You need to wait."

Patrick eased the zipper up and unsecured ties farther up the flap, then rezipped and refastened the tent from the outside. The coyotes hadn't noticed him yet, since he was downwind from whatever it was they were eating. He wanted to scare them off, but not in the direction of the horses or the tent. That meant he needed to circle around them about twenty yards. He moved as silently as he could, tiptoeing through the edge of the trees, hunched low, still downwind. He got as close as he dared—close enough that he confirmed they were coyotes and not their larger, more daring cousins, wolves. *That's a relief.* When he was in position, he cocked the revolver, pointed it in the air, and fired.

The sound exploded into the night, busting the coyotes apart as if it had been a bomb in their midst. The horses whinnied, and he saw them now, restless and milling as far as they could on their lines. But they'd all been trained to tolerate gunfire, so it didn't have the same impact on them as it did the coyotes.

He yelled, "Yah. Get. Yah," and fired again.

The coyotes ran to the edge of the clearing as a pack, but then they stopped and faced him.

Shit. They didn't want to leave their food. He advanced on them and took aim. He wasn't a great shot at thirty yards, but he needed to convince them that leaving was a better choice than staying. He fired into them. Hoped for the best.

There was a pained yelp, and one coyote took off like a streak. The others followed.

Patrick stayed in place for a long minute, listening, before he moved toward the horses. With their excellent night vision, they watched him the whole way. Cindy was pawing like she was trying to dig to the far side of the earth. Reno's flanks were streaked with sweat. Goldie had pulled back, and still had most of her weight hanging against the highline. Only Duke was completely calm. Patrick worked his way from horse to horse, checking for injuries, petting and soothing. They were all right.

The light dimmed, and he looked up. A big mass of clouds had drifted in front of the moon. Too late, he remembered his flashlight, back in the tent. He hadn't wanted to alert the coyotes to his presence, but it would be handy now that they were gone. It would be nice if he could swish the cloud away from the moon with his hand. Or if he hadn't made the bad choice about the flashlight.

"It's going to be okay, you guys." He gave Reno one last pat on the rump and headed to the fire ring.

What the heck had drawn the coyotes all the way into their campsite, and what were they eating? Coyotes weren't as shy as bears, but they still didn't usually come this close to humans. Especially not in areas where they had plentiful food and lots of uncrowded space to hunt and eat, like here. It was hard to be sure. He kept Seton's *Lives of Game Animals,* all eight volumes, on his bookshelf for reference, and he had a passion for wildlife biology, but he wasn't the world's leading expert.

When he reached the fire ring, it turned out he didn't need a flashlight to see what was on the ground. It was a mound of bloody, dirty entrails. He could clearly make out the remnants of intestines and see the ripped-apart remains of the rest of the animal's guts. A big animal, too. Bigger than the coyotes themselves. But where was the rest of it? Coyotes didn't usually drag their kills significant distances. For that matter, they didn't usually kill such big animals. A fawn, yes, but not a full-sized deer unless it was old or sick, and certainly never a grown, healthy elk or moose. He pondered the significance of the entrails. No hide, fur, bones, hooves, skull, or meat. Just . . . what a human hunter would scoop out when field dressing an animal.

"What's that?" Perry's voice was right behind him.

"Their dinner."

Perry leaned into his father and shivered. "It's cold out here."

"Yep. Fall is moving in. Why don't you go back to bed? We'll have a big day tomorrow."

"Are you coming?"

"In a minute. I have to check the camp for more remains. We don't want the coyotes back."

"I have to pee first."

"Stay where I can see you."

He watched his son walk barefoot across the rocky ground to the tree line, wincing and hotfooting, head swiveling to check every sound. Patrick smiled. The kid was tough as nails in some ways, and still such a little boy in others. After Perry finished, he shot his dad a thumbs-up. Patrick joined him and walked him back to the tent, where he repeated the story for Trish, although her questions forced him to focus more on the horses, Goldie in particular. He secured the tent door again, then retrieved his camp shovel, which he'd left near the fire ring. It took thirty minutes for him to move all the entrails into the forest and half-bury, half-cover them. He burned another fifteen minutes scouring the campsite and beyond, searching for the rest of the animal.

He didn't find it.

After he washed his hands with some canteen water, he went back to the tent. How long since he'd slept—really slept? Thursday, he guessed. Between the night in the ER, the emotions of the morning argument with Susanne, and the full day getting here and setting up camp, he was exhausted. Zombie tired. But the harder he tried to fall asleep, the more it eluded him. He counted sheep. He tried deep breathing. He practiced self-hypnosis. Nothing worked. In the end, he stared at the tent ceiling the rest of the night, trying to come up for an explanation for the animal guts in their campground that didn't involve a sick bastard dumping them there.

CHAPTER TEN: TREAD

Buffalo, Wyoming
September 19, 1976, 5:00 a.m.

Susanne

Susanne's eyes were fixed on the shotgun beside the bed. The man snoring in the living room had left it there, along with the phone on the bedside table, after lashing her to the chair Patrick sat in to put on and pull off his boots. She tried for what seemed like the millionth time to escape. She twisted her wrists, trying to slip them out of the rough rope. When that didn't work, she rocked the chair. Its feet were rooted in the deep shag carpeting, and it wouldn't tump over.

Dammit. She was stuck here in this bedroom that she hadn't gotten around to redecorating from Old West rusty barbed wire, cowboy prints, and browns to something softer and more colorful. Her heart was pounding in her ears, sweat dripping down her back, stomach acid-filled and burning. She glanced at the phone and shotgun again.

They were useless. Like her.

At least he hadn't hurt her. In fact, he barely said a word to her, other than to tell her to hold Ferdinand—which she did, although it wasn't easy with the dog going nuts and the man's arm locked around her neck—and ask her where her husband was. She'd been dumb with fear and told the truth. A hunting trip. And when would he be back? She hesitated, then said, "Soon." His eyes bored into hers, then he grunted.

He frog-marched them into the house without turning on any lights. Ferdinand, he made her lock in the laundry room. Her, he tied up in the bedroom. She'd barely gotten a look at him, although she'd smelled him. As her daddy would say, rather crudely, he stunk enough to gag a boar hog and drop it at twenty paces. He wasn't tall, but he was menacing, wiry but strong. Wearing some kind of coveralls. In the dark, she saw only that his eyes and hair were not blond or light, and nothing of his face. He seemed altogether unfamiliar, and she knew for sure she'd never heard his voice before.

Unfortunately, he found a letter on the kitchen table that she'd started writing to her mother earlier. So he'd figured out she was lying. That Patrick and the kids were gone for days. It was lying on the floor beside her now, where he'd dropped it without a word, right before he shut the door to the bedroom, then settled in the living room for his siesta.

Her guess? He was the fugitive they'd been talking about on the radio. Billy Kemecke. The one who'd murdered the local game warden and a Big Horn County deputy.

A ruthless killer.

Downstairs, Ferdinand was keeping up an incessant howling and barking. How he had any voice left, she didn't know. Nor could she figure out how the man slept through it. She wished Ferdinand would save his energy for later, for daytime, when there was a chance someone might come to the door. Although probably no one would. Their mail was delivered to a box a mile away out on Airport Road. She wasn't expecting any friends or deliveries.

She was alone with a killer, and no one was coming to help her.

From the living room, she heard boots hit the floor. The snoring had stopped. She'd thought she was as scared as she could be before, but when, after a moment's silence, his footsteps started down the hallway toward her, she realized she was wrong. She could be a lot more scared. A sound rose from her chest, but her throat closed and choked it off before it became a scream. Her face stretched, trying to get it out. Her cheeks felt like they were on fire, and as the footfalls approached the door, she started to shake.

The doorknob turned in slow motion. Her brain whirred, unable to form any thoughts except one: *escape, escape, escape.* She clenched and unclenched her fingers helplessly.

Escape was impossible.

The door swung inward, and a presence followed it. It was nearly time for dawn, so it had to be lighter outside. But heavy curtains blocked out all the sun, a necessity so Patrick could sneak naps during daylight hours after working nights. The form that walked toward her was a silhouette. If he didn't kill her, she knew that this faceless man would be at the center of every nightmare she had for the rest of her life.

He spoke in a sleep-graveled voice, deep and atonal. "Where did your husband go?"

"Uh . . ."

He leaned down in front of her, so close his breath blew stink in puffs that closed her eyes. "Do you really want me to make you tell the truth?" A finger brushed her cheek, and she shuddered. "I've got no beef with you. You've been real neighborly. I'd like to just grab a few essentials and be on my way, after you answer my questions. But things could go different. It's up to you."

Susanne bit her lip until she tasted blood, then relented. "He told me Hunter Corral. But I went up there last night to take him dinner, and he wasn't there."

The man stood. "How unfortunate."

He walked to the closet, and she heard hangers screech across the clothes rod. Fabric rustled, and something settled on the carpet. The man raised his arms. He was putting on a shirt, she realized. One of Patrick's long-sleeved plaid flannel shirts. Then he opened dresser drawers, shutting them one by one, until he reached into one and pulled something back out. His silhouette stepped into pant legs, then she heard a zipper. He returned to the closet and put on boots and a cowboy hat.

"Why are you doing this?" she asked. "Why?"

The man grinned. It wasn't jovial. "Live free or die."

Susanne stewed on that, then asked, "What do you want with my husband?"

"Do you keep any cash in the house?" he said. "Besides your purse. If I have to look and find out you didn't tell me about some—well, that's not answering my questions, is it?"

She closed her eyes. "Coffee can in the kitchen, up high, farthest from the sink."

He disappeared out the door. She exhaled. She heard cabinets opening and closing and the faucet running in the kitchen. A minute later he was back, standing at her side.

"Take a swallow." He held a glass to her lips. "You'll thank me for this later."

Water ran down her lips, and she shook her head. Some went down her throat anyway, and she choked.

"Come on, now. It's just water. I'm trying to help you out." He tilted it again.

By reflex, she swallowed this time, and kept swallowing until it was empty.

He stepped back and picked up the shotgun. "I'll just grab that money, your keys, and a few supplies and be on my way then, ma'am."

"Let me go." She pulled against her restraints. The rope dug into her abraded wrists, and the pain made her frantic. "Please! Untie me."

But he shut the door behind him without answering her. For half an hour, she listened helplessly to banging and thumping from the kitchen and the utility closet. Finally, she heard Ferdinand's growling erupt into enraged barks as the front door opened and closed. Then the car—her station wagon, not the Porsche, she could tell from the engine noise—started, and its sound receded as it drove away.

She drew in a deep, shuddering breath.

He was gone. At least for now.

CHAPTER ELEVEN: DOUBLEBACK

Southwest of Walker Prairie, Bighorn National Forest, Wyoming
September 19, 1976, 6:00 a.m.

Trish

Why did her dad have to get them up at the butt crack of dawn on vacation, especially after they'd been up half the night with a coyote pack outside their tent? He was always like this. "Hard work never killed anybody," he'd say as he marshalled them for an outdoor work project at dawn. Pulling weeds. Planting a garden. Mending a fence. He never stopped.

This morning he already had a fire going. The

smell was nice. She could hear it crackling outside the tent, along with the clatter of pots and utensils.

"Last one up is a rotten egg," he said now, his voice chipper, as if he'd slept like a baby.

Perry lunged for the tent door. He was such a brownnoser, but she wasn't going to let him beat her. She grabbed his ankles and crawled over him, avoiding his swinging fists as she exited the tent first.

"Not fair," he said.

She reached back in the tent for her boots and jacket. She'd slept in her jeans and T-shirt, but it was cold out, and wet from the rain the evening before. Perry pushed past her, barefoot. One of his elbows connected with her temple as he stood up.

"Stop it, turd breath." She shoved him from behind.

He stumbled forward but kept going without answering.

If Patrick heard them, he didn't give any sign of it. "I need you two to go get firewood."

Trish said, "Can I feed the horses instead?"

Patrick pointed at the grazing horses, their tails swishing and legs hobbled. "You're going to have to get up earlier if you want to do that. They were hungry. So am I, and this fire's going to go out. Get moving."

Trish groaned, but she walked around the edge

of the campsite, gathering twigs and small branches. Nothing more than kindling. "There's not enough. Other people have already gathered it." She dumped her stack beside her dad.

"It's a forest, Trish. There are trees everywhere. You just have to go a little farther."

"Don't worry, Dad. I'll get it," Perry said. In his suck-up voice, he added, "After this rain, the risk of fire is less, isn't it?"

"Yes, it is, Smokey Bear. But we still have to be careful."

Trish rolled her eyes.

"Your sister will help you. Don't forget the carriers." Patrick was referring to their canvas containers for carrying firewood.

"Let's take the horses," Trish said.

"You won't be going that far." But her dad grinned.

She shrugged. "We might. And they can carry more than us."

"Whatever. Just hurry so we can get going."

Perry ran to the horses. They shied away from him.

"Don't scare them." Under her breath she added, "You're such a putz."

"Takes one to know one." He grabbed Duke's lead rope and unfastened his hobbles.

She did the same for Goldie, crooning sweet nothings in the mare's ear.

Side by side the siblings saddled their horses and tied the log carriers behind their saddles. Trish, with ease. Perry, with a monumental struggle. Trish finished first. She brushed Goldie's mane and watched Perry out the corner of her eye. Trish watched Duke's belly expand as he sucked in air. Perry fed the cinch through the D ring, then tried to tighten it.

"Did you get the cinch tight enough?" she asked.

"Yes."

"Do you want me to check?" She stepped toward his saddle.

Perry blocked her with his butt, knocking her sideways. "I've got it."

"Ouch. Okay. Your funeral, shrimp."

He mocked her voice. "Your funeral, Trish."

They mounted and headed into the forest.

"Stay together," Patrick shouted after them. "And don't go far."

She wasn't going far. She didn't know why he wanted all the wood, anyway. They had enough MREs to last the whole trip. Campfire cooking was a major pain. She knew the drill. After gathering firewood, her dad would make them haul water from the stream. Then they'd have to boil it before they could cook, wash dishes, or fill the canteens with it. Her dad claimed the stream water could make them sick, and that the boiling purified it. Whatever. Last time they'd gone camping, boiling was her job. She had filled their canteens with unboiled stream water every day, and no one died. He was such a worrywart. So fat chance she was going to boil the canteen water this time. He'd never know, and it would save her one last haul.

But water wasn't the only problem with cooking out. Everything always had dirt and ash in it, if it even cooked right at all. Half the stuff was burnt or raw or both. The only things good on a campfire were hot dogs and marshmallows, on stick skewers that didn't have to be washed. That was fun.

If Brandon and his friends showed up today, they should do hot dogs and s'mores. She knew the chances of Mrs. Lewis passing on the message she'd left about Walker Prairie were slim, and even if she did, Brandon might not be able to find their camp. Or might not come at all. What if he'd started liking someone else since she left? She hoped that skank Charla Newby hadn't sunk her claws into him.

Goldie snorted. Trish looked around, expecting to see Perry and Duke, but her brother had disappeared. *Great.*

"Good girl," Trish said to her horse.

The forest was eerily quiet. Even Goldie's hoofbeats were muffled—except for the occasional crackling of a pinecone underfoot—by the carpet of browning pine needles and fat tufts of moss over the rocks. What had gotten the mare's attention? She didn't see anything strange, and the horse wasn't acting skittish, so she decided it was probably nothing. Horses acted like total paranoid freaks most of the time.

"Perry, where are you?" she said.

He didn't answer, so she raised her voice.

The only sound in return was the song of a magpie. Goose bumps raised on her arms. It was spooky out here alone. The pine trees blocked what little sun was out, between the stormy clouds and early hour. The tree trunks and boulders provided endless hiding places. It felt like the witch from "Hansel and Gretel" would be jumping out from behind one any second. Every tiny sound made her jumpy. The creak of a branch, the snap of a twig, the chittering of a squirrel. They all sounded ominous.

She'd just get her firewood and return to camp. Perry would probably beat her there.

She hopped off Goldie, who dropped her head to nibble, even though the grass was almost nonexistent back in the trees. Trish picked her way around rocks so splotched with lichen they looked almost like someone had decorated them. Lime green and crackly, forest green and plush, and milky gray with black sporous dots. Threads of green moss wafted in the low fingerling branches of the pines. A juvenile squirrel sprinted up a tree trunk with a pinecone prized in its jaws. Trish noticed it all, but she was too spooked to stop and marvel. Instead, she focused on finding the driest pieces of wood. Big enough to burn, but small enough to put in the bags. It took her five minutes to fill them both. She had grabbed Goldie's mane and put one foot in her stirrup to mount when she heard a CRACK behind her.

She jerked hard, hauling herself into the saddle at the same time that the horse leaped forward. Trish pulled back on the reins, then turned Goldie to face the noise. The horse snorted and took several steps backward.

Trish didn't want to surprise a wild animal. She didn't even want to see one, unless it was Bambi-sized. She needed a noise, so she made one. "Shoo. Yah. Go away."

Nothing moved. Long seconds passed. No more twigs cracked.

Trish exhaled as she patted Goldie's neck. "We're okay, girl. It's nothing."

But she remembered the pack of coyotes. The creepy guys yesterday, on Red Grade and at their campsite. And all that talk on the radio about the murderer loose. If she didn't have the big log loads on either side of the horse's flanks, she would have trotted Goldie all the way back to camp.

Instead, she looked around them. Disorientation reached out and gripped her with icy fingers. She hadn't been paying attention to landmarks on the ride out. But then she saw a trail of hoofprints in the damp pine needles, moss, and dirt. Goldie had left breadcrumbs for them to find their way back to camp. She clucked the mare forward.

Together, girl and horse walked alone through the woods. Trish was still nervous, but she was trying to be brave. If she was scared, Goldie would be, too. The whole way back, Trish called out for Perry, with no response. Goldie's pace picked up the closer they got to the camp. When they reached it, Trish felt weak with relief. There was her dad getting the other horses ready for hunting. But no Duke, no Perry.

She walked Goldie past the fire ring.

"Where's your brother?" her dad called.

"He rode off and left me right when we started. I've been calling for him but he isn't answering. I thought maybe he came back here."

She could see her dad's anger rise. His fists balled, and his lips moved.

Uh-oh. Trish knew she was in big trouble. She hurried to speak before her dad's fury reached the boiling point. "I'm sorry. I can go look for him again."

Just then, Duke galloped into camp, from not too far off the path she and Goldie had taken. Her dad turned toward the horse as Duke clattered to a stop. The saddle was hanging underneath his heaving belly. His neck was lathered, a sure sign he'd been startled and bolted. Without a word, Patrick jerked the saddle from Duke's back, took off his bridle, and fastened him to the lead on the high-line. Then he tightened Reno's cinch and vaulted onto his back with only his halter and, on one side, his lead rope.

Trish untied one log carrier and tossed it to the ground. Goldie jumped away from it. "Shh, girl." She repeated the process on the other side, as did Goldie, then mounted quickly.

Patrick was circling the clearing to find the trail of Duke's flight back into the camp. He was off by about ten yards.

"Over there." Trish pointed and kicked Goldie into a high trot.

Goldie had small hooves compared to Duke. Trish thought it should be easy to tell their tracks apart if their trails had crossed or merged. But it didn't look like that would be necessary, because Duke had left a clear trail of deep, sloppy, panicked prints. Patrick urged Reno forward, smacking his sides with the single line. Trish followed, ducking branches as Goldie wove through the trees. Several still whacked Trish's head and body, but she didn't care. Only Perry mattered. But why couldn't he ever do what he was told? She'd reminded him to tighten that cinch. Her dad had told him to stay with Trish. He always rebelled. Always.

Then she remembered her earlier sensation that she wasn't alone in the woods. The cracking twig. Goldie's nervousness. What if something *had* been out there? What if it got Perry? All the terrible possibilities she'd thought of earlier ran back through her mind, this time with Perry's freckled face and crew-cut hair in the picture. She fought back tears.

In the distance, she saw something moving. "There. What's that?" she shouted.

But her dad must have already seen it. He asked Reno for more speed, and the horse careened through the trees and over the rocks and slippery forest floor at a breakneck pace. Goldie reacted immediately, staying right on his heels. The hooves beat a wicked bass drum cadence. Trish's view of the forest heaved and jerked like a film that had come off its reel. She strained to make sense of the movement she'd seen. What was it?

Perry. It was Perry. Walking. Limping, really, toward them, and rubbing his shoulder.

Her relief was a wave of dizziness that rocked her in her saddle.

Her dad sat back, the lead line in one hand. Reading his body language, Reno slid to a stop. It was an amazing feat for a horse of his size in tight quarters. Patrick was off before the horse came to a stop. He reached Perry in a few running strides.

"Are you okay?" Patrick didn't hug Perry. Instead, he touched him, lifted his arms, and looked him over, checking him for injuries.

Perry's cheeks were stained with tears, but he nodded. "I'm okay. My ankle and my shoulder hurt a little."

"What happened?" Patrick moved a finger slowly side to side in front of Perry's eyes and leaned closer to look at his pupils.

"A b-b-bear scared Duke. My saddle came loose, and I fell off. Duke ran one way, and the bear ran the other. I've been following Duke's tracks back to camp, but it was h-h-hard."

For a moment, Trish felt vindicated. There had been something in the woods. A bear. She wasn't just a fraidycat. But now that she knew Perry was okay, Trish's anger at him returned. "And because you left me, and went way too far, you know. Did you even get any wood?"

"The bear scared Duke before I could get any."

Trish snorted.

Patrick shook his head. "Next time, stay with your sister. And if you get separated, come straight back. You're lucky this didn't end worse." He glared at Trish. "Both of you. You, missy, are older, and that makes you the responsible one."

Trish didn't want to be responsible for Perry, especially not alone out in the scary woods. He was impossible. But she knew better than to argue. "Yes, sir."

He continued muttering under his breath, but Trish heard him, mostly. "Susanne should be here. She shouldn't have sent me off alone with these two." He mounted Reno, then held a hand down for Perry. Perry took it with his good arm, and Patrick hauled him up behind the saddle.

They started the ride back to camp. As she peered behind every tree and boulder looking for the bear, a thought struck Trish. Perry and Duke hadn't been anywhere near where she'd gathered firewood. Whatever had been out in the woods with her and Goldie, if anything, wasn't the bear that had scared Duke. Had there been anything? She kicked Goldie until she was abreast with Reno. Trish wanted to be as close to her dad as possible. Because suddenly she was sure of it. Something had been there. She hadn't imagined it.

She just didn't know what it was, and that scared her most of all.

CHAPTER TWELVE: STUCK

BUFFALO, WYOMING
SEPTEMBER 19, 1976, 3:00 P.M.

Susanne

Every second that passed alone in the chair in the bedroom felt like an hour to Susanne. Her raw wrists burned. Her eyes stung from lack of sleep. She had to go to the bathroom, and her stomach had started to growl. At least her tears had stopped—crying had left her nose first runny and then congested. Ferdinand had even taken a break from his frenzied noisemaking. She'd be completely redoing the laundry room when this was over, if there was any of it left after containing that wild animal for days. The house was so quiet the ticking of the clock in the kitchen sounded like blasts of dynamite.

After hours of rocking and struggling, she'd figured out the reason the chair wouldn't tip. The man —Kemecke?—had used excess rope to secure it to Patrick's gun safe before he'd looped it around her body and feet and tied her arms behind her back. The damn rope must be a mile long. And thick. She needed something to saw through it. But even if she'd had use of her hands, she didn't have on jewelry or hairpins, she had nothing in her pockets or on her shoes, and there were no pieces to the chair that she could break off. As for summoning help, she could scream like mad if someone knocked, but she couldn't make a phone call or even break out the window.

She was stuck. Would she survive until Wednesday when Patrick and the kids got home? It was Sunday morning. She had no idea how long a person could go without water. And pretty soon she'd stink, because there was no way she could go without relieving herself for four days. Who was she kidding? She already smelled bad, from fear and sweat. She'd hold out from wetting herself as long as she could, though, for her own sake.

Occupying her mind would be important, or she'd go crazy. She wasn't used to idleness. She always stayed busy, and if she had down time, she played solitaire or read a book. She was never alone with her thoughts, and she found she didn't like it. Her mind wandered all over the place. To the man who'd left her here. Why had he chosen their house? How had he gotten here? Where was he going? If he was Kemecke—and a merciless killer—why hadn't he hurt *her*? And would he be back? She second-guessed her decision to stay home from the hunting trip. How she wished she was with her family. How a horse sounded better than this chair. That she'd love to have a gun in her hands right now and might never go without one again after this. To where her husband and kids were at this moment, and why they hadn't been at Hunter Corral.

Most especially, she thought about that. Her terror when the man had been in the house had kept her worry about them to a dull roar. Alone in the permanently dark room, it consumed her. She kept picturing horrible things. Their truck and trailer at the bottom of a ravine, with them inside, like the trucker with the nails in his knees. One of the kids bucked off and paralyzed. Patrick gored by an angry elk. One after another, the improbable tricks of her mind tortured her. These things weren't going to happen. She was thinking crazy. But they could have had a wreck anywhere between the house and the campground. Or gotten lost. Been hijacked. She knew the most likely scenario was that Patrick had changed his mind about where to camp. So why couldn't she get her mind to accept it?

Because improbable doesn't mean impossible. Just look at what had happened to her.

To calm herself, she decided to sing. As a child, her mother had sung Susanne and her sister to sleep with hymns. Susanne read to her own kids, since she didn't like her singing voice. Patrick didn't want to sacrifice his rare Sunday mornings off for church, so she only went when he was at the hospital, although she made the kids go to all the children's and youth's programs. She missed the music and the community. The comfort.

That was what she needed. Comfort.

The words to her mother's favorite hymn came to her easily, and with no one to hear whether she was off-key, she sang at a full voice.

"O Lord my God, when I in awesome wonder, consider all the worlds Thy hands have made. I see the stars, I hear the rolling thunder. Thy power throughout the universe displayed. Then sings my soul, my savior God to Thee, how great Thou art, how great Thou art."

Her voice cracked. She cleared her throat and tried again. This time the words came out smoother, and by the time she'd made it through the song one full time, she felt more centered. No one would ever invite her to join a choir, but being on key wasn't what was important. She started from the beginning, now imagining her mother holding her hand and singing with her.

Halfway through the first verse, Ferdinand's barks exploded beneath her feet. She jerked and her voice caught, but she kept going. Seconds later, though, someone knocked on the door.

Kemecke. But no, he had a key. He'd just let himself in. This was a potential rescuer.

"In here. Help. Help. Help me," she shouted. Then, "Shut up, Ferdie."

The dog was so loud, she couldn't compete with him. If anyone was answering her, she couldn't hear it. The tears started again. This was her chance, and the stupid dog was ruining it.

But then Ferdinand shut up, and she heard something else. A female voice. In the house. Murmuring "Wassamatta, boy?"

"Up here," she yelled. "Help me. Help!"

The woman's voice quieted. Susanne strained to hear. Ferdinand whined, and then his toenails scrambled on the linoleum below her, the sound they made when he was winding up his big body to run. Within seconds, his paws were pounding up the stairs. She could picture him, his body nearly as long as the first landing, winding into the turn and covering the second set of steps in a single bound, galloping down the hall to her door, where he bayed like a coonhound. Footsteps followed him, slower, more cautious. They stilled at her door as well.

Susanne's heart hammered. Someone had let her dog out. That was a good thing. But now that they were near, she was scared again. Could it be the man? But Ferdinand would have ripped him up. This had to be someone Ferdinand trusted.

She gathered her courage. "Hello? Is someone out there? Please help me."

The bedroom door started easing open, slower than the passage of a dark Wyoming winter day. Then a blue-jeans-clad figure poked a head inside.

Her neighbor. Ronnie.

CHAPTER THIRTEEN: TRUDGE

Walker Prairie, Bighorn National Forest, Wyoming
September 19, 1976, 3:30 p.m.

Trish

A fly circled Goldie's head, making darting attempts to land in the corner of her eye. The horse shook her head and snorted. The headshaking knocked Goldie off course a little, and then her whole body shuddered. Trish shifted her back on the trail, then turned. A horsefly had landed on Goldie's rump. Trish shooed it with the end of her reins. It flew off for half a second then was back to continue its torment. The one buzzing Goldie's head had never left. Too many flies. Goldie hated flies more than any horse Trish had known, which was a lot, since they were the bane of a horse's existence. The trail they were riding was steep and narrow, too. If Goldie got any more upset, she could fling them both down the incline.

That would suck.

A lot of today sucked. She was riding last in line, for one. Her dad was afraid of Perry getting separated from the group. Again. Neither she nor Goldie were very happy about it. Goldie had nipped Duke's slowpoke butt a time or three, but it didn't speed him up. They'd been riding for an hour, supposedly searching for the perfect hunting spot. She thought they'd found it that morning. It had been good enough for a nap anyway, while her dad and Perry stared through binoculars into nothing, seeing nothing and shooting at nothing. She'd been looking forward to another nap after their picnic lunch, but no, Dad made them pack up.

"I think I see elk over there." Patrick had pointed all the way across the high prairie to a higher elevation, miles north of them.

"That's, like, a long way," she'd said.

"Not for an elk."

"I'm not an elk."

He hadn't replied.

Now the ride back to camp in the dark was going to take forever, which she'd mentioned to him, but had he listened to her? No. If her mom had come, no way would they still be riding out into the great beyond. *God, I miss Mom. How weird is that?*

There had been fewer flies at the morning spot, too.

When they got to his perfect spot, wherever it was—if it even existed—she'd have to walk again. Her boots were pinching her feet, and they'd had to hike into their last spot. She'd be rich if she had a dime for every time her dad reminded them to be as quiet as an Indian. Every time he did his dorky fox walk, she was just glad no one else was around to see him. Worst of all, her hair was gross and dirty. She would have washed it yesterday morning before they left, but her mom hadn't woken her up. What if Brandon came and saw her like this? She'd left him a note pinned underneath a rock between their campsite and the trail, in case he showed up today while they were hunting. It would be awesome to see him, but ew, her hair.

At least she had the small joy of remembering that she hadn't boiled the drinking water that her dad was chugging. She smiled, thinking about what he always told her mom about people at work. "If I want something done right, I guess I just have to do it myself." *Yep,* she thought, *I guess you do.*

Her dad reined Reno off-trail and down a bank to a broad creek. The big horse didn't hesitate, just plunged in up to his knees. *Great.* Reno was a giant. At least six hands taller than Goldie. She'd be swimming. Duke plodded in next. He split the difference in height between the two horses. Perry's head was lolling over. How could he sleep in a saddle on a moving horse in this terrain? Her ass would be on the ground if she fell asleep on Goldie. Perry jerked awake when the cold water splashed on him, and he reacted by sawing at Duke's mouth. The horse ignored him. He might be a puffer, and apparently he didn't like bears, but he was super patient with her brother.

Goldie huffed and pawed at the water's edge.

"It's okay, girl." Trish stroked her neck. "This will get rid of those dumb flies." For a little while, anyway.

Goldie stepped into the water like it might be infested with grizzlies. Trish's feet went under, and water started seeping in. A few steps later, Goldie slipped. Horses have four feet, so normally their balance is pretty good. If things get dicey, they leave three on the ground. But this time, Goldie was in trouble. Frigid water rose up Trish's thigh on one side as Goldie went sideways into the water. Really frigid. Like, breathtakingly cold. Trish grabbed the saddle horn. Suddenly, Goldie was floating, then her front legs were thrashing. Swimming. Goldie was swimming. Trish had never ridden a swimming horse before. Goldie worked hard, but with every foot she gained crossing, she lost another downstream. Trish's heart raced. There were rapids and huge rocks downstream.

"Easy, easy," she said, but her voice had a squeak to it that she knew wasn't reassuring. She tried again. "You've got this, Goldie."

From the opposite bank, her dad looked back as Duke clambered out and shook like a dog. They seemed so far upstream from Goldie and her. Her dad must have thought so, too, because he whirled Reno and rode him hard back into the water. He untied a lasso, and when they were close enough, slung it to Trish.

"Put her head through the loop. Reno and I can haul her out."

Before Trish could do it, Goldie planted her feet and hoisted herself higher in the water. Trish could feel the animal quaking beneath her, and Goldie wasted no more time in the water, now that she had her footing. She scrambled so fast for the bank that Trish worried she would break a leg.

They slipped, slid, and lurched across the rocks. When Goldie reached the short sandy shore, she jumped up the two-foot embankment. There, she huffed and puffed like a steam engine. Behind them, Reno snorted. Patrick led Perry and Duke up a gentler exit from the streambed.

"Good job, kiddo," Patrick said.

Trish glared at him. "I'm not a kiddo. And Goldie is not a draft horse like yours."

"I didn't know it would be so deep. But you did it. And you both learned something."

"Yeah. To stay on the trail on the way back."

Patrick smiled. "You were never in any danger. The Indians rode their horses across rivers deeper than that all the time."

Trish was sick of hearing what the Indians did. "I'm not an Apache." Her dad had written a term paper on the Apache when he was in college at the University of Texas, and he never got tired of talking about it.

"True. And if you were an Indian around here, you wouldn't have been Apache either. They lived in the Southwest. You'd be Sioux or Crow, most likely."

"Don't tell me you wrote a paper about them, too."

"No. But I definitely need to read up on them more."

Perry said, "Your ride across was super bad, Trish."

Trish put her torso and head across Goldie's neck and hugged her lightly. The horse was still quivering. "I'm sorry, girl."

"Now, isn't this better than being in school this week?" Her dad actually looked like he was having the time of his life.

"Tell me when the fun part starts." She clucked to Goldie and let her trot off some of the adrenaline.

She spotted a trail ahead and merged onto it, then let her dad and Perry pass again. Notwithstanding the sheer terror of the creek-crossing, this trip was a snore. Now she'd get to stare at Duke's butt for another few miles. How exciting.

If Brandon didn't come, how was she going to survive two more whole days of this? The only thing worse would be if they actually got an elk. Besides being gross and sad, they were miles and miles from the truck. That's why they'd brought an extra horse even though her mom hadn't come. One of the horses would have the job of carrying the carcass out for half a day before they hauled it down the mountain to be processed. And then? Elk steaks. Elk burgers. Elk sausage. Elk jerky. Chicken-fried elk cubes. Her dad would be in heaven. If Patrick could make them drink elk milkshakes, he would. Every last scrap of meat would be used, no matter how sick they got of it.

She *really* hoped they didn't get an elk.

Which of course is when her dad raised his hand and closed his fist, their agreed speechless signal if he saw big game.

CHAPTER FOURTEEN: FREEZE

Walker Prairie, Bighorn National Forest, Wyoming
September 19, 1976, 5:00 p.m.

Patrick

Hunting with kids is like herding feral cats, Patrick thought. Not for the first time, his irritation with Susanne flared. *She should have come with us.* He'd seen a decent-sized bull elk with what looked like seven cow elk with him, just up the side of the hill in front of them. The animals were in a clearing near a tree line. But they wouldn't be there long. Patrick had shooed the kids off their horses, and they'd tied their mounts to trees. Patrick grabbed the bow and quiver. They weren't in position to line up a shot yet. They had to hike closer. Much closer.

He motioned the kids to follow him. Sighting one last time through the binoculars, he struck off uphill through the forest. The pine needles made for slippery going, especially with the bow and quiver on his back throwing off his center of gravity. The kids sounded like a herd of buffalo. A branch snapped. One of them sneezed. The other said "Ow" so loudly that no self-respecting elk would remain within a hundred miles.

He turned with a finger to his lips. "Like Indians," he mouthed.

Perry nodded. Trish's lips moved, but no sound came out. Her expression left no doubt that he wouldn't like what she'd said, however. Was she talking to herself? Talking back? Or just mocking him? He tamped down another flicker of irritation. This was supposed to be fun. He was going to by-God have fun if it killed him. He felt his lips moving, and he mashed them together.

When the forest thinned, he slowed. By his reckoning, the elk should be on the far side of the next clearing. Behind him, the kids were moving at the speed of turtles. They definitely needed more-active lifestyles. Trish was playing basketball and

Perry played soccer, but the workouts just weren't like they were back when he played in his youth. He tried to be a good example to them. He ran. Lifted weights. Played adult-league sports. And, of course, they all hiked. But he was barely breathing hard, and them? They sounded like the bellows their farrier used. Patrick vowed to do better, to give them more chances to stay fit by having fun. Like this trip.

Movement ahead caught his eye. He held up his fist, then lifted the binoculars to his eyes. The bull was in range, head down as he grazed, and Patrick had a clear shot from downwind. Perfect. If the bull moved away, there were always the cows. Their archery tag was good for any elk. This was Perry's first chance to hunt under his own tag, though, so rather than take the shot himself, Patrick motioned his son forward.

He pressed his lips into Perry's hair, just above his ear. "Yours if you want it. See him?"

Perry nodded, his eyes gleaming.

Patrick lifted the bow out of its rigging, then withdrew one of the green anodized aluminum arrows. He held the arrow while Perry put his hands reverently on the bow. Then he took the arrow, and dropped it. Patrick smiled. The boy's hands were quaking worse than aspen leaves in the wind. He gave him another, and this one Perry knocked without a problem. Patrick picked up the discarded arrow from the ground.

He whispered, "Check to be sure everyone in your party is behind your line of fire and aware that you're shooting, son."

Perry raised his eyebrows at his sister. She shrugged.

"Now show me your stance."

Perry faced his body at a forty-five-degree angle to the elk with his toes pointed straight at the bull. He gripped the bow with his left hand and held it in front of him.

"Loosen your grip. Firm, but not too tight."

Perry exhaled and loosened it.

"Now, don't forget to anchor the string right by your mouth."

Perry pulled the string back. He made it to his chin. It was good enough.

Patrick nodded at him. "Fire when ready."

Perry shook his shoulders and bounced on his toes, then bent his knees. From their left came the sound of loud whoops and pounding hooves. Men. On horseback. The bull elk's head jerked up. Distracted, Perry lowered his bow.

"Take the shot, Perry. You're going to miss your chance."

Perry brought the bow back up, but it was too late. The elk crashed into the woods, followed by the cows Patrick had seen earlier. A keen disappointment cut through Patrick. Two horses burst out of the trees.

Their riders were yelling. "Yah. Yah."

Even over the noise, Patrick could hear the men laughing. He was steamed. More than steamed. "Hey," he shouted. He ran into the clearing, waving his arms over his head.

They saw him and swung around toward him, then stopped. He recognized them. They were the jerks who had demanded Patrick give up his campsite to them. The burly guy with the salt-and-pepper hair and the thinner, white-headed one. But hadn't there been three of them? Anger clouded his vision.

The big man who had taken charge last night took charge again. He guffawed. "It's big bad daddy-o and his wittle bitty boy."

Patrick shook his head to clear his vision. He was so mad he'd forgotten about the kids for a second. Perry was standing in clear view of the men. He scanned for Trish. She was out of sight. Good. He hoped she'd stay hidden. What he had to say might really make these guys angry, but it had to be said. They'd just broken several unwritten tenets of the hunters' code and some wildlife laws to boot.

"You just chased off a herd of elk right as my boy was taking a shot."

"Sorry." The big guy smirked. "Didn't see you."

His buddy laughed.

"You'd be in serious trouble if a game warden had seen you harassing the elk, too."

The white-haired man said, "I don't see any game wardens, do you?"

The big guy was picking his teeth with the tip of a sheath knife. "Nope. Not a one."

As soon as he got back to Buffalo, Patrick would report the incident to Alan Turner with Game and Fish. Not that it would do any good, but it was the right thing. Now, there was nothing else to say. Patrick turned and picked up the bow and the two arrows. He walked down the hill away from the men, Perry close by his side.

The big guy yelled, "My boy is sweet on your daughter, Doctor Dad. Hey, sweetness, you think we can't see you hiding behind that tree? You aren't shaped like a flagpole. Hell, I think we're all sweet on your girl. Unless that's your wife?"

Patrick went from angry to a fearful rage in zero point two seconds. He wheeled. "Leave my daughter alone."

The two men laughed in his face.

The big guy said, "Geez, Doctor Flint. We didn't know you were so sensitive. I guess you're protective of your own womenfolk, then."

Patrick had no idea what the man meant. He

only knew that he wanted his kids as far away from these jerks as he could get them. Who would act this way? They had to be drunk. Or high. Trish came out of the trees and stood by him and Perry. Patrick gave their shoulders gentle pushes, herding them in front of him and blocking them from view.

He glanced back as the hoofbeats restarted, in time to see them leaving the clearing. The big guy waved to him with his middle finger in the air. And that's when Patrick realized the guy had called him by his name. *Do I know that asshole?*

CHAPTER FIFTEEN: RESTART

Buffalo, Wyoming
September 19, 1976, 6:00 p.m.

Susanne

Susanne put her head down on her dining room table. The wood was cold and soothing. The sheriff and deputies had *finally* finished with their questions, and she'd shown them out five minutes before. It had only taken her a hot second to identify Billy Kemecke in the photograph they showed her anyway. Between that, the Big Horn County sheriff's truck parked by Perry's old jungle gym in the backyard, the handcuffs he'd cut off and dropped by the tool bench in their backyard shed, and the orange prison jumpsuit he'd left on her bedroom floor, it had been a pretty solid ID. The only real question was why Kemecke had come to her home.

Unlucky, they'd suggested.

A mild understatement, she'd thought.

The rest of the time they'd spent fingerprinting and documenting everything she'd told them. What he'd done. What he'd said. What he'd taken. She'd started with her drive up to the mountains, and how Patrick and the kids had never checked into their campsite. How she'd come home alone after dark, where Kemecke got her. At first they hadn't seemed very interested in the part of the story about her family, but she'd pressed the issue until they agreed to put out a BOLO and called the Forest Service about it. It made her feel a little better, but not much. She'd never missed Patrick as much as she did then.

Mostly, the day was a blur. People had been in and out of her house since shortly after Ronnie phoned dispatch. Ronnie hadn't left her until the whole posse from her department had arrived, and then only to run next door and change into her Johnson County sheriff uniform and hurry back to help. It had been so busy, Susanne barely had time for her own thoughts. When she did, they weren't about Kemecke or what he'd put her through. They were about Patrick, Trish, and Perry. They were about her fear that something had happened to them. Or would happen to them. She didn't know which, just that she couldn't squash the anxiety. After a full day of this, Susanne was utterly wrung out, and nauseous from hunger.

And alone.

Not that the deputies hadn't urged her to call someone to be with her, and even offered to give her a ride to stay with a friend. They'd been quite kind about it, actually. Briefly she considered calling Vangie. But she was talked-out and peopled-out. She had just wanted food, a shower, and bed. With her husband in it.

Until law enforcement had left. After that, she got rattled.

A door shut somewhere in the house, and it was like a gun had been fired near her ears. The hallway bathroom. She jumped to her feet, gasped, and clapped her hand over her mouth. Her vision tunneled. In a split second, she was at the back door—no keys, no purse—ready to flee across the sagebrush.

"Susanne, wait, it's me."

The familiar voice stopped her. Susanne turned and saw her neighbor. She dropped her hand from the doorknob and lifted it to her heaving chest. Ronnie. The one Ferdinand adored so much that he went to her house for a second feeding every morning, which is why Ronnie had come over at all. To check on her buddy Ferdie when he hadn't shown up.

Susanne's brow furrowed. But she'd thought Ronnie had left.

Before Susanne could ask, Ronnie said, "I didn't mean to scare you. I stuck around to see if you'd let me fix you a bite to eat. And I can stay if you'd like. You've had quite a scare."

Yes, she had. But she wanted to say no. Wanted to say it badly. Only she didn't get the words out fast enough. Ronnie was already in the kitchen—refrigerator open, rooting around—before Susanne moistened her lips to speak.

So what she said was, "Thanks."

"Think nothing of it." Ronnie lifted an egg carton. "How about I make you breakfast for dinner?"

Susanne nodded.

"If I were you, I'd want a shower and jammies. I should have your food ready by the time you're done."

It was less lonely with Ronnie there, but it was also easier to feel everything she didn't want to feel. Mainly, weak. Vulnerable. Scared for Patrick and the kids. They should have been at Hunter Corral. They weren't. That meant they were missing, in her book, even if law enforcement didn't agree. The waterworks started again. She hated this. Hated it especially in front of strong, self-reliant Ronnie. But she couldn't help it.

She nodded again, and a tear slipped down her cheek.

Ronnie cleared her throat. "Don't you worry." She patted her hip. "I'm packing. If he comes back, he won't get past me."

"He won't come back."

"Damn straight. And the rest of it's just stuff. Insurance will cover your car. Even your jacket, the gun, clothes, equipment. You're safe, that's what matters."

"That's not it, either. Not really."

Ronnie looked at her with her head tilted, waiting for an explanation.

"It's Patrick and the kids. I miss them so much. And I'm worried about them." Now the tears fell freely.

Ronnie set the eggs down and came to Susanne. She'd been present when Susanne told the story earlier. Ronnie took Susanne by the shoulders and held her at arm's length. "There are countless places to camp in those mountains. It's going to be all right. Everyone will be keeping an eye out for them, and when they find them, someone will call. Okay?"

"I feel like *I* should be looking for them."

"Well, you can't do that at night. The best thing you can do for them now is rest. You've had a horrible experience. A traumatic one. Let's get you recovered and see how things look in the morning."

Susanne didn't even nod. She just walked down the hall like a zombie. In the safety of her own bathroom, she turned on the shower, stepped under a scalding hot spray, and sank to her knees, sobbing.

CHAPTER SIXTEEN: HALT

Southwest of Walker Prairie, Bighorn National Forest, Wyoming
September 19, 1976, 7:00 p.m.

Trish

Since her dad let Trish take the lead on the way back, they made it in half the time it would have taken otherwise. And they used a designated stream crossing on the trail, one where Goldie didn't have to swim. Duke had to trot to keep up, but so what. Horses liked heading home more than leaving, anyway, so Trish counted him as the lucky one. She gave Goldie a kick, asking for more speed. The sun was setting. It was getting dark, and she didn't like it.

She was still mad at her dad about the whole day, but even more, she was disgusted by the guys who had run the elk off. What kind of people did that? Jerks, that's who. And what was it with guys, anyway? Why couldn't they just be normal, like girls. Non-threatening. Non-mean. Non-whacko. Women didn't have to act all crazy and scary. She just wanted to be zipped into their tent between her dad and Perry. Maybe her dad would take them home tomorrow. Even he couldn't be weird enough to think today had gone well.

They rode the trail in silence, not even passing any other campsites along the way. It was Sunday night. Maybe people had come out for the weekend and had now gone home for jobs and school and stuff.

Ahead, she recognized the last curve in the trail before their campsite. But she also heard something she didn't expect. Men's voices. At first, she was scared, thinking about the jerky elk chasers they'd encountered. But even as those thoughts ran through her head, another one popped in. Brandon! Maybe he found the note she'd left for him. Instead of slowing down, she urged Goldie into a lope. They came around the bend and she saw their tent.

It was dusk, so it was hard to see. But not so

hard that she couldn't make out two guys with shaved heads and beards sitting on the ground cross-legged by the unlit campfire ring.

She stopped Goldie so fast the horse took a few steps backward. "Dad," she whispered. "Look."

Patrick pulled Reno up beside her. He must have still been rattled by the elk chasers, too, because he pulled his .357 Magnum from its holster. Extending it to her, he said, "You and Perry ride back a ways. I'll call you when it's safe."

"What?" Perry said, his voice too loud.

The men's heads turned toward them.

"Go," Patrick said, his voice terse.

Trish tucked the revolver into the back of her waistband. It felt heavy, unbalanced. Awkward. As much time as she'd spent practicing with this gun, her hands still shook.

"Come on," Trish said to Perry.

He didn't argue anymore, *thank God*, and the two of them retreated down the two-track path. They didn't make it far before Trish wheeled Goldie to face their camp. She wanted to stay close enough to see and hear what was going on.

Her dad approached the two men with his arm up, like he was greeting them. She hated that her dad didn't have his gun. What good was it to her? Her hands were shaking too hard to hit anything if she shot it.

"Good evening," Patrick said.

She could just barely make out his words.

"Who are they?" Perry asked.

"Don't know."

"Are they bad?"

"Don't know that either."

"What is Dad going to do?"

"Shh."

There was something familiar about these men. Trish noticed two dirt bikes parked near the trail. She wasn't sure how she'd missed them before. They were dirty, but bright. One yellow, one red. Her father and the two men started talking. Now she could only hear their voices, not their words. The larger of the two men stood up, holding something small and square. Her dad took it, examined it. He turned toward Trish and Perry and motioned them to come back to camp.

Everything was okay. At least she hoped it was.

Perry looked at her. "Should we go?"

She nodded. "We go." She rode Goldie ahead of him again. Her horse's hoofbeats reverberated in her skull. Metal shoes clanking on rock. Or was it her heartbeat?

When she reached the edge of the campsite, her dad smiled and held up what looked like a postcard. "Hey, kids. These guys got some up-close Polaroid shots of a mother moose and her baby."

The older of the two men grunted. "Way close, you know? We were hunkered down, watching for animals. She startled us, man, but she must have been in a good mood, because she didn't kill us."

The other man grinned. "She, like, posed."

"Were you hunting?" Patrick asked.

"Nah, man, we don't kill animals."

Now that she could see them better, she realized these were the guys that had ridden by the day before. They'd broken up the tense moment with the men who had tried to claim the campsite as their own. She relaxed some, until she remembered the note she'd left for Brandon. Had he come to see her? She glanced down at the rock she'd used to anchor it. The note was still there. She dismounted and led Goldie forward a few steps, bending to pick up the rock, and with it, the note, before continuing to her dad and the picture.

"Wow," she said.

It was a great picture. The mother moose's nose seemed only a few feet away from the camera. The baby was gangly and milk- to her dark-chocolate color. *He's probably only a couple of months old*, she thought, knowing that most moose calved in June.

Perry leapt off Duke without falling on his butt. She handed him the picture. After a "Whoa, cool," Perry returned it to the older guy.

They thanked them, and everyone said good

night. The men revved the engines of their dirt bikes, then disappeared back toward the main road.

"Trish, could you get us some water? I need you to boil some for tomorrow, and we're out," her dad asked. "I'll build the fire."

She thought about the bear earlier. Night was falling quickly, and she didn't want to be alone in the dark. Besides, why was he piling all the chores up on her, as usual? Perry needed to pull his weight. "Only if the squirt comes, too."

Her dad squatted at the fire ring and started building a kindling tepee. "Enough with the comments about your brother's size."

"Yeah," Perry said, but he stretched upward on his toes, giving himself another vertical inch or two.

"Take care of the horses first," Patrick reminded them, without looking up.

As they walked away, Trish said, "You're going to need more than your tiptoes."

Perry socked her in the arm. She socked him back. Then he ran ahead of her and she gave chase. He was pretty fast. For a squirt.

After they unsaddled and watered the horses and left them to graze, the siblings took their five canteens down the steep hill to the creek. Perry butt-sledded to the bottom, treating the moss and pine needles like snow. Trish shook her head. If he hurt himself, her dad would probably say she was responsible, but she couldn't control him. He was a reckless little nut.

He stood up and rubbed his butt. "Ow. A rock." The water was low this late in the season, but it was still loud, and he had to raise his voice to be heard.

She pitched her voice low. "They don't call 'em the Rocky Mountains for nothing."

Perry laughed. "Thanks, Dad."

Trish crouched beside the stream and began filling canteens beside her brother. The walk down and the act of filling the canteens wasn't bad. It was climbing back up the hill with five sloshing canteens that sucked. She took a deep breath, savoring the smells. And the taste. The air coming off the water was like moss and sunshine in her mouth.

Perry chattered on the climb back. "Do you think those men were okay?"

"Which ones? Definitely not the elk chasers."

"The ones at our camp."

Trish's breathing grew ragged as they climbed. It made it hard to answer, so she did it in gasps and spurts. "I don't know. Maybe. Dad seemed to think so. Why?" She kind of thought they'd acted like they were high, but that didn't mean they were bad, necessarily.

"I didn't like them in our camp."

"They wanted to show us pictures."

"It's not like I haven't seen a moose before."

"Yeah. Well, I think they were just being nice."

"I wonder if they stole anything."

She pictured the men as they'd departed. "I don't think so. They weren't acting weird."

"Well, I hope they don't come back. I like it when it's just us, you know?"

"Yeah." But Trish realized she missed her mom. It would be even better if she'd come. Or if Brandon or her friends were here.

Still, Perry was creeping her out a little. She didn't want the men to come back, either. They crested the top of the hill. As she saw the camp through the trees, they heard the whine of dirt bikes approaching again.

Goose bumps rose on Trish's arms.

CHAPTER SEVENTEEN: SHOCK

Southwest of Walker Prairie, Bighorn National Forest, Wyoming
September 19, 1976, 7:30 p.m.

Patrick

Two dirt bikes careened around the bend. From first glance, it was clear to Patrick that they weren't the ones with the moose picture. These riders were smaller, and the front rider's shoulder-length hair blew straight back in the breeze. Plus, the bikes were older and both were plain black. Lastly, they didn't handle their bikes as well. The long-haired kid hit the brakes too hard when he saw them. His rear wheel skidded to the side, then regained traction violently. The torque slingshotted the rider up and over the high side, head down and legs up. Somehow, he managed to get his hands down before his head hit the rocky trail.

Behind him, Trish screamed.

The back rider veered, nearly hitting a tree. Patrick sprinted toward the wreck, running through the injury possibilities—*head injury, neck injury, concussion*. By the time Patrick reached the fallen rider, though, he was on his hands and knees. *No paralysis.* He was groaning and making a weird sound. When he flopped over onto his back and stared at his scraped and bloody hands, Patrick realized he was just a kid. And that he was laughing.

"Shit, man. That was far out." The rider sat and rotated his neck. Then he grinned. "Hey, Trish."

"Brandon," Trish said. Or squealed, rather.

Brandon. The Lewis kid Trish had a crush on. Brandon shook sandy brown hair out of his eyes and stood. His ridiculous bell bottoms emphasized his long, youthful frame and nearly toppled him back to the ground. *Was that how I looked to Susanne's father? And what the hell is he doing all the way out here?*

Patrick glared at his daughter. "What a surprise."

Somehow, she didn't look surprised at all.

CHAPTER EIGHTEEN: SPLIT

Southwest of Walker Prairie, Bighorn National Forest, Wyoming
September 20, 1976, 6:00 a.m.

Perry

The first thing Perry heard the next morning was Trish's voice. She was whining. She was always whining.

"Dad, noooo."

"Up and at 'em," his dad said. "Maybe if you hadn't been up giggling with Brandon and his friend last night you wouldn't be so tired this morning."

Perry groaned. Trish had been goofy with

Brandon and the other guy—Todd, maybe?—trying so hard to be cool that it was embarrassing. She talked stupid. Like someone on *American Bandstand*, which he wasn't supposed to watch but did sometimes at his friend John's house. None of what they said on the show made any sense to him. Cool cats, his dad called people that talked in slang like that. More like goofy cats.

His dad had been furious that Brandon and Maybe-Todd showed up. The boys had stayed—Trish had insisted on hot dogs, that was cool at least—but Patrick sent them packing after hot chocolate and s'mores. He was an early-to-bed-early-to-rise kind of dad, and he didn't like the two boys throwing off the schedule.

Plops started pattering the tent ceiling. Within seconds, the plops grew closer together and louder. Rain. A lot of it.

"No way am I going out in this," Trish said. "I'm staying in the tent with my book." She held up her worn paperback.

"I've been ignoring you reading that questionable material since we left, but I'm not letting it ruin our day. Up."

Perry wondered what his dad meant by questionable material. He tried to snatch the book from Trish to see the title.

"Stop it, brat."

Perry stuck his tongue out at her. "Stop it, yourself. I just wanted to look at it."

"Well, it's not your book. Look at your own."

"I didn't bring one."

"Because you're functionally illiterate."

"Enough," his dad said.

"I am not."

"Are too."

"I said *enough*." Patrick raised his voice. "Zip it."

Perry zipped it. Trish did too, but her lower lip jutted out.

Patrick nodded, looking surprised, then satisfied. "Now, get up, get dressed, and let's get going."

Perry jumped out of his sleeping bag. Goose bumps popped up on his arms from the cold. His back hit the tent wall, and water started seeping through.

Trish's voice was a snarl. "Look what you've done. Now it's going to leak on me all day."

"That won't happen because you won't be in here," her dad said. He sounded calm again.

"I said I'd go with you on this stupid trip, but I didn't promise to freeze to death in the rain. I catboxed my own poo yesterday. I haven't washed my hair and it's *gross*. My boots are too tight. My hunting shirt itches my neck."

Perry remembered her taking the overshirt off

the day before and stuffing it into a saddlebag. She'd ridden in only her T-shirt the rest of the day. "How would you know? You barely wore it."

She looked like she wanted to spit at him, her lips puckering and then relaxing. "Anyway, that was the last time I'm wearing that shirt."

His dad closed his eyes. "Do you know how much that shirt cost?"

"No and neither do you because Mom said we weren't supposed to tell you," Trish shot back.

Perry said, "I'll go with you, Dad."

"Kiss-ass."

Patrick's lips started moving. He shook his head slightly from side to side. Perry couldn't understand what he was saying.

"Who are you talking to?" Trish said. "Mom's not here. She can't help you. You just have to do the right thing and let me stay."

Perry smiled. This was getting good. Trish and her smart mouth were cruising for a bruising, as his dad liked to say.

Patrick's lips thinned. "I thought you were scared to be by yourself when you went to get water yesterday."

"That was nighttime. This is daytime."

Perry heard her whisper, "Duh."

Patrick sighed. "Do you promise to stay in the tent?"

Trish's eyes gleamed, and she sat up on her elbows. "Do you honestly think I'm going out in that rain?"

"Promise?"

"I promise. Unless I have to pee. But then I won't go far."

Patrick pulled his revolver out from under his pillow. "Take the gun again." He pushed it toward her.

She sat up and pushed it back, shuddering like a drama queen. "No, thanks. I could never shoot anybody."

It was a super cool .357 Magnum. Perry hoped she didn't take it. Maybe his dad would let him carry it.

Patrick rolled his eyes. "Fine. Use your bear spray, then."

"I don't have it."

"Don't have it in here, or don't have it at camp?"

"In here. It's in my saddlebags."

"We'll leave it with you before we go."

A smile broke out over her face. "Thanks. You're the best dad ever."

Patrick was muttering to himself again when he opened the tent flap for Perry to walk out first. This time, though, Perry could understand the words.

"I hope I don't live to regret this."

CHAPTER NINETEEN: CRASH

BUFFALO, WYOMING
SEPTEMBER 20, 1976, 8:00 A.M.

Susanne

The slump-shouldered Johnson County deputy stared at Susanne like she was a two-headed calf.

And why not, she wondered. She'd shown up first thing on a Sunday insisting that something had happened to her family, with nothing to go on but her intuition. She squeezed her fingernails into her palms. The place was oppressive and depressing. Dark wood paneling, low light, and heavy wooden desks. It smelled musty, too. Like it had been water damaged. It was possible, she supposed, since it backed up to Clear Creek. The whole vibe made her feel claustrophobic. It reminded her of Girl Scout camp. The counselors had taken the girls to hike in an underground cave. In the damp dark, Susanne couldn't escape a feeling like something heavy was crushing her from all sides. Like she felt now.

At least Ronnie was sitting in on this meeting, before her shift. It gave Susanne a shred of credibility, even if it also made her feel like a grown woman who'd dragged along her mama to fight her battles. It didn't make her feel stronger or more capable. And after a night tied to a chair, she desperately wanted to feel stronger, more capable, and in control.

She needed to turn her inner warrior loose. But first she had to find her. Where was the girl that Patrick called "feisty"? When Patrick had to face her father after he and Susanne had eloped, her dad had said, "Son, you know you've got a tiger by the tail, don't you?" Patrick loved telling that story, just like the kids loved the ones about the plates and dishes she'd smashed when she was mad. That girl, the fighter, the tiger. She was the one Susanne needed. So far, she hadn't seen hide nor hair of her.

She glanced at Ronnie for moral support. Ronnie smiled at her.

Deputy Whosit—she couldn't remember his name—repeated what the sheriff had told her the night before. "We put out a BOLO, and we alerted the Forest Service. When did you say they're due back, again?"

"Wednesday."

"Well then, unless we hear something different, they're not missing until then." He added, in a softer tone, "I know it's hard being out of communication that long, but I've been told your husband is a capable fellow. You've got to trust him."

Her ears burned and hissed. Who was he to tell her what she had to do? "He said he'd be at Hunter Corral, and he wasn't. I do trust him. That's why I know something is wrong. And now this madman is on the loose." She refused to say Kemecke's name. Or even think it.

The deputy nodded. "You're sure he's not up at Hunter?"

Ronnie squeezed her knee. Susanne knew a *shut it* hint when she got one. She just wasn't very good at taking them.

She spat her words through clenched teeth. "I told you this already. Someone else was in our spot. I searched for our truck and trailer and it wasn't there. I talked to the person in charge of the campsite, and he said Patrick and the kids never showed up."

"Sounds like you've done everything you can, then. They'll turn up." He pushed his rolling chair back from the table and stood, indicating it was time for her to do the same. And skedaddle.

She got up, adrift on unfamiliar water, rudderless. She thanked the deputy and said goodbye to Ronnie.

"I'll check on you later," Ronnie called, just before the door swung closed behind Susanne.

Angry and distracted, Susanne pulled out of the sheriff's office parking lot in Patrick's stupid Porsche, earning her an immediate honk. What did they need with a snooty car that wouldn't hold groceries or a family of four? Nearly every driver on the road around here reacted to the Porsche. Usually negatively. It made her feel as conspicuous as white shoes in church before Memorial Day. But she had no other option. Driving it made her remember her own car was gone. And it made her think of Kemecke. Just like home did. She didn't want to go to the house desecrated by the fugitive, but what choice did she have? She could stay in a hotel, but that was awfully extravagant. Logic told her Kemecke wouldn't come back. Still, he'd violated her home. It felt dirty and unsafe.

She braked to a stop at one of the two traffic lights in town. Her face gazed back at her from the rearview mirror. Drawn. Eyes with dark circles from her sleepless night. Light brown hair frizzy and wild. It was like staring into the face of a stranger—a crazy one at that. When she found Patrick and the kids, the first thing she'd do, after hugging the breath out of them, was chew off Patrick's backside for scaring her so badly that she'd ended up looking like this. Then she was making him move her back to Texas. She didn't want any more nights than were absolutely necessary in the desecrated house. The good memories they'd built there as a family had been replaced by a faceless man and a night of terror.

A vehicle beeped behind her.

She had an impression of a bronze station wagon in her rearview mirror before she jerked her attention back to the light, letting out the clutch and pressing her accelerator at the same time.

"Hold your horses, buddy."

By the time she realized the light wasn't green, she was already halfway through the intersection in the riding-lawnmower-sized Porsche.

A truck was making a left-hand turn directly at her from her right. She ducked her head into her arm and braced herself. Metal crunched and crumpled on the passenger side. The window shattered and glass pelted her head. Her neck snapped to the right, and her body collapsed over the stick shift. She had a sensation of skidding sideways, until the

Porsche ricocheted off the curb on the far side of the road, catapulting her back in the other direction. She peeked through her fingers into oncoming traffic stopped inches away from her front bumper. Horns blared. *Did they think she ended up in their lane on purpose?*

A weathered face loomed out the driver's-side window, hat askew. "Ma'am? Are you okay, ma'am?"

She pulled her hands away from her face and studied them. They were bloody. His face seemed to retreat from her peripheral vision like he was being dragged into the sky. The inside of the car felt like a bubble, and she heard nothing but her own heavy breathing. Her view changed from bloody hands to dancing lights in a field of black, then to nothing.

CHAPTER TWENTY: SPLASH

Walker Prairie, Bighorn National Forest, Wyoming
September 20, 1976, 10:00 a.m.

Patrick

Patrick guided Reno through a thick stand of trees, hoping for a break from the rain so he could get his bearings. The bad visibility was playing tricks with his eyes. Just a few minutes ago, he could have sworn he saw someone dressed in an orange jumpsuit. No one wore that kind of getup out here to hunt. A vest. A hat. A jacket, maybe. But not head-to-toe. He thought about the escaped murderer. Surely not. He strained to get another glimpse, but whatever it had been was gone, or was never there. It was disconcerting, but he put it out of his mind. *Just an odd hunting outfit.* His mind replaced the orange flash with the face of his wife. It hurt his heart. How could he miss her so much when they'd only been apart two days? It was more than missing her, though. He had a strong feeling that he should be with her right now. That she damn well should have come up here with them, but even more than that, that his *place* was with her, right this minute.

It made it hard for him to think about hunting elk.

But there was nothing he could do about it. The trip had not gone as planned so far, to put it mildly, with Susanne back in town and the horrible weather. Trish wasn't making it any easier. What had she been thinking, inviting those older boys out to their campsite? Brandon and Todd were nice enough, but she was too young for them. For Brandon. Patrick remembered the phone call at McDonald's. Now he understood what she had been up to —calling to let Brandon know where she'd be.

He wouldn't have admitted it out loud, but he was relieved Trish had stayed in the camp today. The break from her back talk and negative attitude was refreshing. *But what if Brandon is coming back today?* He pulled Reno to a stop. The horse snorted in protest. Patrick had been too hard on his mouth.

"Sorry, boy."

That could have been the reason she insisted on staying at the campsite. And if it were the case, well, when he was Brandon's age, he'd had one thing on his mind, and one only.

Beside him, Perry jerked awake. The boy had both an amazing talent for sleep and an amazing ability to remain mounted while he did it. The first time he'd seen it happen was when their family had gone riding with the Sibleys on Piney Bottoms Ranch. Patrick had been shocked and Susanne worried. Henry had laughed it off. He told them about an old horse that had carried him home one night from a neighbor's party when he was passed out drunk. And how Henry's dad used to fall asleep riding fence, and when he'd come back he'd claim the horse did a better job of finding downed fence than he did, stopping any time he found an issue to be fixed.

"Depends on the horse and the rider," Henry had said. "But I think Duke and Perry are pretty well matched for sleep-riding."

After that, he and Susanne had worried about it less. But they couldn't keep the kid awake anyway if they tried. He was practically narcoleptic.

Perry yawned. "What's wrong, Dad?"

Patrick looked at his son. "What?"

"You stopped us, and then you made a funny noise."

"I was just reliving our morning with your sister."

Perry snorted. "Mom would have grounded her."

"That may still happen. Hey, she didn't say anything about that Brandon kid coming out again, did she?"

Perry's eyes popped. "No, sir."

"You didn't hear Brandon or Todd mention it?"

He shook his head.

"Okay. Thanks, bud." Patrick lifted a hand. Rain splashed in his palm. "I don't think this is going to let up."

"Me neither."

"And I couldn't see an elk if it walked in front of that tree to take a leak." He pointed at a large tree ten feet in front of them. "I don't think this is going to work."

"We can fish, though, can't we, Dad?"

Perry insisted on toting fishing gear everywhere they went, by car, by truck, by foot, or by horse. He had it all strapped to Duke's saddle now.

"I guess so. The West Fork of Big Goose isn't too far behind us."

Perry beamed, showing a gap between his front

upper teeth. “Cool.” He kicked Duke, but his short legs didn’t reach the horse’s “go” spot. Duke turned and shot him a look as if to say, “Is that all you’ve got?”

Patrick led out with Reno, whose hooves were thudding a melancholy forest rhythm that matched the rain. Less than an hour later, they made it back to Big Goose and crossed to its east side. Patrick had fished here last year with Henry, although they’d ridden in from a different direction, and he knew there was a two-track running upstream that would give them better access to the creek than they’d get from the west side. Ten minutes and a mile later, the rain had lessened somewhat, enough that they pulled lunch from their saddlebags. They ate under a rock overhang while the horses hunkered, hobbled, under a thick stretch of pines.

“What do you think Trish is eating for lunch?” Perry said. He had pulled his peanut butter and jelly sandwich apart and was eating each side separately, something he’d done since he was a toddler.

“I left her a sandwich.” Thinking about his fussy daughter again made Patrick uneasy. His relief at getting away from her complaining had given way to something else. Guilt. He should have insisted she come, griping or not. It was a family vacation. He and Perry could have laughed about her bad attitude later. She’d have good memories to share someday, even if she protested now. Or she would have. Reading in a tent wasn't a memory. She could do that anywhere.

Perry tossed a crust toward a rock. Within seconds, a chipmunk hopped onto the rock near it. It grabbed the crust, then whipped its tail. It stood tall, feasting on the bread crust.

"It looks like a little bear. Its body, I mean." Perry reached a hand toward it, and it scampered out of sight into the rocks. Perry jumped up, shaking off his slicker. "Okay, I'm ready to fish."

"I have to water a tree."

"What?"

"You know. Answer the call of nature?"

"You've got to pee."

Patrick made a pistol with his finger. He pointed at Perry and bent his thumb like he was cocking a gun. "Bingo. I'll meet you by the creek."

Perry took off, and Patrick walked farther up the two-track, searching for a tree to pee on like a dog in a field of fire hydrants. He stepped off the trail, pushed his slicker up, and unzipped. There was nothing like going outside in the depths of the wilderness. It was freeing. Made a man feel manly. He pressed a palm on the blistered, crunchy bark and immediately into sticky sap. When he was done, he wiped the sap from his hand onto the belly of his shirt and turned back to the trail, with his slicker bunched up, one hand on his not-yet zipped fly, and the other about to tuck himself back in his pants.

A woman was watching him with a surprised but—unfortunately—amused look on her face—what he could see of it under a rain hat and with her hair plastered to her cheeks. The blood drained from his face.

"Barn door's open," she said.

He tucked and zipped so fast he nearly did damage. "Oh God. Oh, sorry. Good afternoon." He was yammering like an idiot. As if he wasn't already embarrassed enough.

She nodded and resumed her walk downstream. He wasn't sure, but he thought he heard her laughing. Not the reaction a man hopes for when he is caught, literally, with his pants down. Especially not when the hiker was the only woman ever to have seen him that way outside of his mother, his wife, and the nurse who assisted on his vasectomy after Perry was born. His ego deflated, he hurried to the creek, feeling chagrined. What was a female hiker doing alone in elk country during hunting season anyway? So much for wilderness. They might as well have been in downtown Denver.

The blood returned to his cheeks slowly as he recovered his equilibrium. For the next few hours, he and Perry fished in companionable silence, occasionally catching and releasing small rainbow and brown trout. The rain continued, but it was sparse, and there was no lightning. They picked their way carefully out into the middle of the stream, moving from rock to rock. In the spring, the level and speed of the water would have made it impossible.

Patrick gazed up at the rock cliffs overlooking them from both sides of the water, their stone faces striking over dark green full-skirted dresses of pines, whose hems ended at the midnight blue of the tumbling water. The cliffs were like a woman and her reflection in a slightly warped mirror. Trish would have loved this, albeit from the bank with her book. Susanne might have even liked it.

Perry hollered from about ten yards downstream. His rod was bent near to ninety degrees.

"Bring it in, buddy. Looking good." Patrick reeled in his line as fast as he could, then hopped along a trail of rocks to go help Perry. "You've got it. It's a big one."

The fish fought, zigging and zagging across the creek. Perry fought, too, his tongue out over his upper lip. Patrick was afraid he was going to trip and bite the thing off. Finally, the fish tired, which was a good thing, because Perry was wearing down almost as fast. His son rotated the reel a few last times, and Patrick scooped the fish into a net from their bag.

"I got it." Perry's voice squeaked, which had been happening a lot lately. Puberty was almost upon him. Then he pumped his fist. "I *got* it."

Patrick wished he had a camera to catch the pride on the boy's face. It was a beautiful fish. "Good job, son." He ruffled Perry's flattop with his free hand.

Perry ducked away from the hair-rustling. "How big do you think it is?"

Patrick held it up to his hand. It extended from the base of his palm, two inches past the tip of his middle finger. "Ten inches or more. A keeper."

A bright light flashed in the sky. Patrick got a sharp whiff of something burning, like plastic, at the same time that a powerful jolt rocked his body and rattled his teeth. Perry screamed and dropped his fishing pole. Patrick looked down and saw the fish and net rush downstream. Thunder shook him to his core. Lightning. They had to get out of the stream, where they were completely exposed electrical superconductors. Then something sharp bit into his arm, then his face, then his shoulder. Hail.

He grabbed his son by the arm and pulled him toward the bank, stepping off the boulders and into the cold water. Running was all but impossible in the rocky stream, but he moved them as fast as he could. Perry tripped and splashed. Patrick bore down and dragged him, with Susanne's face flashing in his mind.

When they reached dry—drier—ground, Perry was sobbing. Hail as big as marbles was pelting them now. Patrick hauled him out of the water and onto the bank, where the kid flopped like the fish that had been in the net only moments before. Another bolt lit up the sky, and Patrick threw himself over Perry. Again, the current rattled his teeth. Maybe a little less than when they were in the water, but it was still jarring, and terrifying. He immediately picked Perry up and set him on his feet.

"We've got to keep moving and find some rocks to get under."

"K-k-kay."

They ran hand in hand as Patrick scanned the rock face in front of them. They were far upstream from where they'd lunched, past where he'd seen the hiker. The horses were nowhere in sight. They'd probably headed for camp as fast as their hobbled legs would carry them.

Ahead, he saw a low overhang. It wasn't big, but it would do.

"There." He pushed Perry under the rock ahead of him, then stuffed his body partway in after him. The space was cramped. Cave-like.

"What happened?" Perry said.

"Don't you know what that was?"

"Lightning. But why did it smell so bad?"

"That's called ozone." Another peal of thunder cracked.

"I thought we were going to die."

Patrick knew well that it could happen. When he was a resident in Minneapolis, he had been working in the ER when a swimmer had been brought in after being struck. He had died. He and Perry had been having so much fun, he hadn't wanted it to end. In hindsight, fishing in the rain was a higher-risk activity than he'd thought. It was probably too much to ask that Perry not tell his mom. But, oh, how he wanted to avoid *that* conversation. "We should let the worst of it pass before we leave."

"Did it hit us?"

"No. We wouldn't be here now if it had. I think it hit a tree or something pretty close to us, though."

"It hurt."

"Yes, it did."

Patrick slipped an arm around his son. The plastic of their slickers rubbed together with swishy noises. They huddled, barely talking. For the first few minutes, Patrick ran through scenarios. Walking back. Staying warm. Keeping out of the hail and lightning. Navigating through the darkness, if it came to that. His adrenaline ebbed, and he tried to free his mind of everything but gratitude, and he prayed, praising God that they survived the close call.

When Patrick hadn't heard any thunder or seen any flashes in the last five minutes, he said, "If we don't want to be walking all the way back to camp, we need to go after those horses. You ready?"

"Is it safe?"

"I think it's moved past us. We'll stay in the tall trees. It's going to strike them before us, if there's any more lightning."

Perry's face looked young and scared, but he screwed his lip and sat taller. "Okay."

Patrick squeezed his shoulder, then bent over and backed out of their hidey-hole. He reached in to help Perry out. Together they slogged along the road, staying under the canopy of trees along the edge. Perry was shivering. They stopped to pick up their tackle box.

"My rod is gone."

"Yes, it is. And the net. And your great fish. Where's your hat?"

Rain was tracing a path down Perry's face, freckle to freckle. He'd been wearing a weatherproof cowboy hat when they were fishing. His head was bare now, and the head loses body heat faster than any other part of the body.

"I don't know."

Patrick took his own off and plopped it on his

son's head. It wobbled, so he pulled the chin strap tight. It was better than nothing. If only he had something thick and dry to wrap him in. Wet hair, wet feet, wet pants. Even his shirt was partially wet under his slicker, from falling in the water. The best Patrick could do was keep them moving fast. That would keep Perry's core warm. They took off at a brisk pace, alongside the muddy prints of their horses' hooves. The hat and hard walking seemed to help Perry, and he didn't speak again for fifteen minutes.

When they came to the uphill turn leaving the prairie, Patrick was relieved to see the hoofprints of the horses heading toward camp. Perry sat down.

"What's wrong?"

"My feet hurt. And my ankle and shoulder a little, from yesterday when I fell off Duke. But mostly my feet."

Patrick felt terrible. Perry had shaken off the injuries and never mentioned them again, so he hadn't asked. The foot issue was new, though. "I'm sorry, bud. Your socks got wet. It's really uncomfortable, I know."

"I didn't wear socks."

"What?"

"I forgot to pack them."

The kid probably had major blisters. He could put his own socks on the boy. But if he took off Perry's boots, he'd have a heck of a time getting them back on raw and ragged feet. Patrick clenched his fists. He'd asked Susanne to get them packed while he worked all night in the ER. A youngster can't be trusted to ensure his own safety, and gear is key to safety.

"I'll carry you on my back." He crouched down, and Perry stood, wincing, and climbed on. He couldn't remember the last time he'd given him a piggyback ride, but whenever it was, the boy had been much smaller and lighter. His legs hung past Patrick's knees now. "Ready?"

"Ready." He felt Perry wipe his eyes, then clutch onto him.

The trudge up the hill was slow and hard, with lots of rest stops. The tackle box cut into Patrick's hand and bounced against his hip. He struggled not to drop it, changing hands frequently. Halfway up, an emotion welled inside him. At first he thought it was frustration over the difficulty of their situation and the disappointing trip. But then he recognized it as a bittersweet gratitude. Almost a longing. Would he ever carry Perry on his back again? He'd blink and the boy would grow out of his undersized preteen body and into muscles and manhood. *He's not heavy, he's my son.*

With this new mindset, he savored every painful step, chanting it to himself.

Perry said, "Hey, Dad?"

"Yep?"

"Those guys at our camp last night were acting funny."

"Brandon and Todd?"

"No. The guys with the picture."

Patrick stopped to catch his breath. "What do you mean?"

"Like, I don't know. Goofy."

Patrick nodded. He'd noticed it, too. "I've seen that at the hospital a few times before. I think they'd been doing drugs."

Perry drew in a quick breath. "Really?"

"I'm not sure, but that's my guess." Patrick started walking again.

"Drugs can kill you. What if they overdosed up here?"

"They'd die."

"Oh." Perry stopped talking, seeming to be digesting the conversation.

Patrick was relieved. It was hard to talk, lug Perry, and breathe at the same time. When they got to the top of the hill, he heard the clomping of hooves. Hope flared in his chest.

A woman's voice called, "Horses got loose." The female hiker he'd embarrassed himself in front of earlier appeared around the corner leading their horses, neither of whom looked delighted.

"Th-th-thank you," he managed to stutter.

"I recognized the big black one from when I saw you earlier. Thought you might like to have them back."

Patrick set Perry down.

Perry limped over to Duke. "Ow."

"We had some lightning strikes near us, and they took off. Obviously they weren't worried about us." He took Duke's lead rope, since he'd removed the bridles and looped them on the saddle horns before he'd turned the horse out in hobbles. "Let's get you onboard and off those feet, son." He bridled the horse and gave Perry a leg up.

The boy's eyes were bloodshot and swollen from crying. He was trying to keep his faced turned away so the woman wouldn't see it, though. Patrick wanted to ruffle the kid's hair again, but that would make things worse.

Patrick turned to her for Reno's lead. "Thanks, again. You really saved us. I wish we could show our appreciation more adequately."

She winked. "You've shown me all the appreciation you need to."

Patrick felt heat rush to his cheeks as he put Reno's bridle on. He turned his big horse so he could mount from the uphill side. Once he was in the saddle, he asked, "Can we do anything for you?

I'm sure you're set back from your hiking destination quite a bit, bringing our horses back to us."

"No, I'm good. I'll camp wherever I get to. I'm hiking down to Sheridan, but I'm taking my time."

"Watch out for hunters."

She pointed to her orange slicker underneath an enormous camo backpack, and he noticed she was also wearing orange rain pants. Had he missed that earlier? He had been a bit preoccupied with his own exposed situation. "Always."

He saluted her, and she waved, smiling.

The horses were as antsy as he and Perry to get back to camp. Normally, Patrick wouldn't let them return faster than they went out. It was a really bad habit, almost impossible to break. But tonight was an exception. He needed light to doctor his son's feet. Plus, he was anxious to check on Trish. He wanted to know whether she'd had a visit from a horny teenage boy while they were gone.

"How do you feel about letting them trot back?" he asked Perry.

"Good." Perry immediately gripped the saddle horn. The boy didn't like horses a whole lot more than his mother did, but at least he saw them as a means to a desirable end.

"Keep your weight off your stirrups. Posting would really hurt your feet right now. It's okay to be floppy for a while. I won't tell your sister." Patrick winked.

Perry gave him a watery smile. "Okay."

Patrick clucked to Reno. The big beast didn't need any more urging than that. He surged forward, almost floating over the ground. Patrick's slicker fanned out behind them. It wasn't far—about two miles—and with the horses eating up the ground at their energy-saving trot, they made it quickly back to their camp.

Or at least they made it back to where their camp should have been.

CHAPTER TWENTY-ONE: RELEASE

Buffalo, Wyoming
September 20, 1976, 2:00 p.m.

Susanne

"I'm fine," Susanne said, again. Being trapped in the ER was making her stir crazy. The exam rooms were like the inside of coffins, tiny monochrome boxes. *How ironic to feel trapped in death in the very place they are trying to keep people alive.* Outside the room, something rolled by with a clanking wheel. Remembering her claustrophobia that morning at the sheriff's office, she thought, *Maybe after a night of captivity I just need to feel free*. She pushed her long hair out of her face. "I've been here for hours."

Wes was leaning against a six-foot countertop covered in stainless steel cannisters and tools of the medical trade—a stethoscope, a blood pressure cuff, a reflex hammer, and a glass jar of tongue depressors—with a sink at one end. He clucked. "Dr. John and Kim could never look Patrick in the eye again if they didn't make double-dog sure."

Susanne liked the X-ray tech. He kept her mostly serious husband more laid back on the job. She pulled the sides of her front-opening hospital gown together so the edges overlapped. "They've done every test known to man. And then some. It's overkill." She'd heard plenty about the expense of unnecessary tests from Patrick a million times.

Wes crossed his arms and adjusted himself into a wide-legged stance. "The Porsche is a pancake. Your face and chest are black and blue. You look like you were shot with salt pellets." He pointed at her cheeks. "And you hit your head and lost consciousness."

"I just fainted."

"Right." Then he smiled. "But despite all that, I have it on good authority you're going to be released into capable hands soon."

She bolted forward, remembering just in time to hold on to the edges of her gown. "Patrick?"

Wes shook his head. His eyes were kind and gentle. "Henry and Vangie."

Susanne slumped back. "How did they find out I'm here?"

"I called them a few hours ago. They're on their way up as soon as the paperwork to jailbreak you is finished."

Tears stung her eyes. She was grateful for friends. Truly she was. But she needed her husband. The blows just kept coming, and he'd always been the one in her corner. Now he was missing—no matter what the deputies called it—and she felt so alone. She choked out the right words, though, because that's what she was raised to do. "Thank you."

Wes patted her shoulder. "You need to take it easy, Mrs. Doc. Stress is a dangerous thing. If you hadn't been so exhausted from your ordeal, I'm sure you wouldn't have run that light."

Susanne had told her story repeatedly. No one believed her. Her voice came out strident. "I didn't run it. Someone behind me honked for me to go. I reacted out of instinct."

He picked imaginary lint from his scrubs. "The police can't find any witnesses that agree with how you remember things. They've said you were alone at the light."

She sucked in a deep breath. That's what the

officers had told her, too, but it didn't change things. "He might have driven off, but he was there."

"He?"

She shrugged. "Playing the percentages in these parts." Maybe the men didn't outnumber the women two to one in Wyoming, but it felt like it.

Obviously whoever it was had fled the scene of the accident, and wasn't the accident itself plenty to distract witnesses from his departure? But who was the mysterious driver? And why had he honked? She thought as hard as her aching head would let her. He could have mistaken the light for green. Maybe he drove away out of fear. He'd caused a serious accident. An expensive one. A Porsche was totaled. A horn once honked isn't a mistake you can undo. But with all that had happened—Kemecke, the wreck—she couldn't help feeling paranoid. Had the driver done it to her on purpose?

A flash of bronze station wagon in a rearview mirror filled her mind, and chills crept up her arms. She'd recalled the car behind her honking, but until that moment, she hadn't remembered what it looked like. Or if she'd really seen it, even when she'd given her statement to the police. Had it really been a look-alike for her own vehicle? Or had it *been* her car? *Oh my God. It could have been Kemecke.* She bunched the gown at her chest in her hand. *Surely not. He'd be heading for the border.*

The cops. She should tell them. But what difference would it make? The witnesses had said there was no car, and law enforcement wasn't going to believe her now just because the car she supposedly saw was her own. They'd think she was just obsessed with Kemecke after what had happened at her house. She closed her eyes, shook her head.

Wes put his hand on her foot. He shook it lightly. "Susanne, are you okay?"

Her eyes flew open. But the entrance of her friends cut the exchange short.

"Oh my gosh, look at you." Vangie hurried through the door and straight to the bed, the scent of sun and hay clinging to her. She kissed Susanne's cheek.

Henry stood behind her, looking like Kareem Abdul-Jabbar to her Dorothy Hamill. Wes greeted them and said his goodbyes at the same time, although he gave Susanne a significant look before he left.

"Call me if you need me," he said from the doorway, then disappeared.

"Thank you." Susanne smiled at Vangie, but it was strained. "Thank you for coming. If I had a vehicle, I could have driven myself home, but mine was stolen last night, and, well, Patrick's is toast." The officers had told her earlier that it had been towed to a repair shop, but that it was likely totaled.

"We heard. You poor thing. Are you okay?" Vangie squeezed her hand.

"Much better than I look."

"Good. Because you look pretty rough," Henry said.

The three of them laughed.

"Just let me get dressed, and we can go." Susanne swung her legs over the bed, holding her gown closed, then groaned. "My clothes. I don't think they're wearable."

Vangie brandished a bag. "Wes told me. I brought you something. Now, shoo, Henry, and let her get dressed."

Henry mimed cracking a whip. "Your wish is my command, Mrs. Sibley."

Vangie rolled her eyes.

After he left, Susanne said, "Thank you. So much. Really."

Vangie put a sweat suit, T-shirt, and undergarments on the bed. "It's nothing. I can't wear any of this for a long time anyway." She patted her flat belly.

Susanne stopped with one foot into the panties. She'd forgotten to ask her about the baby, and she was a terrible friend. "Are you still spotting?"

"Nope. All is well. I have a good feeling about this baby."

"I'm so glad."

Susanne finished dressing while Vangie talked about her shopping trip to Billings. Fifteen minutes later, Susanne and the two Sibleys were on the road for the short ride to the Flint home. Ferdinand met the truck at the end of the driveway and danced around it all the way up the hill. Susanne had hardly had time to tell them the bare bones of the stories about her car wreck and her visit from Kemecke. Enough that they were appropriately alarmed, but she left out her strange feeling that he had caused the wreck. She was beginning to doubt herself about it.

Henry insisted on doing a walk-through of the house before Susanne could enter. Susanne filled Vangie in on the rest of the details while they waited outside. How she'd gone to the sheriff's department to get help finding Patrick and the kids. How she'd visited Hunter Corral and discovered her family had never shown up at their campsite. Despite the horror of all she'd shared so far, it wasn't until she got to this part of her tale that her tears started to fall.

Vangie wrapped an arm around her shoulders. "They'll be okay, sweetie." The words sounded comforting in her soft Tennessee drawl.

Susanne sagged against her. "I'm just so tired, and I can't get it out of my head that I need to go find them."

Henry and Ferdinand joined them in the driveway. "All clear."

Ferdinand pushed up against Susanne's leg. She reached down and massaged his floppy ears. "Thank you."

Vangie released her and turned to her husband. "Henry, Susanne wants to go up into the mountains to look for Patrick and the kids later. They weren't at their campsite last night. Could you give her a ride? She's stranded."

Henry pursed his lips, then nodded. "That should work."

"Really?" Susanne pressed her hand to her throat. "But it could take hours."

Henry widened his eyes at his wife. She nodded.

"No problem. I should be done with our hay deliveries by then," he said. "How about five o'clock tonight or so?"

"That would give you time to sleep some first," Vangie added, giving Susanne a stern look.

"If I knew I was going to look for my family afterward, I could sleep. I don't know if I could otherwise."

"Well then, rest easy. Henry's got you covered," Vangie said.

"Thank you." Susanne felt dangerously close to

crying. She was tired of crying, so blinked the tears back. "I'll see you later."

The Sibleys got in their truck and drove away.

Susanne shielded her eyes and watched the dirt plume that followed them. She felt a tiny flicker of hope for the first time in two days. When the plumes had disappeared, she went into the house with her dog and locked the door. Sleep was going to feel so, so good.

But then she remembered the bronze station wagon. Her mouth went dry. Doubt or not, the memory loomed large, especially now that she was alone in her violated house. Kemecke. Had he been following her? Had he tried to force her into a wreck? *And would he be back?*

All her thoughts of sleep evaporated.

CHAPTER TWENTY-TWO: REVERSE

Walker Prairie, Bighorn National Forest, Wyoming
September 20, 1976, 4:00 p.m.

Perry

Perry had never seen his dad this upset. When they'd ridden up on the camp, it was a mess. Their tent had caved in, and there were food and clothes and sleeping stuff scattered all over the place. His dad hadn't said a word, but he got off Reno and paced around, picking things up, and putting them back down. When he found a piece of note paper, he read it, mouthed cusswords, and wadded it up. Then he changed his mind, flattening it against his pant leg and putting it in his pocket.

It all made Perry's stomach hurt.

"Trish?" his dad shouted.

There was no answer.

He shouted again. And again and again. His voice echoed back to them, but Trish's didn't.

That was when Perry looked for the other horses. "Dad, Goldie and Cindy aren't here either."

His dad didn't respond. He was crouched, examining the ground.

"Dad?"

Patrick glanced up. "I heard you, son. Yes, I know."

"Do you think it was another bear?" Perry asked.

Patrick stood. He rubbed his face, and Perry was startled to see his father's hands shaking. "No."

"What did this, then?"

"People, I think. Hard to be sure."

"Like, a prank?"

Patrick leaned over and started scavenging MREs. "I hope so."

"Where's Trish? Do you think she's hurt?"

"I don't know, son. Let me concentrate. I need to get us some supplies."

Perry's stomachache spread until it was hard to draw in a breath. "Supplies for what?"

"We have to go find her."

"You don't think she'll come back?" His voice cracked and squeaked. He hated it when it squeaked. "Maybe she just got scared and ran off to hide and wait for us."

Patrick stuffed MREs into his saddlebag. Then he pawed through the sodden mass of clothing options. He came up with a pair of Trish's wool socks, her slicker, her winter jacket, and three extra sweaters. They dripped water in steady plop-plop-plops. "You have your gloves and wool cap? And your heavy coat?"

"In my saddlebags." Why hadn't his dad answered him about Trish?

Patrick added the wet clothes to Reno's packs. He patted the bows, quiver, sheath knife, the pocketknife Wes had given him, and his holstered revolver, then rummaged in the rest of the saddlebags, mouthing out his finds. Extra canteens. A compass. The first aid kit. Ammunition. Matches. A flashlight. Rope.

Finally, he spoke to Perry, pointing at hoofprints on the tent. "Look at that."

"Did our horses do that?"

"Can't say for sure. I don't think so." He turned to face Perry, hands on his hips. "Do you need to go to the bathroom? We're going to move out fast."

Perry hopped off Duke. His dad stepped over

and caught him before he butt-planted. Then Perry walked a few feet away. He'd just water a tree, like his dad. "Where are we going?"

"We're going to follow any trail we can find. Footprints. Hoofprints." He frowned. "That's assuming the horses didn't just spook and take off."

Perry wanted to cry, but only babies cried. Instead, he fastened his pants and returned to his dad, his shoulders back. "I don't think they got loose. The tack and saddles are gone, too."

Patrick's stony face softened. "So they are. Good point, son. So let's start by me circling the campsite to see if we can figure out which direction they went. You hold Reno. I don't want to add any more prints to this mess than I have to."

Patrick helped Perry back onto Duke, then handed him Reno's lead and started slopping around the campsite. Perry almost hollered out, "Like an Indian," but something made him stop.

He kept the horses still but looked around as best he could. The whole area was muddy and trashy, and now that his dad had pointed out the hoofprints on the tent, Perry could see the edge of the camp was chewed up with them. It was dotted with manure piles, too. More prints and piles than there'd be from just Goldie and Cindy. He tried to figure out how long the piles had been there. Because of the rain, it was hard to tell. He and his dad had left camp early. Right after breakfast. And now it was dinnertime. That was bad, because Trish could be a long way away if she'd left then, too. But the manure smelled fresh to him. Maybe they hadn't left long ago, which would be better, so he and his dad could catch up.

Perry knew Trish's friends wouldn't come up here on horseback, but maybe Brandon would. She acted dumb enough around him—she could have just gone with him. "Maybe she went somewhere with Brandon."

Patrick froze. He touched his pocket. "You said they didn't talk about plans."

"They didn't. I didn't hear them if they did, anyway. But Trish told me that Brandon ditches school sometimes."

Patrick frowned, nodding, then went back to tracking. Reno nickered at him. Perry wrapped the lead around Duke's saddle horn, in case Reno decided to try to catch up with his dad. He clenched the line, and his knuckles whitened. Trish was mean to him half the time. She was always running off and leaving him and calling him stupid names. Just last week he'd asked her to let him come when she was going into town for ice cream with Brandon and his friends, and she'd said, "This isn't for babies, shrimp." He'd been so embarrassed that he'd balled his fists, wanting to punch her. And he would have, if they'd been at home instead of the parking lot at school. But he wasn't mad at her anymore. When she was being half-decent, he liked her, sort of. His eyes burned. He didn't want anything to happen to her.

Duke sighed and shifted. His head drooped, like he was falling asleep, but Perry saw the old guy's ears swiveling, following every noise, no matter how tiny, and he wasn't fooled by the horse. Duke was on alert, he was just conserving energy, as his dad liked to call it. He must be worried about Trish, too.

Patrick's pace slowed. "Horses moved off in this direction. I'm not sure how many." He followed something Perry couldn't see. Then Patrick's shoulders slumped. "Headed back toward Ranger Creek."

"That's good, right? That you can see which way she went."

"Yeah." Patrick said, but he didn't meet Perry's eyes. "We'll be headed toward the truck, so I'll just grab the keys." He hurried back over to the piles of their gear and supplies. He dug through them, over and over. Then he repeated the process, carefully going through every item and putting them in a pile. After three times through their gear and poring over the campsite, he stood. His face was white as a ghost.

"What's wrong, Dad?"

"I can't find the keys."

"Maybe Trish took them."

Patrick nodded. "Probably so. We've got to get going. Only a few hours of daylight left." He returned to Reno and remounted. "Follow me."

"Aren't we going to take all our stuff?" Perry asked. They couldn't just leave a mess like this in the mountains. Woodsy Owl's words ran through his head. *Give a hoot. Don't pollute.* He felt dumb for thinking of it. Woodsy was for little kids. Still, his dad had taught them to leave things like they found them, or a little better.

"We'll come back. After we find your sister."

Perry shivered. Something about his dad's voice was off, way off, and suddenly Perry knew what it was. His dad was scared.

So was Perry.

CHAPTER TWENTY-THREE: SWERVE

BUFFALO, WYOMING
SEPTEMBER 20, 1976, 5:00 P.M.

Susanne

A loud ringing noise startled Susanne. She gasped and reached for the bowie knife she'd stashed under the pillow. Then she heard the noise again. *Brrrrrrng*. She laughed in a massive release of tension. It was just the phone. Which meant she'd fallen asleep, despite her fears about Kemecke. But only after she'd checked all the locks, pushed the chest of drawers against the bedroom door, and retrieved the bowie knife Patrick kept in a sheath between the mattress and box springs. It was the only weapon Kemecke hadn't found and taken with him. Susanne had lay down on top of the covers, with her clothes and shoes on, ready for anything. Except the telephone, apparently. *Brrrrrrng*.

She snatched it up. "Hello?"

For a split second, she was optimistic. It could be Patrick calling from a pay phone at a gas station in Buffalo or at South Fork Lodge up in the mountains to let her know he was on his way home. Or it could be her mother or sister. She needed to tell them about the last forty-eight hours. And have a good cry.

It was none of them.

"Susanne? It's Henry."

She was disappointed. Still, hearing from Henry was good. Maybe he was leaving to pick her up. She checked the time. Five o'clock. He should have already been here. "Hi, Henry. Are you running late?"

There was the briefest of pauses, the kind that precedes the bad news someone is reluctant to announce. "About that."

"What?"

"I've been held up, and I can't make it."

Susanne leaned back. Her head thumped hard against the wall. "Okay." She almost grilled him about what he found more important than the safety of her husband and kids. But she didn't. She knew he didn't understand her fears. It seemed as if no one did.

"But I have two pieces of good news."

Downstairs, she heard knocking on the front door, then her doorbell rang immediately. "Oh God."

"What is it?"

"The doorbell."

"Well, that could be my first piece of good news. I found a replacement. Someone to take you up to see Patrick and the kids. She should be there about now."

"Who?"

"Ronnie."

Susanne almost growled. She couldn't get away from her uber-capable neighbor. But that explained why Ferdinand wasn't barking. Since he dined with Ronnie every day, she'd expect the big mutt to treat her like a long-lost member of the family. Sure enough, she heard him whining and pawing at the door.

"Hold on a second." She put the phone down and scooted the dresser back into place. Then she picked the phone back up. "I have to go answer the door."

"Okay, don't keep her waiting, but don't hang

up on me either. I have one more piece of good news."

"Be right back."

Bowie knife in hand just in case, Susanne ran down the stairs and looked through the peephole. She saw Ronnie's blonde braids. She put the knife behind her back and threw open the front door. Ferdinand pushed past her to his buddy. He stood on his hind legs and planted his feet on her shoulders. Ronnie went down on her rump, landing on a railroad tie that Susanne used as a border to her landscaping. Half the year, the yard was covered in snow. But for the three months the flowers bloomed in Wyoming, they were spectacular. Especially the Mississippi irises that the women in the family raised from bulbs and passed along to each other from her grandmother's growing-up years there. How could they take to this climate when it was so hard for her to do the same?

Ronnie was laughing as Ferdinand slathered her face with kisses. "I missed you, too, boy."

Susanne said, "I'm on the phone with Henry."

Ronnie didn't get up from the railroad tie. She scratched behind Ferdinand's ears. Susanne felt a stab of jealousy. Ronnie knew his favorite scratching spots, too.

She said, "Take your time."

Susanne sprinted back up the stairs. In her bedroom, she put the knife on the bedside table and picked up the phone. She said, "I'm here," out of breath. "What's the other news?"

"Vangie told me that you'd expected Patrick to be camping up at Hunter Corral."

"Yes. He wasn't there two nights ago."

"I know. I saw him in Sheridan on his way up to Walker Prairie on Saturday. I told him about my favorite area for camping when I go elk hunting. He was headed there."

Susanne sat down and put her head in her lap to ease the sudden rush of blood. "You're kidding."

"Nope. So there was good reason you didn't find him at Hunter. I suspect he's just fine."

"Thank you." Susanne was relieved. More than relieved. There was a good explanation for why they weren't at Hunter Corral.

Yet the underlying anxiety was still there. This gut feeling that something was wrong. Not being at one place didn't mean they'd made it to the other. As paranoid as that sounded, it was also true. She needed to see her husband. Put her arms around him and feel his around her. Be reassured that he was okay and let him soothe her. With two near-death experiences in the last twenty-four hours, she didn't feel like she could let another minute of their lives go by without it. She bit her lip, glad for the pain. What had she been thinking? She should have gone on the hunting trip. The most important thing was that they be together.

Henry said, "I hope this puts your mind at ease some."

Susanne cradled the phone between her shoulder and ear. She stretched the cord between her hands then released it. It rebounded into its curlicue shape. Her funny feeling might not be about the safety of Patrick and the kids, or it might be. Maybe it could even be about her own. Whatever the cause, she was going to head up to Walker Prairie, as fast as she could. And she needed information from Henry to make that happen.

"Can you describe exactly how to get to where they're camped?"

"You take Red Grade up from Big Horn to Forest Road 312. Then you ride in toward the good camping spots from that direction."

"Ride? Don't you mean drive?"

"Nope. Ride. It's a couple miles past where regular-sized vehicle access ends."

"Ride," she repeated.

Ronnie knocked on the door frame. In normal decibels, she fake-whispered, "I followed you in. Sorry."

"Thanks, Henry. Tell Vangie hello for me."

"I will. Bye, now."

"Bye." Susanne hung up and turned to Ronnie. "He had news."

"So do I. A kid named Brandon Lewis called in to the sheriff's department today right before I got off shift."

"Brandon." Susanne rolled her eyes. "Our daughter has a crush on him. I think he's too old and too experienced for her."

"Well, he heard about your wreck, but he was scared to call you directly. He wanted someone to tell you that he saw your family camped last night up on the southwest end of Walker Prairie, in case you needed someone to go get them for you."

Susanne tapped a finger on her lips. "Hmm. Maybe the kid isn't all bad."

"That's it? I thought you'd be excited to hear where Patrick and the kids are. You aren't acting surprised."

"Henry just told me something similar."

"So, they're okay."

"I guess."

"You're not convinced?"

Susanne suddenly felt like she couldn't sit in her bedroom doing nothing a second longer. She rose and walked to the kitchen.

Ronnie shadowed her. "Talk to me, Susanne."

Susanne went to the window. She pressed her

fingertips into the frame, eyes glued to the mountains. "I need to see them."

She didn't want to elaborate. She didn't know what to say. What could she tell Ronnie that didn't sound nuts? I've had a bad premonition and knowing where they are hasn't resolved it? Ronnie would just think she was crazy. Maybe that she'd injured her head in the wreck. She might even cart her back to the hospital.

So Susanne held her tongue.

Ronnie came to stand beside her. They gazed into the Bighorns together. Then she nodded. "I get that."

Susanne swallowed. She was jealous of her neighbor's capabilities. She felt like a vacuous Southern belle next to her, and she didn't like it. But she needed help, and here Ronnie was, offering it, over and over. It would be shallow and shortsighted not to take it. Before she could second-guess herself, she said, "Could you take me there?"

"I've got the day off tomorrow. No problem."

"I was hoping we could go now."

Ronnie flipped around and leaned against the window frame. She crossed her arms over her chest. "Now? But it'll be dark in a few hours. And where they are, we'd have to haul in horses and ride to reach them. Maybe camp overnight if we don't find them and try again in the morning."

Susanne tasted bile in her mouth. Riding horses. In the mountains. In the dark. With Ronnie instead of Patrick. It was bad enough with Patrick. Bad enough in daylight. But she would do whatever she had to.

She drew in a deep breath. "I know I'm asking a lot. But I can't do it alone." She could mention the lack of truck, trailer, and her horse, Cindy, but that didn't begin to explain all that she couldn't do. She'd never even saddled a horse by herself, something she would be embarrassed to admit in public in Wyoming. Patrick was always there, taking care of whatever she needed to make her life easier.

"Jeff and I packed up to backcountry camp with our horses last weekend, then decided not to go at the last minute. Left everything in the trailer. With that head start, we could be on the road in an hour. If you're sure." Jeff was Ronnie's husband. He worked two weeks on, two weeks off in the oil fields.

Susanne wasn't sure about riding, but she was sure about what she needed. It felt like all the demons in hell were swirling around her, launching attack after attack. She needed her family, and she needed them now.

"Absolutely," she said.

CHAPTER TWENTY-FOUR: BACKTRACK

RANGER CREEK, BIGHORN NATIONAL FOREST, WYOMING
SEPTEMBER 20, 1976, 6:00 P.M.

Patrick

To Patrick, the ride out seemed to take forever, and his guilt and terror swelled with every passing minute. How was he going to tell Susanne that Trish was missing? Of course, if Susanne had come, Trish wouldn't have been alone in the camp. Dammit. How could things have gone so wrong? If only he hadn't let Trish skip hunting today. She stayed by herself all the time, though, even babysat. He and Susanne let her ride out alone on Goldie at least once a week. She'd be gone for hours. He never worried about her, had never dreamed something like this could happen. He wanted to go faster, to catch up to her. The trail was too rocky and wet to even trot the horses, though, and their lack of speed frustrated him. At least Trish and whoever she was with were facing the same conditions.

When they reached the stretch of the road where vehicular traffic access was permitted, he pulled his watch from his pocket. He'd stashed it there to keep it dry. It was only six o'clock. Not as late as he'd feared. Night hadn't fallen, but with the clouds and precipitation, it was like permanent dusk and hard to judge time.

As they rode, he'd gotten better and better at differentiating the hoofprints, despite the water dripping in his eyes off his bare head. Cindy had tiny hooves, almost donkey-sized. She was easy to follow, especially in the muddy trail, which she didn't deviate from. Goldie's tracks were even more distinctive, since Trish had sweet-talked their farrier into cutting a deep G into the freshly forged metal. Each step in the mud was like a personalized stamp. Together, they'd left him a neon sign to follow.

After a while, he realized that their tracks were on top of the others, too. If the Flint horses were in the rear, maybe that meant Trish had spooked and fled for the truck. She could be traveling of her own free will, and alone. Maybe they'd get back to where Patrick had parked the truck and trailer, and he'd find her, horses loaded, huddled in the cab with the heater on full blast.

He prayed that would be the case. If it was, he'd stick Perry in there with her to warm up, too. The storm had passed, and with it, the north wind. Still, the light rain was steady and cold. Perry's teeth had chattered for the last hour. The kid kept a stiff upper lip, though. He was damn proud of the boy. Not a single whimper. Not about his feet, his ankle, his shoulder, being hungry, being scared, or the cold.

"I see a truck," Perry said.

Patrick strained to see farther. "Me, too."

The horses picked up their pace. It was impossible to tell exactly how much farther down the forest road they'd parked, but Patrick didn't recognize the first setup they came to. Rig after rig, the trucks and trailers seemed unfamiliar. Goldie's and Cindy's prints were harder to follow now. They ended, along with the others, at an empty parking spot. Tire marks gouged the earth over the hoofprints, headed out and down the road toward Red Grade.

Their truck and trailer had been moved. *Shit.* A buzzing started in his ears.

"Wasn't this where we parked?" Perry asked.

"Maybe. Let's keep going."

He and Perry rode on in the dismal rain, far past where he thought he remembered parking, with no sign of their truck. He realized that he hadn't seen the silver trailer with the blacked-out windows, either—the one that belonged to the Harley riders who harassed Trish. They kept going, all the way down to the intersection with Red Grade at Ranger Creek. They stopped the horses. Patrick looked up Red Grade one way and down the other. There were no other vehicles or people in sight.

His empty stomach churned with fear and acid, and the buzzing in his ears intensified. The trail had ended. Trish was gone, and so were the truck, trailer, and horses. The world suddenly felt like an impossibly large place, spinning helter-skelter on its axis.

"Dad, I didn't see our stuff." Perry's voice vibrated like a high-tension wire.

"Me either, son."

"What's going on?"

Patrick imbued his voice with a positive, hopeful note. "I'm thinking your sister got scared and drove out."

"She doesn't know how to drive."

Patrick didn't correct him, but that wasn't technically true. He'd been giving her driving lessons—part fun, part battle of wills, all to a soundtrack of Janis Joplin and the Rolling Stones blaring from the eight-track—but in addition to that, she'd been driving on his parents' Texas farm since she was younger than Perry. Her grandfather would ride beside her on the bench seat in his pickup, down the dirt roads along his peanut fields. Susanne hadn't liked it, but Patrick hadn't seen the harm. It had made the recent lessons easier. Trish was a little immature to make good decisions, but she knew how a car operated, and she could judge distance, stop-time, and turns. Enough to drive a truck down a mountain pulling a horse trailer, though? He tried to remember if he'd left the truck facing out, or whether she would have had to back the trailer out, and he was almost certain it required backing. That she couldn't do. Even if she hadn't had to back it, there was the descent down the face, a muddy, dark drive on Red Grade with a trailer full of horses. It wasn't something he wanted to do himself, and he sure as shootin' didn't want his unlicensed, inexperienced daughter doing it.

"Let's ride back a ways and ask around," he said. "Maybe someone saw her."

Within minutes, they'd ridden back to the first truck and campsite. All the lights were out, and it didn't look like there was anyone there. At the next vehicle, a group of men were leaning over a fire, drying themselves. One was whittling a stick. Another was puffing on a pipe. Patrick asked about Trish and the truck, but they said they'd just arrived and hadn't seen anyone.

At the third campsite a tarp was erected beside a fire, with a tent behind it. A woman was stirring in a cast-iron pot suspended on a tripod over glowing coals and flickering flames. The scent of tomatoes and sautéed meat wafted toward Patrick.

"Hello there," Patrick called.

A man was chopping—onions?—on a camp table beside her, and it was he that answered. "Good evening. Rough weather for a ride."

"It is, but we're looking for someone."

The man and woman glanced at each other and shrugged.

Patrick said, "A girl. She would have been in a white Ford truck pulling a red four-horse trailer, or maybe riding a Palomino horse, possibly ponying a stout little sorrel. She's fifteen, with blonde hair. Long. Probably in a ponytail or a braid."

The man shook his head. "Haven't seen her."

The woman stopped stirring, her head cocked. "I might have. At least I saw a truck and trailer go by that looked like what you're describing."

"Huh," the man said.

The buzzing in Patrick's ears was a whine now,

like a giant mosquito. His eagerness transmitted to his horse, and Reno moved closer to the man and woman. Patrick looked down to make sure the animal's big hooves weren't crushing anything important. Rivulets of water coursed around them. "How long ago?"

"An hour or two."

The horse shifted from foot to foot.

"Whoa, boy," Patrick said. "Was she in the truck?"

"Maybe. It was a boy driving. There was definitely a female in there with him, but with this rain." She lifted a ladle and pointed at the sky, splashing out liquid.

"Do you know which way they went on Red Grade?"

"Toward Twin Lakes."

It didn't make sense. Into the mountains—not down toward Sheridan. Patrick backed Reno up, preparing to leave. "Thank you."

The man said, "Awful dark and wet to be out looking for someone. Do you have a camp?"

"No."

"Well, why don't you hole up under our tarp here until dawn?"

"Because it's my daughter. I think something . . . bad . . . has happened."

"Shit. Whyn't ya say so? I've got a CB radio. Let's see if we can raise a forest ranger."

"That would be great." Patrick snuck a glance back at Perry. The boy's eyes were like full moons in the light of the campfire.

"I'll be right back. It's in the truck."

The man got in his vehicle and started it up. They watched as he leaned over and fiddled with something, scowled, and smacked the dashboard with his hand. He swigged from a flask, then he came back outside with it in his hand.

"Can't get the blasted thing to work. Why don't I drive over to the ranger station and let them know about your problem while you ride after your daughter? I expect they can catch up with you easy enough."

Patrick reached to touch the brim of his cowboy hat before remembering it was on Perry's head. "I'd appreciate it." As a flatlander heading high into the mountains, he could use all the help he could get.

The woman called, "Need anything for you or the youngster?"

Patrick shook his head. "We're in a bit of a hurry."

The woman smiled. "I understand." She leaned over a cast-iron skillet on the ground beside the fire. "At least take a hunk of cornbread. You can eat that in the saddle if you're fast enough."

"Thank you."

She brought one to him, and one to Perry, shielding the cornbread from the rain with her jacket.

"Thank you, ma'am," Perry said. He tipped his cowboy hat to her, and water ran off onto Duke's back. The horse didn't seem to notice.

"You're welcome. Good luck finding that girl of yours. I'll be praying for the good Lord to lead you right to her and that she'll be safe and sound."

For the first time since he and Perry had come upon their own desecrated, empty campsite, Patrick's eyes watered. He held the tears back, though. "We'll take those prayers, for sure."

He wheeled Reno.

"Wait. What's your name?" the man asked. He had one hand on the door handle to his truck. The flask was now in his breast pocket.

"Flint. Patrick and Perry. My daughter is Trish."

The man nodded. "Flint. Any relation to the young doc in Buffalo?"

"That's me."

"You saved my brother's leg when he had a logging accident. We're very grateful to you."

Patrick remembered the logger. "I hope he's doing well."

"He is, and he'll be real happy we were able to

help you out. I'll get to the ranger station quick-like."

"Could you ask them to call my wife?" His heart spasmed. He hated for her to get that call alone.

"Can do."

He hopped in his vehicle and pulled out ahead of the horses, accelerating so fast his truck fishtailed and sprayed mud. Patrick and Perry were back to Red Grade in minutes. The road ahead and to the right was smooth and relatively rock-free. Patrick couldn't be sure, but it appeared that there was more than one set of tracks heading to the right in the mud. Definitely at least one truck and trailer, more likely two of each. Which was theirs? It didn't really matter until one made a turn. Until then, he had a good trail.

"Hold on tight," he said to Perry.

"Ready."

"Yah," Patrick said firmly.

Reno responded with his usual understated power, and Duke clattered along behind them. Trish was up ahead somewhere, with God knew who. Patrick's need to find her and protect her was so overwhelming that it was all he could do not to ask the horse to chase after his daughter at a full gallop into the gloom.

CHAPTER TWENTY-FIVE: FUMBLE

UNDEVELOPED FOREST AREA NEAR WOODCHUCK PASS, BIGHORN NATIONAL FOREST, WYOMING
SEPTEMBER 20, 1976, 7:00 P.M.

Trish

Rain—almost sleet—was blowing in the open truck windows, along with the nauseating smell of exhaust. Trish put her hand under her nose. Without sight, her other sensations were too much. Sounds were louder and clearer. The slap of the windshield wipers and the booming kicks of Cindy in the trailer felt like they were pressed up to her ears. The taste of the salty tears on her lips was sharper, and the chapped skin felt like razors to her tongue. And her sense of smell —she'd never experienced anything like it. She could smell everything, the good and the bad. The horse manure in the trailer. The chemical scent of the vinyl seats. The clean moisture in the air. All of it. She was disoriented and terrified.

Everything since the men blindfolded and kidnapped her had been surreal.

In the tent, Trish had dropped her book on her stomach. She was thinking about Brandon, and rebraiding her dirty hair. She held the smiley-face hair fasteners in her mouth while she worked. Last night had been amazing. Brandon had really come all the way to Walker Prairie just to see her. Brandon had slipped her a note before he left. It was so romantic she couldn't stand it. He'd even suggested that he could follow her into the woods just to sneak a quick kiss. But she'd been too scared of her dad catching them. She regretted it now. Trish fastened the first braid, then plaited the other side quickly and refastened it, too.

She pulled the note from her pocket, smoothed it, and reread it. *I can't wait to see you again. Next time alone. And soon.*

Swoon.

But then she'd heard hoofbeats and men's voices on the trail. She was glad the tent was zipped and tied, since there'd been strange people around. The ones who'd argued with her dad about the campsite. The elk chasers. The weird ones who had harassed her on the drive up. Even the dirt-bike guys with the moose pictures, who'd dropped one with her just that morning, "for your family, since, you know, they appreciated them so much." It was a close-up of the mother and baby. She'd thanked them and tucked it in her jeans pocket, then they'd left. Thank goodness.

One of the men outside whooped. "See those horses? Someone's here. Come out, come out wherever you are."

That was her introduction to the voice of the man she now thought of as the ringleader.

"It's the girl. I saw her on that palomino," a second voice said. It was creepy and made her skin crawl. "We can work with that."

She heard boots hit the ground and footsteps coming toward the tent. The bear spray. For a moment she looked for it in the tent. She couldn't find it. Where was the dumb thing? Then she remembered. She'd taken it with her outside earlier when she went to the bathroom and checked on the horses. She'd laid it down in the grass by a tree. And left it there.

A quiet but authoritative voice said, "Gloves, everyone." It was flat and toneless.

Gloves? Her heart lodged in her throat. Why did they need gloves? And how could they "work with her"—and why? She couldn't think of a single good answer.

There was a wet-sounding SPLAT on the ground, and then the ringleader said, "I'll bet she's in the tent. Are you in the tent, sweet thing?"

"No," she prayed, mouthing the words. "Please, God, no." She dropped Brandon's note and buried her face in her sleeping bag. This had to be a bad dream. It was too late to run, too late to hide, and she had no weapon.

"I'll just have to take a look inside."

The tent zipper ripped open. She didn't dare turn around, afraid of what she'd see.

"Well, well, what do we have here?"

Big hands grabbed her shoulders. A knee dug into her thigh and a weighty leg trapped hers. *Fight, fight, fight,* she heard in her mind. She kicked, thrashed, and screamed. Footsteps stopped at the mouth of the tent. She screamed louder. The man on her legs struck the side of her head, so hard it was like her brain rattled inside her skull. It hurt, a lot, and she stopped screaming. Stopped everything. He leaned over and pinned her wrists. Something wet and warm dripped onto her neck. He was so heavy, she was afraid her bones would break. Her dad's self-defense drills had seemed so simple in their living room, but there was nothing easy about them.

"That's better," the ringleader said near her ear. "It won't do you any good anyway."

"Fresh meat," the one with the creepy voice said.

The scary voice said, "None of that. She's payment for a debt—no more, no less."

She glanced at her hands. The ringleader's hand was covered by black work gloves. Above them, his wrist was as red as a ribeye steak, like he'd been burned, but covered in thick, curly hair. Her stomach turned. He smelled worse than Ferdinand had after he'd been skunk-sprayed. An awful stink cut with a nauseating sweet mintiness. The stench then made her eyes water. It did now, too.

The scary man said, "Put this over her eyes."

There was a rustling sound, then the ringleader released her wrists and lifted his knee. He straddled her, putting his bottom where his knee had been, and pulled her head up by the back of her hair. Her head throbbed from his blow. She whimpered, trying not to cry. Fabric slid across her face. It felt like flannel and smelled like her dad. His shirt? At first, she thought the ringleader was going to suffocate her. That it was all over for her, and the last thing she'd have seen was the note from Brandon. Then the ringleader jerked the fabric and tied it around the back of her head. He flipped her body until she was faceup and he was straddling her from the front. She panted inside the fabric.

"What do you see?" the man with the scary voice asked.

"N-n-n-nothing." She hated that her voice cracked. But if he was asking what she saw, then maybe the shirt over her face was just a blindfold, and they weren't going to kill her.

"Good."

"Get her out of here," the ringleader said. He got off her by crawling over her face on his knees. The smell was even worse. She gagged.

Instead of yanking her up, the men dragged her out of the tent feetfirst. Her shirt rode up and rocks dug furrows through her back. The ringleader crawled out behind her. She struggled to breathe. Her own hot breath was suffocating her inside the flannel.

"Stand up," he said.

She did, after several unsuccessful efforts. Rough hands tied her wrists behind her back.

"Hold her for a minute."

A tall, bony body grabbed her from behind and pulled her close. He pushed his personal parts against her hands and she cringed. She tried to pull herself away from him, but it didn't work. He breathed heavily in her ear, and it didn't seem like it was an accident. She concentrated on getting enough air. Pots and pans began hitting rocks. Softer items landed in a pile near her feet.

"Who can pony out the girl and the horses?" the ringleader asked.

The creepy-voiced man's lips brushed her ear. His breath was hot and damp. "I can."

Trish shivered.

The ringleader grunted. "Good. I'll ride ahead and make sure we don't meet people on the trail. We can't let anyone see her with us."

She heard a jangle of metal.

"I found their keys." It was the scary voice.

The ringleader laughed. "Jackpot. And now we have an easier way to move the girl and the nags."

"We need to move fast and put some distance between us and her dad."

"That fancy-hands flatlander? He's going to run for help. We'll have a day's head start before the knuckleheads with the sheriff's department get their shit together."

Pony her and the horses out? Move them in her family's own truck and trailer? Put distance between her and her dad? That sounded bad. Her dad's voice rang in her head. "Whatever a bad guy is going to do to you somewhere else is always worse than what he is going to do to you right here." Really bad. Trish didn't want to leave. Her dad wouldn't know where to find her, or who she was with.

"Please," she'd said, her voice loud and at the same time muffled inside the shirt. "Please, no."

But they'd ignored her, and she'd zoned out, trying to imagine herself somewhere else. Anywhere, with anything else happening. Doing algebra problems under her mom's watchful eye. Eating canned asparagus. Even hunting in the rain with her dad and Perry. She didn't care. Anything would be better. Time passed, but she lost track of it.

Sometime later, the ringleader said, "Get her up on her horse."

New hands took over for the creepy guy. He was gentle and kept his body at a distance from her.

"Now, son. Don't be such a pussy about it."

The man holding on to her moved faster. He tapped her left leg, then she heard a creak of leather. She lifted her leg. His hands caught it and shoved it into a stirrup. With a quick grab and lift, he got her to stand in it. He didn't let go of her waist. She swung her leg over and landed in the saddle like a sack of potatoes. Goldie snorted. The man's hands released her, and she swayed, alone and unsteady. If Goldie spooked, she had no way to hold on or break her fall, except for her legs, so she gripped tightly with them.

The ringleader said, "Move out."

Over the next few hours, she'd ridden Goldie with Cindy ponied behind her. Her head was killing her. The lead rope cut into Trish's thigh. She weighed out possible escape scenarios. Without her hands or her eyes, though, she had no options. She needed to keep from freaking out and pass the time until she had a real chance at it. So she made lists of her favorite books. *Black Beauty. The Black Stallion. Blue Smoke.* Lately mystery series. Trixie Belden. Nancy Drew. Even the Hardy Boys. And, of course, everything by Judy Blume.

The mental exercises had worked, mostly, and she breathed easier and thought about her aching head less. When they reached the truck, the ringleader started issuing orders again.

"You're with her, son."

One of the men shoved her up onto the bench. He removed the rope from her hands and used it to bind her feet. She heard the other men talking and the horses being loaded into the trailer behind her. It all happened so fast, she didn't have a chance to make a break for it.

Who was she kidding? She was too scared to try.

The driver's door slammed. She heard clanging of hooves that sounded like someone was loading horses into a trailer next to them. An engine fired up. Then their truck started, backed up, and pulled away. As they rolled down the forest road, she peppered him with questions. Who was he? Where were they going? Why had they taken her? She was embarrassed to think about how she'd babbled, really. The only time he'd even responded was when she said she couldn't breathe through the blindfold. He'd stopped the truck and fixed it, rolling the shirt into a band and retying it. Then he had started driving again without a word. That was it. Nothing else.

And now she was careening blindly up a mountain with him, kidnapped.

Wind buffeted through the open windows. Her head throbbed, and her ears rang. She pressed her hands against her ears but it didn't help, so she put them back in her lap. Why hadn't she put up more of a fight? Her parents had trained her better. And when it had happened, what had she done? She clenched her fists, frustrated and disappointed in herself. She'd screamed. Screamed like a little girl. Then gone limp as a rag doll when the ringleader hit her. Whimpering. Cowering. Defeated.

Well, she was done with that and ready to fight now. More than ready, when she got the chance. It had taken her a while to get her wits about her, but her thinking was clear now. No one in the world had any idea where she was. She didn't know what the men wanted with her. What they planned to do to her. But she knew it wouldn't be anything she liked. Help wasn't coming. She might only be fifteen years old, but it was up to her to figure her way out of this.

She needed a way to signal rescuers where she'd gone. To signal her dad. What did she have? She thought about the moose picture in her pocket. There was nothing else. No wallet, so she couldn't use her learners permit or library card. She didn't have on any jewelry. But she did have the smiley-face hair fasteners at the end of her two French braids.

Moving like one of the giant tortoises she'd seen at the Dallas Zoo, she pulled one off a braid and slipped it even more slowly into her pocket. Immediately the wind tore a few strands out of the braid now that it was untethered. They whipped around her face, tickling her and sticking to her lips. She waited a few minutes, then repeated the process on the other side. The driver didn't seem to notice, or if he did, he didn't say or do anything.

What else could she do? If she'd gotten herself together sooner, she could have been memorizing the turns the truck was making. But come to think of it, she didn't need to memorize them. They'd only made one turn. After that, the truck had driven a long time. At least half an hour. It had been going mostly up instead of down. Her ears had even popped a few minutes ago. She concentrated, trying to visualize the mountains and the roads. That meant that when they made their first turn onto Red Grade, they'd gone in the opposite direction from where she and her dad and brother had driven in two days before. To the right. Into the mountains.

So, they were heading higher. Much, much higher.

Suddenly, she heard a vehicle honk from far to her right. *Bom-bom-ba-bom-bom, bom-bom.* A signal. The driver heard it, too. He swung the truck toward the sound. The road was bumpier, and the tires crunched dirt and rocks. Trish was ready, had been for miles. She dropped one of the two smiley-face hair fasteners out the window. She had one left, plus the moose picture. Two more turns she could mark. It energized her to be doing something.

"Where are we going?" she asked. She fought to keep a quiver out of her voice and almost succeeded.

He veered the truck, and the tire noise changed from dirt crunching to foliage crushing. He didn't answer her.

"You can't drive on the grass. It's against Forest Service rules."

Not that rule-following seemed to be an issue to him so far, given that he was helping kidnap her.

The only rule he seemed to follow was "Do what your daddy tells you to." Because she might not know who he was, but the ringleader had called him "son." Twice. So she was pretty sure that her driver was the ringleader's son. And that his daddy was a big-time jerk.

The truck lurched to a stop, backed up, then made a turn and kept going. The ruts and rocks were getting worse, and Trish bounced so high off the seat that she had to catch herself on the ceiling. After a few more jarrings that made it feel like her tailbone was jamming into her neck, the driver—the son—parked. Outside, Trish heard the rumble of an engine and the familiar voices of the other men. Her mouth went dry. Was this it? Was whatever bad thing they planned to do to her going to happen here? The son stayed in the driver's seat. Cindy was kicking the inside of the trailer, over and over.

The ringleader spoke through the open driver's-side window. "We were talking about whether to ride out from here or drive up to the pass."

Trish heard a splatting sound as something hit the ground. The son grunted. Trish guessed that meant, "Yes, sir." Cindy kept kicking.

"Jesus, what is wrong with that animal?" the ringleader asked.

Scary Guy said, "It's a longer ride from here."

Creepy Voice whined, "But we're hidden better

here."

Cindy's kicks intensified.

"We only need one of those damn horses," the ringleader growled.

Trish heard him stomp away. The horse trailer opened and hooves clattered.

"I don't want any gunshots," Scary Guy said. "Use a knife."

"No," she said, her voice choked. "No," she repeated, louder.

Someone pulled a knife from a scabbard, the noise unmistakable to Trish. It was just like the sound her dad's made.

"Use this one," Creepy Voice said.

Trish scrambled for the door handle, screaming. "Don't hurt her. Please don't hurt her."

Just as she found it and wrenched it open, the son yanked her back in the truck by her other arm. "Don't do anything stupid."

Trish stiffened. His voice was familiar. Then she heard a horse bellow and a loud thud as if something heavy had hit the ground.

She dropped her face in her hands. Sobs racked her body.

The ringleader came back to the son's window. "Well, that's settled. We don't want to leave our trucks by a dead horse. We'll meet you up at the pass."

CHAPTER TWENTY-SIX: CHANGE-UP

Undeveloped Forest Area Near Woodchuck Pass, Bighorn National Forest, Wyoming
September 20, 1976, 7:30 p.m.

Trish

Less than ten minutes after the murder of her mom's horse, Trish realized they were driving back the way they'd come. The bumps still jarred her, but she didn't care. She was leaden. Her aching head didn't even matter anymore. They'd slit Cindy's neck, just for kicking the trailer. What kind of sick assholes did something like that? She heard a familiar and welcome sound.

A horse neighing. Her poor Goldie, who must be scared out of her mind. She didn't understand. Not any of this. Why they killed Cindy, why they had taken her, and what she was repayment for.

"Why?" she said, her voice a croak. "Why did they kill our horse?"

The truck and trailer turned onto a better, less bumpy road. The one where she had dropped her hair tie earlier, she figured. Her bad luck. She'd finally got her courage up to do *something*, and it was a dead end to a dead horse.

"Aren't you going to answer me? I know who you are." She didn't, of course, but she should. That familiar voice. It probably meant he knew her, so maybe he'd fall for the bluff.

But he didn't say a word.

He turned the wheel abruptly, and Trish slammed into the passenger-side door. They were making a left turn. She hadn't been prepared, and she had to mark it. Trish pretended she was just slow sitting up, as she pulled her other hair tie from her pocket. With only the moose picture left, she could only mark one more turn after this one. She dropped it out the window. She'd wanted to leave it visible from the main road, but they'd already traveled a good bit past it. *God, please let my dad find it.*

Ahead, she heard the sound of rushing water. The brakes screeched and the truck slowed, then descended. Water splashed through the window onto Trish's face, so cold it was like an electric shock. It dripped down her nose. She didn't react.

The truck bounced and dipped side to side as the son maneuvered it over creek-bed rocks. It felt strangely light to Trish, almost as if they were floating downstream, like when Goldie had swum the deep section of the creek. Had that only been yesterday? It felt like forever ago. The weightless sensation ended, and the truck started the climb out the other side, engine whining under the strain of the trailer, which was still splashing through the water. The downhill force of the current felt like it was twisting the trailer on the hitch and pulling the back end of the truck with it. But a long second later, the truck's engine noises eased. The trailer was out. They were free from the power of the water.

Trish wrapped her arms around her body. "Can we roll the windows up now?"

The son didn't answer. She didn't know why she bothered. She stuck a hand out the window. The rain had stopped, but the temperature was dropping fast. The smells were changing too. Somehow, the air was crisper and cleaner. Her dad had taught her the difference in the scents of the evergreen trees. The pine was herby, almost grassy, and better than the Pine-Sol her mom used on the kitchen floor. Spruce was intense and kind of fruity. She breathed the sweetness in.

She tried to visualize her surroundings. The road was super rough. She could walk faster than the son was driving the truck. They were still going uphill, but it wasn't steep. She heard tumbling water out the driver's-side window. It all seemed familiar. "Where are we?"

No answer.

Natch. She was sick of it. "It's too late to give me the silent treatment. I told you. I know who you are. I've heard your voice."

When the son spoke, his voice was soft and raspy. *Had he been crying?* "Woodchuck Pass."

She knew it. Her dad had brought the whole family here a couple of times. It was one of his favorite places, and her mother liked it, too. Her dad had been trying to convince her mom that when they died, they have their ashes scattered in the pass off the top of Bruce Mountain, which was totally gross. Who did they think had to do the scattering? Her. And Perry. She didn't want to get the ashes of her dead parents blown back in her face. That was what would happen here, too. It was always, always windy, and it seemed to come from every direction at once. The hike up would be hard, too. Bruce Mountain was over ten thousand feet high, which was above the tree line. The pass was pretty, though. Lots of moose, elk, and deer. In the summer, it was blanketed with wildflowers. Lupine. Columbine. And balsam root, which were like short mountain sunflowers. They were the reason her mom liked the pass.

But those things weren't what was important now. The son was talking. He was *talking*. She needed to ask him questions while she could.

"Why Woodchuck Pass?"

He cleared his throat. "It's close to where we're going."

His voice wasn't mean like the ringleader, or scary, or creepy. It didn't sound old like theirs did either. In fact, it was young, like the kids she went to school with, and sort of *nice*. Maybe even a little frightened?

"Which is where?"

"Into the wilderness."

That didn't narrow it down much. Cloud Peak Wilderness is huge. And high. Her dad called it the spine of the Bighorns, and she imagined the mountains as a stegosaurus—like the dumb rubber ones Perry used to play with—with a slightly humped back and the wilderness as its chunky spikes pointed up at the sky. The wilderness is where all the peaks are, tons of lakes, and even a glacier. They'd hiked and ridden in the wilderness before, and her dad had gone hunting for bighorn sheep in it once, although he didn't get one. That secretly made her happy. The whole area was rugged and primitive, with no vehicles or buildings. She didn't want to go there in the middle of a cold, wet night with anyone. Going with these horrible men was unthinkable.

She shuddered. She had to get out of this truck, away from the men and what was coming. "You could take me back, you know. Drop me off by Ranger Creek, then just keep driving."

His voice came out tight. Higher-pitched and strained. "I can't. They'd find me. Somewhere, sometime, they'd find me, and they'd make me pay."

She was right. He was scared. She softened her voice. "You can't let them do this."

He didn't answer.

"Hello?"

"If you know who I am, then say my name," he said.

Her mind raced, searching for a face or a name. She didn't really have any idea who he was. But she decided to try to fake it, based on what she did know. He was young, like her, and while she recognized his voice, it wasn't one she'd heard much. "I don't remember your name. But you go to school with me. You're older."

Again, he said nothing. The truck started up a steeper hill. He downshifted. It was rockier too, and

Trish bounced in her seat. Tree branches slapped the windshield and sides of the truck. A slim branch sticky with pine resin reached in and smacked her arm. One scratched along the top of the trailer, screeching. Then, to her horror, the son parked the truck. *I'm out of time.* He left it running and didn't move.

"You're not like them. I know you're not. Don't let them make you do this."

The son turned off the truck. He grabbed her by the arm. "Come on. Get out on my side."

She jerked away from him. Bracing her back against the passenger-side door, she lifted her bound feet onto the bench seat, then kicked at him with all her strength.

The son grunted. "That's not going to do either of us any good." He tackled her legs, but not before she connected with his nose. "Ow."

She bucked her legs, but the weight of his body made her efforts futile. She swatted his face, then clawed at it. He drove his head into her chest, knocking the wind out of her. By the time she recovered and drew in a painful breath, he had immobilized her in a bear hug.

Trish knew he'd won this round. She needed to save her strength for when the time was right. Thanks to the altitude, the short fight had winded her. She struggled to catch her breath, uncomfortably aware of his body heat and dirty-gym-sock scent. She'd never had a boy lie on top of her before, for any reason, and she was mad that this was her first experience with it. She'd never forget it, and it was nothing like what Judy Blume had written about in *Forever*.

The fight went out of her. She let her body go limp. "I'll stop."

"You promise?"

"I promise." *For now*. Her ankles were crossed, so she didn't feel guilty lying.

He sat up, sliding backward out the driver's-side door. He pulled her after him, not roughly, but her arm and shoulder banged on the gearshift and steering wheel. She didn't cry out, though. When her legs were clear, he dropped them and grabbed her elbows. He sat her up on the edge of the seat. "Hop off."

She did. Then she heard something sliding. Something slick against fabric? A few seconds later, he looped whatever it was around her wrists and snugged it tight. It felt like Ferdinand's leash. Nylon. It had to be his belt. The son untied the rope around her legs. A tug on her wrists told her to follow him. She did, to the back of the horse trailer.

"I'm hooking you to the trailer. Don't try anything."

She nodded. But of course she'd try something

if she got the chance. Especially while they were alone. Where were the others? Maybe they'd driven off a cliff and died, if she was lucky. She heard nylon rubbing against metal as he threaded the belt through something. He pulled it so hard that it lifted her arms. *So much for him not wanting to hurt her.* Her body weight tightened the noose around her wrists. *The tie ring on the side of the trailer,* she thought. He'd looped the other end of the belt above her head through the ring.

The son moved away and opened the latch to the back door of the trailer. Goldie nickered. It was a nervous sound. She didn't like strangers.

"It's okay, girl. I'm right here," Trish called to her.

She reached her fingers and hands in every direction, trying to get a grip on the belt. On anything. If she could only loosen the tension, she could enlarge the noose and maybe slip her hands out. She stood on her tip toes, but it didn't create enough slack.

"I can see you," the son said.

Trish didn't answer. It didn't matter. She couldn't get loose anyway. The trailer door opened with a long squeak, releasing the scent of wet horse, manure, and sweat. Goldie's hooves chattered on the edge of the trailer as she balked at the step down.

"Get on there," the son said.

Trish heard a rope pop Goldie. The horse hopped down from the trailer. She rubbed her velvety nose against Trish's neck as soon as she was out, talking to Trish with the funny noises in her throat that Trish loved. Her wind-loosened hair fell forward, creating a cocoon of their faces.

Trish breathed it in, savoring the sweet-smelling horse breath and the warmth. "Good girl, Goldie. Good girl."

Goldie's metal lead-rope buckle clanked. She swung her head in the direction of the son and moved toward him. Even though she couldn't see Goldie, Trish could hear and smell the entire process as the son saddled her up. The flop of the blanket onto Goldie's back, the creak of leather, the whistle of the cinch through the D ring, the clank of bit against teeth. Leather, drops of water, and more horse sweat.

Quicker than Trish liked, Goldie was ready. The wind had grown colder. Trish shivered, wet and exposed to the chilly air, unable to huddle herself in her own arms.

Hoofbeats approached. Then men's voices, a thump, and footsteps.

The ringleader's voice and minty stench announced his presence. "You two are going to ride her horse."

"What happened to mine?"

"Funny thing. We got ready to go and heard something fall in the trailer. We opened it up, and he was down. Took all three of us to drag him out."

"What happened?"

"I think he hung himself in his lead rope."

"My horse." The son sounded like he had something in his throat.

Trish felt numb. Two dead horses. There was a SPLAT on the ground near the ringleader.

"Yours. Get over it. It was just a horse."

Trish could hear the son swallow.

"Yes, sir. Where did you park?"

"Across the road, down in the trees by the little creek. We're completely hidden. You did a good job parking here, too."

The son didn't respond.

"Your uncle is in a big hurry to get this show on the road. And you don't ever want to piss him off." The ringleader cackled.

Uncle. So either Scary or Creepy was the son's uncle. One big, happy, criminal family.

The son didn't laugh. His voice was cowed. "No, sir."

His daddy's boots crunched rocks as he walked back to his horse.

She whispered, "I'm sorry."

"Thanks."

Trish's brain felt like it was overheating. She had to figure out a way to escape these psychopaths or leave another clue for her dad. Anything to help him find her. The truck and trailer would have been a clue, except they were hidden up here in the trees. She had the moose-and-baby picture left. Thank God the son had tied her wrists in front of her. She'd drop the picture when they were clear of the trees and moving out.

The son said, "Time to mount up."

"I'm really cold. Do you have a jacket I could wear?"

The son called out, "Dad, do we have an extra coat?"

"For who?"

"Her."

The voice drew nearer again. "You'll keep her plenty warm riding double."

The son said, "But what about when we get up to the camp? It will be colder up there. Especially at night."

The ringleader leaned into Trish's face. He smelled like foul breath, earthworms, and mint. She nearly gagged. "You just let me know if you get too cold, honey. I'm sure one of us will be happy to warm you up."

Trish tried not to shrink back, but failed. She couldn't stand the smell. "I'll be fine."

Trish heard the sound of a hand slapping a back. The ringleader laughed. "Son, your uncle has been without female companionship for a while. I think we should give the job to him."

Scary Guy's voice came out of nowhere. "I've been without the companionship of a woman. This one is a child. Real men don't hurt women or molest children."

The ringleader stopped laughing. Trish could feel a sudden tension fall over the men.

"I was just kidding."

Footsteps moved away so quietly that Trish understood why she hadn't heard Scary Guy walk up.

"Shit," the ringleader said. His voice was jittery. "He's always been a sneaky bastard, ever since we were kids."

Trish heard horse hooves against rock, moving closer. Then Scary Man's voice rang out. From its trajectory, she knew he was back on his horse. "Time to go."

Someone—the son, she hoped—unfastened the belt from the tie ring on the trailer. Blood rushed into Trish's hands, and she fell on her butt.

"Get up," the ringleader said, his voice coming back to her as he was walking away.

"Here." The son put a hand under her armpit and lifted her back to her feet. Then he took her by the belt and pulled. She stumbled after him, pitching forward into Goldie's side when the pressure stopped. A sharp buckle edge bit into her cheek, and unyielding leather jammed her nose. Her eyes watered.

The son moved her to the side by her shoulders. Another man took her by the upper arm as soon as the son released her. Leather creaked, a body plopped onto the seat of a saddle, and Goldie huffed.

"Ready," the son said from Goldie's back.

"Lift your left foot, blondie." The voice belonged to the creepy guy, and it was in her ear again.

She lifted. She wanted to get away from him as fast as possible. He let go of her arm and grabbed her foot with his hand.

"You know how to get on with a leg up?"

"Yes. When I can use my hands."

The son said, "I'll help you."

Trusting Creepy Voice not to launch her up and over Goldie's back wasn't easy. But Trish didn't have a choice. She stepped down in his hand and jumped off the other foot. The son caught her around the waist. Awkwardly, she swung her leg over Goldie's rump. The horse snorted and shifted. She'd never liked double riders. Trish leaned away from contact with the son.

The son unfastened the belt around Trish's wrists. "Put your arms around my waist."

"I can balance on my own."

"Do what he tells you." It was Scary Guy.

Trish nodded, then thought of her moose photo. She only had a split second to retrieve it from her pocket, moving fast while trying not to look like she was moving at all. She used the hand on the opposite side of her body from Scary Guy. Was he watching? Did he see what she'd done? She crushed the picture in her palm to hide it, and put her hands in front of the son, palm and picture down, still holding her body as far back and away from him as she could. The son looped the belt around her wrists again, but left the opening slack. Her wrists landed in a humiliating location on the son's lap. She flopped and wriggled her arms to find a different resting spot, but it only made matters worse. The ringleader and Creepy Voice hooted.

Trish felt tears threatening. Heat flamed from her chest up to her forehead.

"Sorry," the son whispered. "Hold on to my shirt."

"I can't. My wrists are turned wrong."

"Can you reach the saddle horn, if you lean forward?"

Trish tried, and her body pressed into the son's back. She flinched, wanting to jerk away, but her hands found the horn, and she decided that of two evils, this was the lesser one.

The son kicked Goldie's sides. The mare ducked her rump and scooted forward.

Trish held on with her legs, careful not to dig into Goldie's flanks. "She doesn't need to be kicked. Just cluck to her. Or squeeze her a little."

"Okay."

The other horses surged ahead of them. Their hoofbeats were muffled by grass. The son turned Goldie uphill.

It was now or never. She wished she knew whether this was a decent spot to leave her clue, but what choice did she have? Trish relaxed her palm and the picture expanded. She maneuvered one of its edges between her fingers like a card trick, then flicked it away from herself, the son, and Goldie.

In her head, she sent up a silent message. I left you a clue, Dad. Please find it. Please hurry.

CHAPTER TWENTY-SEVEN: SPOOK

Red Grade Road, Two Miles South of Woodchuck Pass, Bighorn National Forest, Wyoming
September 20, 1976, 9:00 p.m.

Patrick

Patrick slowed Reno to a walk to give both horses a breather. The slow trot he'd been asking of them is the most efficient gait for a horse, but they'd been working hard all day. The animals needed rest, food, and most of all, water—more water than the mouthfuls they were slurping out of puddles. His own stomach had gone past growling to roaring and now was silent, and his mouth was parched. But it was up to him to find Trish, and that desperate fact had been driving him onward.

He couldn't believe the horses had been so willing, actually. After a full day, they had given him fifteen more miles by his reckoning, in less than three hours at an ever-increasing altitude. They were close to Woodchuck Pass, so he estimated they were at nine thousand feet. It was too much, and he had no idea how much more he would have to ask of them. But every moment that passed was one where his daughter was missing, and anything could be happening to her. Tired horses and people were the least of his problems.

He groaned aloud, and Reno's ears turned toward the sound. Patrick was the one who had let Trish stay alone at the campsite. It didn't matter that he had almost without fail found people in Wyoming to be kind and helpful. She was gone. His guilt was soul-crushing. Who was she with? And why take the horses, truck, and trailer, too? It was brazen. Taunting. Or just very foolish. And if it were foolish, that meant it could be the act of teenagers. He prayed that it was just Trish and Brandon. The crumpled-up note in his pocket gave him hope, even though it made his blood boil. *I can't wait to see you again. Next time alone. And soon.* He'd ground her for the rest of her life if she'd run off with that kid, after he hugged her and kissed her and gave her a thorough injury check.

But what if she wasn't with Brandon? He had to face facts. It was a really bad sign that their campsite had been trashed. Something had happened there. He just hoped it was unrelated to her whereabouts.

Hope. He couldn't let go of hope. As long as he didn't know otherwise, his daughter was alive and well, and he would be hopeful. Hopeful and determined. If someone had taken her and he found them, God help the bastard, because Patrick didn't plan to hold back. There was no way he was leaving this mountain without her. No way he was telling his wife that Trish was gone.

He angled his head and scanned the road ahead of him. The tracks were still easy to follow. *Owl eyes,* he thought. That's what the Indians had called the expanded periphery of night vision. As a doctor, he'd learned that the eyes primarily use cones in the light and rods in the dark, and that the difference changes not only how the world looks, but how the eyes are even used. Cones see straight ahead, in full color, and with detail. Rods are for peripheral vision, with no color or detail. The adjustment to darkness between the two takes about half an hour, so his eyes were now fully adapted and nearly a hundred thousand times more sensitive to light. Because of this, he moved his eyes slower than he would have in daylight, blinked to refocus frequently, and forced his eyes to view the world off-center. He couldn't see as well as the horses, especially with them moving so quickly, but he could see well enough.

Perry mumbled in his sleep. Patrick looked back at him. His son listed in the saddle, head flopping down. Then he jerked upright. How was the kid still onboard? Luckily, Duke would follow Reno to the ends of the earth, so Perry's dead weight and lack of direction didn't slow them down. Patrick was keeping Duke on a loose pony line with his lead rope, just in case.

An owl hooted, and Patrick flinched. Branches snapped beyond the reach of his vision. The wind played tricks on his ears. Was that a growl or a gust? He was glad the boy was asleep. He needed rest. Plus, the night sounds in the dark were spooky enough that they even had Patrick on edge.

Perry's head lolled forward, and the cycle of list and jerk started again.

Patrick wished he'd left him at Ranger Creek. But where, alone on the side of the road? Or with strangers? At the time, those options had seemed like bad ideas. If Susanne had come, he could have left him with her. Although knowing her, she'd have insisted on coming, too. Now, in the dark—facing unknown dangers—he worried that what they faced ahead would be worse. And when they found Trish, what would he do with Perry then? He'd be putting one kid at risk for the sake of another. The boy slowed him down, too, which left Trish out there longer. A Hobson's choice. A nightmare for a parent.

He pulled his eyes away from his son to recheck the truck and trailer tracks in the mud. The rain had slowed to a drizzle, giving them a small break. Enough wet to be miserable, but not enough to wash away the tire marks. He nudged Reno with his heels, asking for a trot again. Reno complied a little more slowly after each break. Duke's resistance was more active. Patrick wrapped the pony line around his saddle horn. He hated putting the burden on Reno, but Duke had to pick it up. Reno leaned into the drag without faltering. Duke's head wagged and his front legs splayed, but it was useless. Reno outweighed him by nearly a thousand pounds. With a snort, Duke gave in, but without enthusiasm or a slack lead.

The jerky-gait transition wrested Perry from sleep. "What is it?" His voice sounded startled.

Patrick turned to check on him. He looked good enough. "It's okay, son. We're still riding after your sister."

Before he could say anything further, Reno

snorted and exploded sideways. Then he rolled back and bolted in the direction they'd come. For a moment, it was all Patrick could do to stay on his horse. Duke was a few beats slower, and the pony line wrapped around Patrick's back.

"Hang on," Patrick shouted to Perry, without turning around.

He didn't dare compromise his balance while Reno was in a blind panic. Reno wasn't speedy, but neither was he smooth. Riding him at a gallop across rough terrain was like riding a truck with no shocks across a boulder field. The pressure of the rope on Patrick's back eased, then hit his saddle horn at full force. He had to release Duke. Perry's horsemanship skills weren't up for a midnight rodeo. Thank goodness Patrick had wrapped the line without tying it off. He shifted his reins to one hand and unwound the lead rope, then let it fly.

He turned his attention to his own horse, shifting his weight and pulling back on the reins. "Whoa, Reno. Whoa."

The horse ignored the pressure on his bit. Whatever was behind them, Patrick had to get the horse under control and get back to his son. He slid his hand down one rein, gripped it, and pulled it straight back to his hip while pressing one heel into Reno's side behind his back cinch. Reno stretched his neck out, resisting the one-handed stop maneuver. Patrick held firm and shifted his weight again, using his body to interrupt the horse's forward propulsion. Reno's gait became even choppier and harder to ride, but the big beast kept rocketing forward, his head and nose turned to face the opposite direction. But Patrick didn't give in either.

After fifteen yards, Reno submitted to the turn, rearing a little with each step. Patrick circled him until it was too hard for the horse *not* to walk. Reno huffed and snorted.

"Perry?" Patrick shouted. "Are you okay?"

Duke trotted slowly up beside them. Perry was bouncing in the saddle like a dead fish, legs flapping. The boy could never quite get the hang of posting—standing in the stirrups in rhythm with a trotting horse. And with his sore ankle and blistered feet, he didn't even seem to be trying anymore.

"I'm okay, Dad."

"Did you get a look at what scared Reno?"

Perry grinned. "It was a moose. A big one, with a giant set of antlers."

"Uh-oh." Reno hated moose. His fear of them was irrational, since he was bigger than any he'd ever encountered. That fact didn't compute in his brain, though. Like most horses, Reno thought of himself as a helpless kitten when confronted with a perceived threat. The curse of the prey animal.

"He charged you guys for a second, then he ran into the trees." Perry pointed to their left, uphill.

"Did Duke do okay?"

"Duke acted like he didn't even see him." Perry patted Duke's withers.

Duke is too wiped out to care. "All right—you're sure the moose didn't come back?"

"I'm sure."

Patrick leaned over Reno's neck. "Did you hear that, boy? There's nothing to be afraid of."

"You dropped a canteen."

Patrick nodded. He clucked and squeezed Reno with his heels. The horse backed up instead of going forward. "Come on, Reno. Don't be a baby. The big, bad moose is gone."

He kicked Reno's sides, wishing he had his spurs. He'd left them in a compartment in the horse trailer, since they weren't a good match for elk hunting. Reno backed up faster. Patrick untied the lariat he always carried on the saddle. He waved it over Reno's backsides. The horse stopped backing up but still refused to walk forward. Patrick smacked the saddle with the rope. It made a loud thwack. Reno shook his head up and down.

"You've left me no choice, bud." Patrick thwomped the rope across the horse's rump.

Reno did an Olympic-record-breaking standing long jump, tail swishing, then started walking, cat-footed. Patrick knew they were still one moose breath away from another bolt. Duke brought up the rear.

"Did you see where the canteen fell?" Patrick asked.

"Uh, not really."

Patrick felt stupid for asking. He knew exactly the type of answer he'd get from a kid Perry's age. He started scanning the ground. When Reno wheeled, he'd taken Patrick off-road, so looking for a canteen in a camo-patterned burlap pouch in the dark should have been a challenge. But Reno made it easy. He snorted and sidestepped. Patrick looked down to see what his horse had shied away from this time, and there was the canteen.

"Whoa." When Reno was almost stopped, Patrick hopped down.

The impact of feet to ground was painful after a day on horseback. He hobbled back to the canteen like a broken-down cowboy and grumbled as he leaned over to get it. Beside the canteen, he thought he saw a line of crushed grass. Tire tracks? He knelt, running his hand across the grass and tilting his head to the side. There were faint tire tracks across the virgin grass. There was no road here, but there were definitely multiple sets of recent heavy-vehicle tracks. Two, three, maybe four sets? He followed them back toward the main road, leading

Reno by his reins. The tracks connected with yet another road, this one faint, but clearly an established thoroughfare. Tire tracks stretched out before him and met up with Red Grade, one hundred feet away. He walked the tracks all the way to the road, keeping Reno and himself in the grass, with Duke and Perry close behind them.

When they were near the edge of Red Grade, something beside the tracks caught his eye. It was light, and an odd shape. A piece of bone, maybe. Or granite. He'd passed it by when a thought struck him like a fist to the jaw.

He whirled and scooped the object off the ground. He squinted as he rotated it. Two balls with smiley faces on them, connected by a figure eight of elastic. A fastener, like girls used in their hair.

"Trish wears some like that," Perry said.

Coincidence? The odds of another person dropping a hair fastener in the middle of the Bighorn National Forest near where Trish had disappeared were almost nil. And hope flamed, a red-hot poker to Patrick's chest. "Come on." He vaulted onto Reno and traced his steps back to where he'd found the canteen, then followed the faint tire tracks toward the forest.

"This is the direction the moose went," Perry said.

Patrick choked up on the reins a little. Tough luck for Reno. Patrick was finally hot on the trail of his daughter.

Even as he was tracking and talking to his son, Patrick's mind was racing, and not to good places. If Trish was traveling of her own free will, she'd have no reason to plant a hair tie along her path. It was unlikely she dropped it by accident. Not at the first turn the truck had made off Red Grade. His daughter was signaling him. She was helping him find her, because she needed him.

He had to face the most likely scenario. She'd been taken and finding her might be the easier part of his mission tonight.

Reno snorted, and Patrick realized he was urging the horse forward at the same time that he had pulled back too hard on the reins, confusing and frustrating the animal. He had to stay calm and focused. He tried to relax. They were so close to Trish now. Of course, that meant they were close to whoever had her, as well. And that meant the danger to Perry was increasing. He had to find someplace safe for Perry to wait this out. Things were likely to go south in a hurry once they found Trish.

He pulled up at the edge of the trees. "Wait for me here."

"Why?"

"I need you to be safe and out of my way, in case there's trouble."

"I can stay out of the way." Perry's voice was wheedling.

"Yes, you can. Right here." Patrick looked at him sternly. "I mean it. It's for Trish's safety, and yours."

"Dad, what if that moose comes back?"

"Duke's not scared of any moose."

"How long?"

"Ten minutes. Count it out."

"What if you're not back by then?"

"I will be."

"Okay." Perry's voice was lackluster.

He took off at a high trot on Reno, not giving Perry any more opportunities to argue. He pulled his revolver out of its holster and held it down at his side. He'd never fired from Reno's back before, and he didn't want tonight to be the first time. It was a long way to fall if Reno tossed him. But he'd rather get thrown than be taken by surprise. Or worse, miss his chance to get his Trish back.

The woods grew thicker. A branch came at his neck. He ducked just in time to keep from being clotheslined off Reno's back. He pulled the big horse back to a slow walk and dodged branches. It was darker in the trees, but the tracks were still visible, just barely, thanks to all the rain. As they went deeper into the forest, the pine needles piled up on the ground, though, and the tracks started to disappear.

Patrick was afraid he'd lost their trail and was about to circle back when Reno let out a whinny that was almost a shriek. He'd never quite recovered his equilibrium from the moose encounter, and his fall back into panic wasn't a long one. He started backpedaling, nearly falling as his rear end slid under him. Branches whipped Patrick in the back of the head and torso. Straining to see into the distance, Patrick caught a quick glimpse of two large mounds. He had the impression of a sorrel colored animal before he turned all his attention to Reno. He had to regain control of his horse before one or both of them was seriously hurt.

"Whoa, boy. It's okay."

Just as he was about to force Reno to reverse his backward plunging, he changed his mind. Maybe Reno knew something he didn't. He decided to trust his horse and let him have his head. Soon Reno had backed off his panic, and as he slowed, he nearly ran into Duke and Perry. It startled Reno again for a moment, and he reared. Patrick hung on to the saddle horn with one hand and put his weight over Reno's neck until the horse lowered his front feet back to the ground.

Patrick held a finger to his lips and shook his

head. Perry didn't say a word, and neither did Patrick.

Patrick let his rattled horse catch his breath. As Reno's lathered flanks heaved, Patrick tried to figure out what had just happened. His mind's eye returned to the two lumps. The sorrel animal. What about it had been so terrifying to his horse? And then suddenly he knew.

Cindy. The lump was Cindy.

CHAPTER TWENTY-EIGHT: STARTLE

Big Goose Ranger Station, Bighorn National Forest, Wyoming
September 20, 1976, 9:30 p.m.

Susanne

After Ronnie drove them up Red Grade, Susanne was close to barfing up the potato chips she'd eaten in the truck on the drive from Buffalo. It had been past sundown, but not so dark out that Susanne couldn't see the sheer drop on the side of the road—or fail to see the guardrail, had there been one. The truck tires had spun repeatedly—sending her heart on a hundred-yard dash each time—struggling against the weight of the trailer, the loose surface of the dirt roadbed, and the steep grade.

Fifteen minutes of much smoother, less steep roadway later, Ronnie let off the gas and braked to a stop in the middle of the road.

"What is it?" Susanne clutched the armrest on the door. She was jumpy. No, that word wasn't strong enough to describe her current emotional state. She tried again. *I'm coming out of my skin.* She'd lost a few years of her life to that climb, she was sure, and a few more to Kemecke and to her wreck. Would she have gray hair next time she looked in the mirror?

"Just the turnoff to the Big Goose Ranger Station. See it?"

She relaxed, some, and tried to spot the ranger station. There were no streetlights, so she couldn't see anything past the reach of the headlights. Well, not even that far, really. Her nighttime vision was the pits, and she was half-blind in daylight.

"No," she said.

They rolled forward another hundred feet, then Ronnie eased the truck and trailer into a wide turn. They bumped over a cattle guard.

In the near distance, Susanne saw dark humps. "Is that it?"

"Yep. And a couple of cabins. I like to check in

with them when I'm here on official business. I'm hoping there's someone up here."

"But this isn't official business."

"I know. But I want to do it anyway. As a courtesy."

Susanne wanted to keep going, to get to Walker Prairie, wherever that was. Get there *yesterday*. But she didn't say so. Ronnie was the deputy, and she was the one going out of her way to help her neighbor. Susanne would defer.

No sooner had Ronnie put the truck in park than a silhouette loomed in the headlights. Susanne yelped. Ronnie smiled. The figure grew larger and more distinct as it approached Ronnie's door. A man, in civilian clothes.

Ronnie rolled her window down. "Hey, Chuck."

"Hi, Veronica." He grinned at her.

Veronica? How . . . feminine.

"You know it's Ronnie." Ronnie grinned back at him.

Chuck leaned down and propped an arm in the window. "Not between old friends."

"Especially then."

"What's up—did you miss me and come all this way to tell me you've dumped Jeff and want me back?"

Susanne's frustration level was increasing. At

this rate she and Ronnie wouldn't get to use the sleeping bags they were packing in to camp with Patrick and the kids tonight. It would be dawn before they even got there. But she was also intrigued. Tough Ronnie—who never wore makeup, dresses, or loose hair—a breaker of men's hearts? It was like Wyoming was on a different planet than the South.

Ronnie turned back to Susanne and made a face.

Susanne studied her. High cheekbones. Icy-blue eyes. Pale pink lips. Thick blonde hair that Ronnie could barely contain in her braid, with curly wisps around her nape and face. The woman was strong, with muscular arms and shoulders, but she had a trim waist and a flare to her hips. Okay, Susanne could see the raw material was there. In Texas, Ronnie would have to work harder to be noticed, but here in Wyoming, she was like Lauren Hutton on a catwalk.

"Hush that. I'm up here with my neighbor, and you're going to give her the wrong idea."

"Or the right one."

Ronnie shook her head. "Chuck Baxter, this is Susanne Flint. Susanne, this is Chuck."

He nodded his head at her. "Charmed, I'm sure."

Susanne didn't feel charmed or charming. She

felt anxious. "Nice to meet you. We're looking for my husband and kids."

"Oh?" Chuck said, his thick eyebrows lifting an inch. "Are they lost?"

Ronnie joggled her hand. "They were supposed to be at Hunter Corral, and then today we heard they might be camping near Walker Prairie. Susanne wanted to check on them, so we decided to ride up 312 together. And I'm just dropping by to let you know I'm playing in your sandbox."

The raised brows dipped in a V, furrowing the space between them and above his nose. "What was that last name again?"

Susanne leaned all the way into Ronnie's lap. Had Johnson County even called the National Forest Service like they'd said they would? "Flint. F-L-I-N-T."

Chuck cleared his throat and looked into the distance. "Well, strangely enough, I just tried to call your home, ma'am."

"What? Why?"

"I'm sorry to tell you this, but a man walked all the way down here from near 312 after his truck broke down. He'd talked to a man named Flint who was riding north on horseback with his little boy. They were looking for his truck, his trailer, some horses, and his daughter."

"My daughter is missing?" Susanne went from

worry to hysteria without stopping to collect two hundred. She'd been right. Her premonition that something was wrong had been right. She felt like a pawn in a chess match between good and evil.

"Honestly, ma'am, this is secondhand from a man who'd been nipping from a flask the whole walk here. He said the girl drove off with a boy about her age in a truck, pulling a trailer. I can't say whether she's missing or just taking a joyride."

"She's *fifteen*, and she's gone. In the mountains. That's missing."

Chuck looked taken aback. After a moment he said, "No offense meant, ma'am. We just have our fair share of teenagers giving their parents a chase up here."

Ronnie gripped Susanne's hand in a bone-crushing squeeze. The *calm down* gesture reminded Susanne of home, of her mother, who'd always told her she'd catch more flies with honey than vinegar. So Susanne stopped just short of the ass-chewing she wanted to give Chuck.

She took a deep breath. "Please tell me what you are doing to find my *missing* daughter."

"After I ran the drunk gentleman back to his camp, I radioed out for everyone to Be On the Look Out." He shook his head, and his voice betrayed his irritation. "For the father and son, too. Because two flatlanders riding out in the dark on horseback with no map or destination means we'll be looking to rescue them next."

Susanne lunged at Chuck. *How dare he. How* dare *he!* Her daughter was missing, and her husband and son were out looking for her, and he was mocking them?

Ronnie put an arm out, restraining her. "Chuck, I know this kid. She's a good girl. She was out hunting with her brother and her daddy. It sounds like this needs to be reported as a missing-child situation to the local sheriff's department."

"Sheridan and Big Horn Counties were the first calls I made."

"And the status?"

"I'm waiting to hear back."

Ronnie put her hands on the steering wheel and pushed her shoulders back. "Okay . . . so in the meantime, what can the Johnson County sheriff do to help you find her?"

He crossed his arms over his chest but stayed close to the truck window. "I'll be honest, we're a little shorthanded. We've also had another couple of campers high on speed that had to be taken down to the emergency room. I think we've got a speed lab operating up here somewhere. We're doing the best we can do to take care of everyone and everything in the whole national forest. Any personnel the sheriff can spare for a search would be appreciated."

"I'll call and see what I can do."

"When can you start looking for her?" Susanne asked. Terror was overtaking her anger. She felt short of breath. Her baby. Her firstborn. Her precious daughter. Missing.

"We can organize searches and get started just as soon as we have the manpower."

Susanne didn't let up. "Which is when?"

"Hopefully pretty soon after the sun comes up."

"That's not good enough."

Chuck bristled. "I'm afraid it's the best we can do. I literally just got off the phone from making these reports. It takes people, and a plan, or bad things happen. Do you *realize* how much wilderness there is out there?"

"Do *you* realize how much wilderness that is for my daughter to be lost or hidden in?"

Ronnie turned to Susanne, her face inches from her. Her voice was calm, firm, and determined. "He understands. So do I. I expect his phone is ringing off the hook in the station. We should let him get to work."

"Don't they need things from me? Pictures, descriptions, information about our truck?"

Chuck backed away from the vehicle. "Yes, we do. Please. Come on in."

Ronnie turned off the ignition. "I'll radio my department while you work with him, Susanne."

Susanne reached for the door. Her hands were shaking so badly it took her three tries to open it. She stepped out onto wet ground, and the cold seeped through her boots and into her bones. She pressed a fist to her mouth. The three people she loved most in the world were out there somewhere, in bad weather and total darkness, and no one was going to look for them until dawn.

It was almost more than she could bear.

CHAPTER TWENTY-NINE: GATHER

Woodchuck Pass, Bighorn National Forest, Wyoming
September 20, 1976, 10:15 p.m.

Perry

Perry woke with a jerk. Duke was standing still. He scrubbed at his eyes, his arm bumping the brim of his dad's hat. The chin strap bit into his throat, so he loosened it. It was pitch dark, and he was so, so sleepy.

"Dad? Are you there? Where are we?"

"Woodchuck Pass. We followed all those sets of tire tracks to here," his dad said from just in front of him. "You've been asleep nearly the whole ride, kid. I don't know how you and Duke do it."

It all came back to Perry with a jolt. Trish missing. The long ride. Cindy dead. He wanted his mom, only he didn't want to see her face when she learned about Trish and Cindy. It would make her really sad, unless he and his dad could find Trish and bring her home.

Perry stretched his eyes open wider, but it didn't do any good. All he saw was darkness, except for one little patch of stars high in the sky. He knew there should be a creek and a valley between two mountains. He even knew their names. Woodchuck Creek. Dome Mountain on one side, Bruce Mountain on the other. His family liked this place. They didn't come very often, because the crossing over the East Fork of the Tongue River was too high until nearly July, from snow melt. Then, by mid-September it would start snowing again. He knew this firsthand because it had started snowing on them about this time last year when they were hiking near the pass. By the time they got back to the truck, there was two feet of snow piled up on the road. It took all of them digging together for the rest of the afternoon to get the truck out of the pass. His mom had grumbled a couple of times that hiking was a summer sport, but his dad hadn't let it bother him.

Perry really hoped it didn't snow this time. That hadn't been fun at all.

He yawned. When his eyes opened, he realized he was starting to see a little better. "Is Trish here?"

Patrick got off his horse. "I don't know. But the tracks from our truck and trailer led here." He pointed up an incline. "They head that way. Into the trees. I think. Something else drove in here after our truck, but they kept going."

"How do you know it's our truck?"

"The two sets of tracks are different. But I don't know for sure until I check it out."

Perry's back tingled like someone or something was watching him. If there was, he couldn't see them, and that freaked him out a little. His dad always said animals were more scared of him than he was of them, but he didn't buy it. He moved Duke closer to Reno. Reno flattened his ears and pulled his lips back at Duke. Duke ignored him.

His dad turned to Perry, a scowl on his face. "Don't mess up the tracks, son."

"It's scary out here. I can't see."

The scowl softened. "I know. But you'll be fine. Try turning your head a little to the side and using your peripheral vision. The Indians called it their owl eyes. It works better in the dark than looking straight ahead."

Perry tried it. It was a little better. "A flashlight would help more."

"And ruin our night vision. We'll only use one if we have to." Patrick handed Perry his reins. "Hold Reno."

"Here? I thought you wanted me to hide and stay out of the way."

"I'm not going far. And I don't hear anything that makes me think we're near people. But if things go wrong, take the horses and ride back out to the main road."

"I can't leave you."

"You can. But you won't have to."

Perry was afraid he'd cry if he said anything else, so he stayed quiet. He darted glances left and right. It was so *big* out here. His ears tuned in to the night sounds he hadn't heard moments before. The tumbling creek. The whine of insects. A jet airplane far overhead. The breathing of the horses. None of them should have bothered him. They wouldn't have, normally, but nothing was normal. Nothing. His bed in his own room in his own house would feel so good right now. Pancakes in the morning. His mom would ask whether they wanted sausage, bacon, or Lit'l Smokies. Trish always wanted Lit'l Smokies. He got really sick of them, but he wouldn't argue when she demanded them like some kind of princess.

"I'll be right back," Patrick said.

His dad drew his revolver and took a few steps forward. He scanned the ground, then leaned over to pick something up. Perry could see him pretty well from the side, at least when his dad was moving, but it got harder as he moved farther away. Something cold landed on Perry's face. His first thought was that it was raining again. But it wasn't rain. It was soft and light. Snowflakes. He lifted his face. Millions of flakes were passing through the tunnel of starlight. It was hypnotizing. He leaned back, his head almost on Duke's rump, and watched the snow float down at him.

Patrick's voice ripped through the stillness. "Son of a bitch."

Perry shot up in the saddle. Were things going bad? Was he supposed to ride away? "What is it?"

Patrick walked back to Perry, shaking something and holding it up. "It's a Polaroid of a moose and its calf. The same one those guys on the dirt bikes showed us."

Perry put both reins in one hand and took it from him. "The dirt-bike guys were here? Maybe they dropped it." Perry held the picture where he could see it. His arms were bulky with the layers of shirts his dad made him put on under his jacket, back when they found Cindy. The picture was familiar, although damaged by water.

Perry handed it back to him.

Patrick paced and scanned the ground again. "Either them or Trish. My money's on Trish. She's been leaving us clues the whole way. You were asleep when I found the second smiley-face hair fastener at the turn off Red Grade to here."

Maybe his dad was right that Trish left the picture, but that didn't mean Trish wasn't with the dirt-bike guys. Perry hadn't liked them. His stomach started to hurt again, and he clutched it with one arm. He hoped they hadn't taken her. Then Reno snorted. Perry heard the trees rustle where his dad had said the tracks led. He gripped his saddle horn and bit his lip. He tasted blood in his mouth.

His dad drew his revolver. Two men rolled dirt bikes out of the trees. They waved when they saw Patrick and Perry.

"What the hell?" Patrick said under his breath. Then, louder, he said, "I'm armed."

Perry's stomach cramped so hard he nearly hollered. He'd known it. The dirt-bike guys were bad. Bad, bad, bad.

"Hey, man," one of the guys said. "We come in peace. No need for guns."

He stopped his bike about ten feet from Patrick and Perry. Close enough that Perry could see snowflakes landing in his long beard and the bandanna covering his head.

Patrick lowered his revolver but didn't holster it. He held the moose picture up in his non-gun hand. "Is this yours?"

"What?" the bandanna guy said.

Both men set their bikes up on their kickstands and walked to Patrick. The younger one had a stocking cap on his head. He took the picture first, squinted at it close to his face, then handed it to the guy in the bandanna.

The bandanna man rocked side to side as he talked. "No, dude, we gave it to a girl this morning."

Patrick snatched the picture back from him. "Where is she?"

He shrugged. "Back on Walker Prairie, I think. With some old dude and kid."

"I'm the old dude and this is the kid."

He squinted at Patrick, then Perry. "Whoa, yeah. I remember you now. Sorry."

"When did you say you gave it to her?"

The stocking cap man was wringing his hands, then rubbing them together, then wringing them again. "Like, this morning. Pretty early."

"Why?"

"Why what, man?"

"Why did you go to her camp?"

His dad sounded like a cop. Perry sat up straighter in his saddle.

"We didn't, like, *go* there. We were driving by

on our way here and she was outside. She liked the picture." His voice was defensive, and his hand-rubbing grew faster.

"Was anyone else with her?"

The bandanna guy cut in again. "Just a couple of horses. If you count them, which we do."

The two men grinned at each other.

"What have you been taking, gentlemen?" Patrick's voice cracked with authority.

The bandanna man stepped back. "Whaaat?"

"Drugs. What drugs are you taking?"

Perry's jaw dropped. His dad thought these men were on drugs? His mom had told him only bad people did drugs, and that the worst of all were drug dealers. His pulse pounded in his throat. Were they drug *dealers*?

The stocking-cap man's face cracked into a smile. "You can get speed from the dudes from California in the silver trailer back by Ranger Creek, man. Cheap." He frowned. "Except I think they're gone. We're running low and were going to restock, but they weren't there when we drove through."

"They were *selling* speed there?"

"Making it, too. Great shit, man."

"What time was it when you noticed they were gone?"

He laughed. "Don't be so intense, man. Relax."

Patrick cocked his pistol but didn't raise it. "My

daughter is missing. You have no idea how intense that makes me."

Four hands lifted in the air. Two heads dipped.

The stocking-cap man shrank back. "Dad, you handle this."

Dad? Perry couldn't believe a father and son would do drugs together. It was so wrong.

The father—bandanna guy—said, "Uh, missing what?"

"Missing. Gone. Disappeared. We're trying to find her."

"Shit, man. We didn't know. That sucks."

"Yes, it does."

"Sorry." His brows collapsed in on each other, drawing a straight line above his eyes. "What was the question?"

Patrick spoke through clenched teeth. "What time did you notice the silver trailer was gone?"

"Oh, maybe around noon. After we gave that picture to your daughter."

Patrick gestured at the woods where the men had appeared with their dirt bikes. "What were you doing back there?"

"We were going to take a siesta. After the, uh, last round of speed wore off, we were pretty beat. But since the spot is already taken, we just took a leak instead." He grinned.

"Was anyone else back there?"

"Nah, just a truck and trailer way back in the trees." He laughed. "Like, how they got them in there is a mystery."

Patrick holstered his gun. "If you see that girl again, her name is Trish Flint. Let the Forest Service know immediately."

"Okay. And if I were you, I'd be looking for that silver trailer."

Patrick walked back to Reno. He took the reins from Perry and handed him the picture. "And that stuff is bad for you. I'd lay off of it."

The stocking cap guy laughed. "Says who?"

"Says me. I'm a doctor, and we've had way too many people in the emergency room lately coming down from it."

The father didn't look convinced. "Okay. Listen, we've got to boogie. Find a place to catch a little shut-eye. I hope you find her."

Patrick didn't answer. He just watched the two men drive out toward Red Grade. Patrick and Perry didn't speak to each other until the sounds of the dirt bikes were faint and distant, but Patrick's lips were moving the whole time.

Perry said, "Well, at least Trish was here."

Patrick nodded. "But there's no one here now. Let me just go check to be sure it's our truck back there. Give me two minutes."

"Do you want the picture back?" Perry still had it in his hand.

"Stick it in your pocket. We need to keep it."

Perry lifted his slicker and stuffed the picture in his jeans pocket. It didn't fit very good and folded where his hip and leg met up. His hand felt slick. He wiped it on his jeans. It didn't help much since they were damp, too.

Patrick mounted and rode Reno into the trees. Perry didn't want to ride out to Red Grade alone, and he silently urged his dad to hurry. He started measuring seconds like his mom had taught him. One one thousand. Two one thousand. Three one thousand. Four one thousand. His dad was back before he reached one minute.

Patrick was nodding. "It's ours. And no one is there."

"Where do you think they went?"

"Let's see if we can figure it out. Starting from where Trish left the picture." Patrick paced back and forth, his head tilted as he examined the ground. "Lots of hoofprints." He walked to the right then the left, then faced hulking Dome Mountain, which Perry could see now that his eyes had adjusted. "I think they went this way." He crossed the road, his steps slow and careful, and his full attention on the hoofprints. "This is definitely the trail. But it isn't going to be easy, son."

"Why?"

"I think they're headed up into Cloud Peak Wilderness." Patrick pointed to the right of Dome Mountain.

Perry bit the inside of his lip. He was tired, he was thirsty, he was hungry and sleepy, and he needed to pee. Duke probably felt the same way. All except for the peeing part, because he could go anytime he wanted to. Horses were luckier than boys in some ways, but then again, they had to carry people and gear on their backs and boys didn't. Perry didn't mind short hikes or rides, but this would be way more than that. And there were no beds, food, or bathrooms up there.

Patrick was already in the saddle. Perry decided to hold it until their next stop, since he couldn't get on Duke by himself. His dad made him practice holding it all the time, anyway. On road trips, Patrick wouldn't stop except when they needed gas. He carried a mason jar which he'd offer to anyone in the family who asked for extra stops. Perry had used it once, but Trish and his mom never had. His dad could be kind of a hard-ass. One time he'd refused to pull over for his mom until she started crying. Come to think of it, when they'd gotten home, that was one of the times she'd thrown a coffee mug at him. It had missed his dad and shattered against the wall. "Look at your mother throwing a temper tantrum," he had said to Trish and Perry. She'd thrown another cup, which only missed his head by a hair, then had grabbed the keys and driven to her friend Vangie's house. The next day, a delivery van pulled up at their house with a dozen yellow roses for his mom. Perry had snuck and read the card. *I promise we can stop whenever you need to, for the rest of our lives. I love you. Patrick.*

Perry decided he could tough it out. Whatever or whoever came their way. Trish needed them, and he was no baby.

He touched his pocket, where he'd stashed the moose picture, and tried to push the two dirt-bike guys from his mind. "No problem, Dad."

CHAPTER THIRTY: PURSUE

Big Goose Ranger Station, Bighorn National Forest, Wyoming
September 20, 1976, 10:30 p.m.

Susanne

Ronnie put the truck in reverse as soon as Susanne opened the door. Susanne had to jump and pull herself in to keep from being dumped back out and left behind.

She used both hands to wrestle the door closed. "Hey, what's going on?"

Ronnie glanced in her side-view mirrors and frowned. "I thought you wanted the search to start tonight."

The truck whirled around to face the other direction so fast it reminded Susanne of the teacup ride at Disneyland. She and Patrick had taken the kids there last year to break up the harsh Wyoming winter. Southern California experienced record low temperatures and rain the whole time they were there—so much so that they slept four-in-the-bed under all of the blankets in their unheated beach bungalow—but they by-golly rode every ride anyway. The spinning teacups had made Trish motion sick.

"I do," Susanne said.

The truck heaved forward with the trailer and horses, gathering speed quickly. Susanne caught one last glimpse of the blurry humps of the ranger station. Ronnie didn't slow down for the cattle guard, and the truck jittered to the side and almost went airborne. She turned north on Red Grade, accelerating. Gravel shot from under the back tires. Susanne heard it ping against the trailer, which was pulling on the truck as it fishtailed.

"Sorry, horses," Ronnie muttered. The truck found traction and the trailer stabilized. To Susanne, she said, "Well, if you want us to search tonight, we've got to get moving."

"Us?"

"See anyone else in the truck I could be talking to?"

"But what about the search party? The plan?"

"Let's leave that to the Forest Service and the counties with jurisdiction here. I've got a lifetime of experience in these mountains, two good horses, and you, the expert on your family. We'll start tonight."

Susanne felt a lightness in her chest. "Thank you."

The truck and trailer rattled and skittered over the washboards in the road. Ronnie seemed to have the route memorized. In the pitch dark, she raced up the straightaways and anticipated the turns just enough to careen around them.

Susanne steadied herself with her feet on the floor and hands on the dash and door. "You're going to kill us. Or the horses."

"I'm going to catch up to your husband and son."

"But we don't know where they are."

"We know he went north on Red Grade. On horseback. Following your daughter in your truck pulling your trailer."

"True."

"And we know their trail starts at Forest Road 312. We're almost there now. I'll stop and get a good look at the ground."

"The ground?"

"Yep. Tracking in the dark isn't easy, but it's not impossible."

"I didn't know you were a tracker."

"I'm a little of everything. I grew up on a ranch, fishing, hunting, and trailing cows. And I've had training since I started up with the county. I can track good enough." Ronnie pulled the truck over in front of a forest road sign with the number 312 on it. She positioned her lights across the road where it T-ed into Red Grade.

She got out, then leaned back in. "The fewer footprints the better. Could you stay inside?"

"That's fine."

Ronnie used a flashlight to study the ground. She traipsed about one hundred feet past the intersection, then doubled back. Susanne bounced her knee. The windshield wipers were off because the rain had stopped, but she noticed damp spots on the glass. She leaned toward the dash to get a closer look. Fat snowflakes were wafting into the beams of the headlights. She wrapped her arms around herself. Patrick. Perry. Trish. In this weather. Soon she'd be out with Ronnie, riding in this, too. She shivered.

Ronnie hopped back in the truck. "Patrick's on that big-ass horse of his with hooves the size of dinner plates. Perry's horse wears toe-clip shoes. Lotta tire tracks, but I actually noticed something the other day at your place. Your truck has different tires on the two front wheels. Hence, different treads. It's definitely one of the sets I saw. Piece of cake." She threw the truck into gear, and they shot forward.

"In the dark?"

Ronnie pointed ahead of them. "We have headlights. We'll do fine as long as nothing comes along to mess up our trail."

The truck's lights illuminated a tiny cone in front of them, with the night pressing in hard from all around it. The snow was light and intermittent, but not sticking. Yet. *That's good.* But they were driving on the left.

Susanne said, "You're driving on the wrong side of the road."

Ronnie nodded. "Their prints are on right. I'm not going to be the jackass that messes up the trail for the rest of the search party."

Neither woman spoke again, and as fast as Ronnie drove, it still felt to Susanne like they were frozen in time, making no progress. Around every corner, she braced herself for mayhem. An overturned truck and trailer. A man with his arm around her daughter's neck, with a gun to her head. Her husband and son, shot and left for dead. It got to the point where she dreaded every new straightaway. Forget the teacups. This was like the Runaway Mine Train rollercoaster at Six Flags Over Texas. She'd vowed never to ride it again after her first time, but it seemed like every year they lived in Irving one or both of the kids would go on an excursion that needed a chaperone. She somehow always ended up the sucker that signed up for heart-stopping dips, neck-jarring turns, and plunges into darkness.

Now here she was, doing it one better, in the dark with no rails.

After about thirty white-knuckled minutes, Ronnie slammed on the brakes.

Susanne put her arms out too late and crashed into the dashboard. "What is it?"

Ronnie put the truck in reverse and backed up twenty yards. "Something happened here."

"What do you mean?"

"The horses. Wait here." Ronnie jumped out of the truck and slammed the door. She lifted her flashlight to her shoulder overhand and examined the tracks. The floating snow was spooky in the headlights and flashlight beam.

"Okay," Susanne said in the suddenly empty truck.

Her worries about her family intensified with each moment alone in the truck, until she felt like a powder keg. She wished she understood tracks and that she knew what Ronnie had seen and what that meant. Zoning out as she recycled on her fears, she lost track of time. A light in her eyes blinded her. Startled, she looked up. Ronnie was stalking back to the truck, hunched against the cold. She switched the beam off and got in.

"Are they okay? Where are they?" Susanne demanded.

Ronnie wiped melted flakes off her face, then shook her hand. "I can't answer those questions. But I can tell you the horses bolted off the road that way." She pointed to her right, then moved her hand in a loop. "They circled around but didn't come all the way back to this road." She eased the truck forward.

"Where'd they go?"

"It appears they joined a little two-track that cuts back into the woods."

Susanne's voice pitched up. "Aren't we going to follow them?"

"We can't turn here. There's a gully. I'm looking for a place to cross. Vehicles have to get over there somehow."

"How do you know that?"

"Because I saw the truck tracks, too."

Susanne turned to Ronnie, bouncing a little on the seat. "They're up there! They're all up there!"

Ronnie held up a hand. "We don't know that." Then she swung the steering wheel to the right.

"Here's the road. And those, my dear, are the tracks to your truck and trailer. See them?"

"I do." Susanne leaned onto the dash, trying to get a closer look and urge the truck to go faster.

Once they were on the little road, Ronnie stopped again. "I have to radio this in. And we need to get our weapons ready."

"I didn't bring a weapon." Kemecke had taken everything except the bowie knife. But honestly, it wouldn't have occurred to Susanne to pack weapons anyway.

"Lucky you're with me." Ronnie smiled at her. "Because I have two guns." She spread a Bighorn National Forest map out on the seat between them and played her flashlight over it. She nodded, then snatched her radio from its holster. "Deputy Harcourt to Base. Come in, Base." Silence. She repeated her call. Still silence.

To Susanne, she said, "I may be out of range. Let's try one more time." Which she did.

Scratchy sounds filled the air, then a likely-male voice said, "This is Base. Come in, Deputy Harcourt."

"Virgil, I'm off of Red Grade between FR 520 and 226, following the tracks of a truck and trailer and some horses, along with a teenage girl, Trish Flint. They've been reported missing by the Forest Service to Sheridan and Big Horn Counties. Coincidentally, I'm with the mother, Susanne Flint, who is my neighbor. The father, Patrick Flint, and the brother are in pursuit, but we are not in contact with them yet. The tracks turn off to the right on a little unmarked road. I'm going to take it a little ways and provide some backup to Dr. Flint."

"Copy that, Deputy Harcourt. We have personnel en route to Big Goose Ranger Station to assist in that search now. Hold on."

More scratchy sounds. They grated at Susanne's ears. Then the man came back on. "The sheriff has asked that you return to Big Goose to meet the team."

Susanne grabbed Ronnie's wrist. "No."

Ronnie bit her lip. To Susanne she said, "We'd be better off with more people, in case there's trouble."

Susanne shook her head. "Please. Patrick and Perry don't have anyone with them. And Trish . . . it could be too late by then." Her voice broke.

Ronnie locked eyes with Susanne, then clicked the radio's speaker button several times. "Hello? Hello? Come in, Base. Come in, Base." She clicked again. "I think I've lost you. Deputy Harcourt, over and out." Then she replaced the radio mic in its holster and reached under the seat. "If that didn't work, I may be back to working as a cashier at the supermarket. This is for you. A Thirty-eight Special." She showed Susanne a revolver that looked a little like the one Patrick used. "Do you shoot?"

Susanne waggled her hand. "I can aim and pull the trigger. I haven't done much more than that."

Ronnie checked the cylinder. It was full. She popped it back into place. "It's a long-pull trigger. No safety. You've got six rounds. Does that make sense?"

"Yes, I understand you."

"Don't shoot unless you're close, say ten to fifteen feet. I know that sounds scary, but most people can't hit the broad side of a barn from any farther away than that, much less in the rain and dark, under pressure."

"Ten to fifteen feet." Susanne took the gun and held it in her lap pointed straight ahead of her. It felt heavy. "Okay."

"And be sure not to point it at me or anyone you care about."

"Of course." She had trouble swallowing. What was she getting herself into? *Anything for my family*, she told herself. *Anything*.

"There's a holster under the seat. You'll want to wear it."

Ronnie started forward, only to stomp on the brakes, then arm-wrestle the truck into an immediate turn. The trailer bore the worst of it. "This is getting a little too interesting. I'm afraid of getting the truck and trailer into something I can't get them out of. We're going to need to go overland from here."

Susanne wasn't sure she was ready to be exposed to the dark and the forest, but she didn't see a choice. "Should we take the horses?"

Ronnie screwed up her mouth, thinking. "Let's just go take a peek in the woods. I don't want to take the time right now. We can always come back for them. I can't imagine they got much farther than we did with the other truck and trailer."

Susanne pulled a rain slicker on as she exited the truck, careful not to get the revolver stuck or point it in the wrong direction. Wet snow splatted on her face and hood. The women walked single file with Ronnie's flashlight to guide them. Susanne stubbed her toe on a half-buried rock. She pitched forward and dropped the .38 Special before going down on her hands and knees. The flashlight beam swung over to the gun.

Ronnie made a "huh" sound. "You didn't bring the holster."

"I forgot."

"Why don't you stick that thing in the back of your waistband. We'll both be a lot safer."

Chagrined, Susanne took her advice. The barrel of the revolver felt cold and hard against her skin. "Sorry."

Ronnie was leaning over to get a better look at the ground near where Susanne had fallen. "That's odd."

"What?"

"The tracks are real messed up here, like there was some kind of commotion. What, I'm not sure. But the tracks keep going into the forest, so we'll follow."

In the trees, the snowfall lessened, and Susanne dropped the hood on her slicker. Outside the narrow beam of the flashlight, she was night-blind. Spooky turned to downright scary, and the night sounds didn't help. They walked onward for a few minutes. Then, ahead of them, something creaked and snapped. Susanne muffled a squeak.

"Probably just the wind," Ronnie said.

She didn't stop.

Susanne stayed frozen in place. She heard tearing, snapping, and growling. "Ronnie," she whispered.

Ronnie held an arm out low.

Susanne moved in close, almost hiding behind Ronnie like her friend was a human shield. "It sounds like something eating."

Ronnie nodded. "Yes. And we don't want to get in the way of that."

"Can we go around them? Or could you shoot your gun and scare them off?"

"No, and no. But let's see if we can get a better look."

Ronnie lifted her flashlight toward the animal sounds. She tiptoed forward. Susanne stayed glued to her. After about fifteen feet, shapes emerged, but Susanne couldn't make out anything distinct. The eating sounds paused. Something growled in their direction, and Susanne's blood turned to ice.

Ronnie drew in a breath. "Wolves. A whole pack. I haven't seen one in years."

Wolves. Susanne closed her eyes and tried to stay calm. With her bad vision she couldn't see the wolves, but she'd never been this scared in her life, not even when she'd come upon a rattlesnake in Texas and had to back away slowly, all the while waiting for it to strike. Every childhood story casting a wolf as the bad guy came back to her in a flash. "Peter and the Wolf." "The Three Little Pigs." "Little Red Riding Hood." She longed for the protection of the truck.

"What do we do?" she whispered.

"Let me think," Ronnie said.

She paused. The sounds of animals tearing into flesh started up again.

When Ronnie spoke, her voice was fraught with tension. "Oh my God."

"What's wrong?"

"They're eating a horse. Well, two horses,

actually."

Susanne's legs were shaking. She steadied herself by grabbing Ronnie's arm. "What do they look like?"

Ronnie wasn't listening and didn't answer. "Shit. I get it now."

"What?"

Ronnie pointed at the ground with the arm Susanne wasn't attached to. "The oddness about the tracks I mentioned earlier. They had doubled back. They're not here anymore. We're standing where they turned around."

This meant they could leave? Susanne wanted out of here, so she was glad to hear it, but she was still fixated on the horses. "What do they look like?" she repeated.

"What do what look like?"

"The horses. What do the horses look like?"

"It's hard to say for sure. One is maybe sorrel, the other is white?"

Susanne pressed her hand over her mouth, then talked through it, her voice muffled. "Cindy and Goldie."

"Who?"

Susanne dropped her hand. "Our horses. I think the wolves are eating our horses."

And then Susanne vomited on the toes of her own boots.

CHAPTER THIRTY-ONE: CLIMB

Southwest of Bruce Mountain, Cloud Peak Wilderness Area, Wyoming
September 20, 1976, 11:00 p.m.

Trish

Trish loved to ride, but riding double on a horse scrambling up a steep, rocky trail was not her idea of a good time. Goldie was slipping and tripping all over the place. The horse had been jittery at first, but she grew calmer as she got more tired. Trish felt sorry for her. Carrying two people uphill, one off-balance and with heels in the ticklish part of her belly? It had to be super hard. Not to mention that it was snowing. She could feel the flakes on her chin and hands. Funny—the ringleader had been right about one thing. The son's body was keeping Trish warm. Not that she was touching it. She was keeping herself rigidly away from it, in fact, which she could only do by holding the cantle at the back of the saddle. And that she could only do because she and the son were last in the line of riders. The son had taken the belt off her wrists as soon as the others turned their backs. It was a relief to have the use of her hands and an even bigger relief not to have the eyes of the men on her.

"There's nowhere for you to run," he'd said as he eased the belt off.

"I know. I won't." Of course, she would, if she thought it would do any good. But where would she go?

He hadn't spoken since then.

They continued climbing. Trish's arms were tired from clinging to the cantle, fighting the gravity that threatened to pull her backward off Goldie's rump. She swayed. Goldie stumbled sideways. Trish had gotten used to riding blind, but it still wasn't easy.

The son reached around toward her head. She sensed it coming. At first, she shied away.

"I'm not going to hurt you. I'm just going to take off your blindfold. You'll balance better if you can see, and then maybe you won't get us killed."

Was he really going to take off her blindfold? She held still. He grasped the flannel shirt and lifted it off her head. *Oh my God. Oh my God.* She could see. Her hungry eyes looked around her. She couldn't see much better in the dark than through a blindfold, but her eyes started adjusting quickly. Soon she could tell that they were on a narrow trail through truck-sized boulders, with nearly sheer drops over more of the same. The giant rocks were like a jumbled chimney piled all the way up to the sky. She followed the chimney up, then lifted her eyes skyward. Swirls of snowflakes danced down and landed on her face.

But these weren't the things she needed to see. She needed to see *him.* The son.

She tried to get a look at him, but he kept his face turned away from her. All she managed was his hair—dark and curled to his collar—and his height. Her head barely came to his shoulder. She ducked around his shoulders to stare after the men ahead of them. With their backs to her, she couldn't see their faces. They were only dark cutouts against a darker background.

They rode on through switchbacks back and forth across the boulder field. She saw movement and spotted animals huddled together under a rock overhang. Was it her imagination, or did she see the curved horns of bighorn sheep? She peered harder into the darkness. Yes! A small herd of them. Tears pooled in her eyes. How happy this would have made her dad, to see these creatures. How much she wished they could have seen it together. With her mother and Perry, even. And how guilty she felt for the way she'd treated her dad back at Walker Prairie. She hadn't even passed along her mom's message that the coroner had called him. It wouldn't have cost her much to do that. Why hadn't she? But she had no answer. They climbed closer to the bighorn sheep, and the animals scattered. Trish gaped as they hopped away, surefooted on wet, narrow rock faces. Then they were gone, like they'd never been there at all.

Time flew by even as she begged it to slow down. She didn't want to get wherever these men were taking her. The snow stopped. The stars came out. Millions and millions of stars against a velvet sky that seemed just a shade bluer than black. The star glow highlighted the silhouette of the mountain to her left. Dome Mountain, she assumed, if her reckoning was correct on their direction since they crossed Woodchuck Pass. In the near-dark, the colors around her ranged from dark blue to purple to gray. A bruised world, beaten by the fists of weather, moisture, and time. It was like something in a dream, and like nothing she would have ever seen in her life. She would have said "no way" to a ride in these conditions for fun. Yet, she knew no matter how long she lived, this picture would remain one of the most achingly beautiful things she'd ever seen.

She couldn't let this dreamscape be one of the last things she saw. Her dad's advice rang again in her ears. "Whatever a bad guy is going to do to you somewhere else is always worse than what he is going to do to you right here. So fight, fight, fight." She was glad her mom had insisted he teach them self-defense. She would use it. She flexed her fingers and rolled her shoulders. She would be ready, and she would use it.

Goldie stumbled. The son reined her to a halt. He handed the flannel shirt back to Trish. "Put this back on." His voice was a whisper.

No. Something in her wailed and begged her not to do it, but she had to. Now was not the right moment to fight. There was nowhere to run and hide. The men could overtake her easily in the boulder field. So she pulled the shirt over her head and twisted it around until her eyes were covered, leaving a sliver of sight out of her left eye.

The son said, "Do you have it on?"

"Yes."

He turned toward her. She leaned away. She

felt the shirt slide around as he adjusted it. The sliver of sight disappeared. She heard the nylon belt slide through his belt loops.

"Wrists."

Putting on her blindfold was hard enough. Giving him her wrists was hard like she imagined it would be to jump out of an airplane with no parachute. The belt drew tight around her wrists. She grasped the saddle horn, fighting back revulsion as her body was forced to lean into his back again.

He clucked to Goldie, who sighed heavily. "We're almost there."

Goldie shuffled forward. Trish closed her eyes inside the blindfold. She wasn't ready to die. There were so many more things she wanted to see and do. It was time for her to fight. That's all there was to it. It was time to fight. Goldie stiffened, almost as if she felt Trish's intention, then her pace picked up. The trail leveled off. Goldie's hooves clacked against rock. After another five minutes, they stopped.

Footsteps approached. Heavy. Purposeful. Cocky. Her mouth went dry. The ringleader. *Fight, Trish, fight, fight, fight.*

"Tie her up, then put up the tents," the ringleader said. His words sounded soft at the edges.

"Are you drinking?" the son asked.

Trish heard liquid slosh.

"What are you, a spy for your mother?"

"Just wondering." The son untied Trish's wrists and then refastened them when her arms were no longer around him. "Get down. I'll hold on to you."

Trish slid off the back of Goldie's rump. The belt jerked out of the son's hands, and Trish fell onto her tush. Goldie didn't kick. Trish heard the son dismount. As Trish leaned over to push herself up, her blindfold dislodged just enough that she gained a narrow view of the world around her from one eye. Could anyone tell? She ducked her head to hide her eye, just in case, but not so much that she couldn't watch what was going on. She stood stock-still while she took a moment to get her bearings.

They were in a clearing in the midst of a ring of stumpy trees. Ringleader spat a thick, brown stream of tobacco juice on the ground. Some of it dribbled into his beard. He was continuing to chew out the son, this time for letting go of the belt, so she was able to put the voices to the faces. Her stomach fell like the time she'd jumped off the high dive at the city pool in Irving. She'd seen them before. The men who harassed her dad at their campsite—the ringleader was the one who'd been in charge then, too. He also might have been one of the two that chased the elk, she thought, although she wasn't as sure about that. But the son she'd seen many times. He went to her high school. He was a senior. Quiet. A loner. She tried to remember his name. Ben something. With a J, maybe? Ben Johnson. Ben Jenkins. No, Ben Jones, she realized. But where were the other two men? Scary and Creepy?

Then a thought struck her. She had to control her facial expressions and body language. She couldn't let them know she'd seen them, recognized them. She relaxed her face. Her dad had taught her self-hypnosis in seventh grade. She was getting nervous stomachaches all the time, being the new kid in her class in Buffalo. It was all about breathing and telling the thoughts in your mind to go away while you relaxed every muscle in your body. She couldn't make her brain stop, but she started coaxing her body to relax, beginning with her face. In a few seconds, she felt the muscles relax and droop. She dropped her shoulders. Released her clinched fists. Forced herself to breathe normally.

Better.

With no warning, a wiry body pressed into her from behind and pushed her all the way to the ground. She landed on her hands and knees. Under the weight of the body on her back, she collapsed to her belly.

"Still cold, little girl?" Creepy Voice's breath was boozy and foul. Her dad didn't drink much, but she had sleepovers at a friend's house whose parents drank a lot. Creepy Voice smelled like they did when they'd come to tell the girls goodnight. Only Creepy Voice smelled even worse.

"I'm fine."

He snorted. "Yes, you are."

"You're hurting me."

"It only hurts the first time."

She thought about *Forever*. The characters talked about sex hurting the first time in the book. Creepy Voice had to be talking about *sex*. Fight, fight, fight. She thrashed and raised her voice. "Get off of me."

"I'll get off on—"

Suddenly his weight lifted from her body. She scrambled forward on her hands and knees, away from the spot where he'd pinned her. Her blindfold fell off around her neck. She turned and saw a man she recognized. The white-haired man from her first night on Walker Prairie. His body was writhing, and his chin was hanging over a forearm, but she'd never seen the man who held Creepy Voice in the choke hold.

When the fourth man spoke, it raised the hair on her arms. The uncle. Scary Guy. "I already told you, we don't hurt women or molest children. Are you a slow learner, cousin, or a bad listener?"

Creepy Voice's eyes bulged. He looked like he was trying to answer, but all that came out of his mouth was spit bubbles. The uncle looked Trish in the eye, and before she realized he even had a knife in his hand, he slit his cousin's throat and dropped his flopping body to the ground. Trish stared at the body. She screamed so hard it hurt her throat. The flopping stopped. Creepy Voice's throat gaped open in a drooling red clown-smile.

Ringleader shouted, "Why'd you go and kill Larry?"

"I don't think you want to be next, do you, Chester? Just think of it as one less person to split the payment with."

"What payment?" Chester sounded almost whiny.

The uncle pointed at Trish. "She's seen us. She can identify us. We need cash to make a getaway. We can't leave her up here to walk out. Scaring her dad isn't good enough anymore."

Trish buried her face in her shoulder. She hated that she'd seen them.

"But how?" Now Chester sounded interested.

"We still leave her here, but we don't let her loose. We call her dad and make him drop the ransom before we'll tell him where she is. Then we hit the road."

Ben said, "When do we tell them where we left her?"

The uncle's voice was chilling and final. "We don't."

Trish's head jerked up. The uncle locked eyes with her again. Whimpering, she broke eye contact. He laughed and turned away. Something in her snapped. She scrambled to her feet, then she ran as fast as could, blindly, straight into the dark heart of the forest.

CHAPTER THIRTY-TWO: SCREAM

SOUTHWEST OF BRUCE MOUNTAIN, CLOUD PEAK WILDERNESS AREA, WYOMING
SEPTEMBER 20, 1976, 11:00 P.M.

Patrick

Patrick doubled over onto his saddle horn. His abdomen was cramping like a woman in labor. Or so he guessed, having only witnessed it before himself. His guts had been fine while they were riding up the valley and over the other side of the pass. Everything had been easier for a while. The light snow was much less unpleasant than the rain had been. His extra layer of flannel shirt was even feeling a bit too much for the weather. He felt better about catching up with Trish now that he was chasing horses instead of a truck. And he was finding it surprisingly easy to follow a herd of hoofprints, even though the group wasn't following an established trail. He kept his mind busy trying to guess how many. More than two. Three? Four? Five? Was one of them Goldie?

He glanced back at his quiet son. Asleep. Again.

A cramp rocked through him. Sweat beaded on his forehead. Dear God, he regretted the MREs he and Perry had scarfed on the ride out of Woodchuck Pass. One of them must have been spoiled. Or maybe it was the water? He groaned. The water. He'd been careful not to consume any water that hadn't been purified. Not even when he brushed his teeth. He'd washed and rinsed the dishes with water that had been boiled. Or so he thought at the time. But had it been boiled? He had trusted Trish with the job. Last night she'd been distracted by Brandon, to put it mildly. Now that he was connecting the dots, he was sure he was developing a wicked case of giardia. But it was quick for him to be symptomatic—could it really have been just from last night?

It didn't really matter, because—however and whenever he'd gotten it—he was sick as a dog now.

The trail grew steeper, and the ride rougher.

The only sound was the creaking of leather and heavy breathing of horses. Patrick emptied the canteens one by one as he rode, and Reno ignored the little waterfall beside him. Perry wasn't showing symptoms. Hopefully the kid wouldn't get it, too. If they had to camp tonight, he'd boil fresh water in the pot in Duke's saddlebags. And rinse the canteens good with the purified water before refilling them. Another cramp raked his guts. A wave of dizziness wobbled him in the saddle. He just had to ignore the pain and press on after his daughter.

And Patrick couldn't let Perry sleep anymore. The farther back into the wilderness they rode, the more certain he was that there was no way Trish was with a teenage boy. This was no joyride. Cindy hadn't died by natural causes. Bad people had taken his daughter. The group would have to stop for the night. He and Perry could overtake them and be in a boatload of trouble before they knew it. The mountain itself was a threat. Not only was it steep, but the horses were picking their way through sharp, wet rocks. Small boulders. It wasn't a place to get thrown.

"You back there, Perry?" Patrick's guts rolled, and he clutched his stomach. He repeated himself, louder. "Perry?"

The voice that answered him was weak and thick with sleep. "Yeah."

"You okay?"

"Yeah."

"Hang in there, buddy. You're doing great, but I need you to stay awake now. Can you do that?"

There was a long pause. He heard Perry shifting in his saddle.

"Yeah."

"Thanks, bud."

They rode through a stand of trees, then the trail opened onto a towering field of boulders. *No, a waterfall of boulders, cascading off the top of a ridge high above them,* Patrick thought. At first, he couldn't imagine they could get through them. Then he saw the hoofprints led below and around it, then into it. The starlight now provided a little illumination, and he saw a game trail cutting switchbacks through the strewn rock. As long as there was no earthquake or some kind of shift, they would be fine, he decided. He wanted to believe the rocks were stable, but he'd seen the result of slides across the mountain roads too many times to delude himself.

They'd just have to move briskly. He nudged Reno with a knee in the direction of the hoofprints, even though the horse didn't need to be told where to go. He knew they were following the other horses, and he occasionally stopped to sniff their droppings. But if nothing else, Patrick occasionally wanted to remind Reno that he was still on his back and in charge. Patrick heard the distinctive chirping of a yellow-bellied marmot. The rock chuck's sounds grew louder and closer together as Reno moved forward, until it escalated into full-blown trilling. At its crescendo it was almost like a human scream. Hair rose on Patrick's neck.

"What is that, Dad?" Perry's voice sounded scared, but at least he was still awake.

"Just a rock chuck. He doesn't like us invading his territory."

"Okay."

Patrick's painful stomach made another series of loud noises. *Mind over matter.* He had to give himself something else to think about. A distraction. Something constructive, though. No wallowing in his fears of worst-case scenarios about Trish. Or about Perry. He started mentally rehearsing fighting tactics. If only he hadn't quit the martial arts training he'd started when he was a resident looking for a way to stay in shape. In college and even medical school, he'd played on a soccer team. That schedule became impossible, and the martial arts studio had been open 24/7, which fit his unpredictable hours. He'd treated it as nothing more than a stopgap. He should have taken it seriously. But he forced his rusty memory back through fighting moves, defensive and offensive. He segued into self-defense tactics along with things he'd picked up from short stints in boxing and wrestling. When he'd exhausted his hand-to-hand combat repertoire, he visualized knife thrusts, then gun draws from all angles and directions in his head. He tried one for good measure, aiming uphill without firing.

As his eyes followed his draw, his jaw dropped. Above him, nearly camouflaged into the rocks around them, a herd of bighorn sheep was making its way onto the boulder field. An enormous ram stood in the rear of the herd of ewes and their offspring. His horns were curved into nearly a full curl. It was hard to tell from this distance, but he could be four hundred pounds or more. He pawed the ground. Then, as if cued by some silent signal, the whole herd started running through the boulders. Their leaps were death-defying, their balance and purchase on the rocks were unbelievable. Reno lifted his head, and they watched them together. The sheep stopped all at once, perching on rocks, looking down on the horses and their riders as if daring them to try to follow. An intense longing stabbed his heart. He wished Susanne had experienced this with him. Susanne and Trish. He wished he hadn't come on this trip. That he'd kept his family together.

"Do you see that?" Patrick whispered to Perry.

"Huh?"

"The bighorn sheep, do you see them?"

The sheep disappeared into the night.

"Uh-uh."

Patrick shook his head. The horses needed a break, and this was as good a place for a rest stop as any. And Perry was awake. It was time to talk seriously with his son about what came next.

Patrick turned toward him. "When I give you the signal, Perry, I'm going to have to have your word that you'll stay hidden this time, wherever I put you."

Before Perry could answer, a scream echoed across the mountainside.

"Was that a rock chuck?" Perry asked, eyes wide.

Patrick wanted to scream back. *Trish. Trish.* He swallowed hard. "No, son. That was a girl."

CHAPTER THIRTY-THREE: DOWN

Southwest of Bruce Mountain, Cloud Peak Wilderness Area, Wyoming
September 20, 1976, 11:15 p.m.

Trish

Trish's breaths were coming in searing gasps that blocked out all other sounds. Even without the blindfold, she was running almost blind in the dark. Branches whipped across her face. Bushes tore at her jeans. She kept her arms in front of her, to break the collision or fall she knew was coming. The terrain up here was rugged and dangerous. Cliffs. Boulders. Thick-trunked trees. Tufts of grass where there were no rocks. She wanted to slow down, but she couldn't. She had to keep going. But going to where? She hadn't found the trail. Surely if she just ran downhill, she'd end up back in Woodchuck Pass sooner or later. From there, she could find her way back to the main road and go for help. She latched on to the plan. It was all she had.

Then it happened. Trish's shin smacked into a rock. She flew forward, reaching out desperately with her hands. They met with solid rock and broke the worst of her fall, but her elbows collapsed. She skidded to a landing with her face hanging over the far side of the rock.

"Ow," she moaned.

She sat up, not knowing which part of her body to cradle first. Her bloody palms? Her throbbing leg? Her smarting elbows? But then she thought about the men. They wouldn't let her run off without going after her. She had to keep going, as fast as she could. She hopped off the rock, her adrenaline surging so hard that her ears burned and her head buzzed. After a few limping steps, she took off downhill again. She knew she should be tired, but she wasn't. She could do this. She could do this.

She ran onward for another minute. Her eyes were adjusting enough that she could see about ten feet ahead. It wasn't much, but it helped. She sped up. Then something jerked her head back. It wrenched her neck, and she fell to the ground. She just had time to roll away from the person, then a body landed on top of her back. This one didn't stink of booze and chewing tobacco. So not Chester, the ringleader. Not Larry, the Creepy Voice, because he was dead, his throat slashed open and his blood all over the ground at the camp. Ben, or the uncle?

A scream rose in her throat, but a hand clapped over her mouth, muffling it.

"Shh. Stop. You're going to make them hurt you. Please stop." It was Ben, and he sounded genuinely concerned.

She was relieved it wasn't the uncle. This meant she had a chance. Ben wouldn't hurt her. She bit down.

Ben's body stiffened. His voice was strained. "Dammit, Trish, stop it. I'll move my hand if you won't scream."

She nodded.

He moved his hand.

Her words tumbled out in breathless pants. "Let me go. You've got to let me go."

When he didn't release her, she thought, *Fight, fight, fight.* She slammed her head back. Something cracked. *Good.* Bone. Warm liquid ran around her neck. *Ugh, nosebleed. On me.* It made her queasy, but only for a second. She didn't have time for weakness right now.

"ARGG. Crap." He released her.

His weight kept her body and legs immobile. But not her hands. She swung wildly, trying to connect with any part of him she could find, but her angle was wrong. Time for a change in tactics. She dug her fingers into the pine needles, grass, dirt, and rocks. Rocks. Moving fast, Trish selected the biggest, sharpest one she could identify with her fingers.

"I think you broke my nose." His nose sounded plugged up.

"I think you kidnapped me."

"They made me go along with it. I didn't want to."

"I don't care what you wanted. I only care what you did, Ben Jones."

His head dropped into her neck. She felt his shoulders lift and fall, over and over. Was he crying?

"I'm sorry." He lifted himself up and pulled her arms behind her.

She writhed and donkey-kicked, but it did no good other than slowing him down. In the end, her wrists were bound once again in his belt.

"I really am sorry." He scooped her around her waist and set her on her feet.

She'd been right on multiple counts. Ben was very tall, his nose was bleeding, and he'd definitely been crying. He held on to the belt near her wrists with one hand and scrubbed his shirt back and forth across his face with the other, smearing the wetness.

"Come on," he said.

She hung her head. She had no choice. She'd have to wait for a better time to try again. To fight again.

But she had her rock. She squeezed it in her palm, appreciating its sharp edges and the way her hand barely closed around it. It was a good rock. Now she just had to keep it out of sight. The dark was in her favor, but the lack of access to her pocket was not.

The hike back to camp seemed to take forever, all uphill. More than once she slid and fell. The first time, she landed face-first without her hands to catch her and split her chin on a rock. She didn't even care. After that, Ben moved her bound hands in front of her and kept a finger through one of her belt loops. She took the opportunity to stuff the rock into her pocket. Then she fell again. This time, Ben caught her before she hit the ground. It just made her madder at him. Being nice didn't do her any good. She needed him to help her escape. How could she get him to do it? Then she had an idea.

Trish squashed the fiery anger inside her and

used the sweetest voice she could muster. "Ben, we could escape together. I know we could do it. My dad would help you. He's a doctor. He has money. And my mom is really nice—she'd help, too. They wouldn't let your dad hurt you."

The ground leveled off for a moment.

Ben kicked a rock. "I'm not scared of my dad. He's just a bully. I'm scared of my psycho uncle."

The uncle had just saved her from being raped. True, he'd slit the throat of his own cousin, but it had been to help her. She shook her head. How messed up was her brain if she was excusing someone for cold-blooded murder? And if it was that messed up, how would it ever help her get out of this mess alive?

CHAPTER THIRTY-FOUR: BREAK

Woodchuck Pass, Bighorn National Forest, Wyoming
September 20, 1976, 11:15 p.m.

Susanne

Susanne was listing against the window, caught between wired and wiped out. Wanting to close her eyes and not being able to. Ronnie was driving through Woodchuck Pass—where she had tracked the truck, Patrick, and Perry. The truck went through a rut in the road. Susanne's head knocked against the window. She sat up, rubbing her head. Then the headlights illuminated an odd sight. Dirt bikes lying on the far side of the road, with two men sitting beside them. Was she hallucinating? What were the men doing here, in the middle of nowhere, in the middle of the night?

A man in a red bandanna raised two fingers to his forehead in greeting.

Ronnie braked. "I'd better make sure they aren't having a problem."

"Are you sure that's a good idea? We're two women. Alone."

Ronnie patted the gun at her hip. "Don't worry. You're with an armed law enforcement officer. Besides, it's kind of my job."

"Are we in Johnson County?"

Ronnie sniffed. "Details." She stopped beside the men. "Everything all right?"

The bandanna man stood up and walked to Ronnie's window. He brushed snow from his eyebrows and beard, then nodded. "Dude, I mean, ma'am, are you out here looking for the missing girl?"

Susanne's scalp tingled. She reached for Ronnie's hand.

Ronnie shared a look with Susanne before answering him. "We are." She drew the words out, emphasizing *are*. "Have you seen her?"

The man pulled up a sleeve and started scratching his forearm. "Not tonight, you know, but I saw her dad and her little bro."

"Where'd you see them? And when?"

"Like, an hour ago, maybe." He stopped tearing at his skin long enough to hitch a thumb up the road. "By the communication tower. They asked us to, you know, keep an eye out. She's a nice girl."

Susanne frowned. The men looked rough. But they did seem to know her family. All of them, except Susanne herself. "How do you know my daughter?"

He propped his arm inside the window frame, and his scratching intensified, leaving white, flaky trails over reddened flesh. "Whoa, you're the mom? I'm so sorry. You must be, like, totally freaking out."

Susanne couldn't take her eyes off the damage he was doing to his arm. "I am. Which is why I want to know how you know Trish."

Tiny flecks of blood seeped to the surface of his skin. "We met her at Walker Prairie. Showed her some pictures we took of some moose."

"She was by herself? Where were her dad and brother?" Susanne tore her eyes from his arm long enough to glance at his friend. The man had his hands on his head. He was scrunching a black wool cap and shaking his head, like he was telling someone no. It made his beard wag.

The bandannaed man glanced down and saw the blood on his arm. He pulled his sleeve back down. "I dunno. Like, they were there the night before, but they weren't there when we came back."

Susanne pushed her hair back in frustration. They weren't exactly founts of the information she needed. The bandanna man sounded like he was high. The other guy was in worse shape. "Listen, mister, I—"

Ronnie leaned forward, blocking Susanne from the guy. "Do you have any idea where she is or who she's with?"

Susanne folded her arms across her chest. This was getting to be a bad habit with Ronnie. But the man was answering. She unfolded her arms and peered over Ronnie's shoulder.

"My money's on the guys dealing speed by Ranger Creek, but I don't know for sure." He rocked forward on his toes, catching Susanne's eye. "Whoever it is, your family took off after them going that way." He pointed across the valley and up the mountains.

"From the communication tower, the one about a mile up this road?"

"Yeah."

"Do you know how many people were with her?"

"I dunno. I didn't see them. But there was a truck and horse trailer back in the woods by where we saw her dad. A lot of horse shit, too. Jason stepped in some." He thumb-pointed at his silent buddy.

Ronnie said, "And Patrick and Perry rode out after them."

"The man and the son?"

"Yes."

"Yeah. They took off after her. Hey, that dude is intense."

Susanne raised her eyebrows.

"Sorry, missus. No offense."

Ronnie and Susanne shared a look.

Susanne addressed the other man. He'd stopped tearing at his hat, but he looked like he was going to throw up. "You have anything to add?"

He shook his head, then winced. He pressed a hand to his temple.

"Are you okay, sir?" Ronnie asked.

The man with the bandanna said, "A deer ran in front of us and he, like, wrecked."

"You should get that looked at."

The man with the bandanna laughed. "I'm sure an ambulance will be right along."

"Go down to the ranger station at the East Fork of Big Goose. There's an emergency team there. That's only a half hour away."

"I'm fine," the guy in the knit cap said.

Ronnie nodded. "Okay, then. Thanks, gentlemen. We've got to get moving."

"Good luck."

Susanne waved as Ronnie accelerated, but her mind was already racing ahead toward her family. "We have the faster method of transportation. We're getting closer. We should be able to catch them."

Ronnie cocked her head. "Not where the *dude* pointed, we can't."

"Why?"

"Because no motor vehicles are allowed in the Cloud Peak Wilderness area. Or off the road at all up here, except for campsites within certain restrictions."

"Is there a trail?" Susanne had hiked in the wilderness before. The most-used trails were narrow, at best. Some got hardly any usage and were little more than game trails. Most of the wilderness had no trails at all.

"I don't know. But don't worry. You can go anywhere on foot or horseback."

Lack of access hadn't been her worry. The horses were. When she'd asked Ronnie to bring her to see Patrick and the kids, she'd made the leap to riding a horse along the relatively wide Forest Road 312 up to Walker Prairie. Striking off into the wilderness at midnight after kidnappers, on a horse —a strange horse at that—set butterflies loose, churning in her stomach. Narrow-to-nonexistent trails, rugged terrain, big predators. It was a daunting thought. But if riding in those conditions meant they'd find her family, she was on board.

"Where will we park?"

"Up at the communication tower. I'll radio the troops to meet us there."

"I thought they weren't coming until daybreak."

"Correct."

"But we can't just let them get away. They have Trish." Her fear about the upcoming ride evaporated.

Ronnie smiled. "Exactly." She picked up her radio and barked into it, giving Johnson County their location and plans. "Susanne Flint was insistent on following her family. I couldn't stop her. I've got no choice but to go after her."

The response was immediate, predictable, and absolutely unsatisfactory. "Wait for backup."

"I can still catch up to her."

"Then arrest her if you have to and come back to meet the group."

Ronnie turned the radio off abruptly. The sudden silence was ominous until she clapped her hands.

Susanne jumped. "What was that for?"

Ronnie looked sheepish. "I don't know. We always did that and then yelled 'break' when we came out of the huddle and back onto the court in high school basketball."

"Are we about to play ball?"

"Oh yes, Susanne Flint, that's exactly what we're going to do." Ronnie grinned. "Let's go find your family."

Susanne grinned back, but her cheeks were tight. She wanted to be confident and optimistic, but she wasn't. However, she was determined, and every step forward took her closer to Patrick and the kids. "Break," she said.

CHAPTER THIRTY-FIVE: REGROUP

Southwest of Bruce Mountain, Cloud Peak Wilderness, Wyoming
September 20, 1976, 11:30 p.m.

Trish

Ben led Trish back into the camp by the belt, like a dog on a leash. It was demeaning. She huddled in on herself, trying to shrink—better yet, to become invisible—and trying to stay warm. The wind had driven the cold to the center of her bones and lodged it there, even on the hard walk back to the camp. It was painful, like her whole body had an ice cream headache.

From the other side of the fire, Chester said, "Didn't get very far, did you?"

She swallowed, eyes fixated on the flames. She didn't want to see their faces again, or the macabre red smile in Larry's throat.

"Where do you want her?" Ben asked.

The uncle answered, from her left, nearer the tent. "By the fire, where we can keep watch on her."

Ben led her close to the campfire. The heat teased her. Better, but not enough to overcome her single shirt. Without use of her hands, she lowered herself Indian-style, shivering. It made her think of her dad. She wondered where he was. Honestly, she'd been so sure he'd rescue her. She couldn't believe he hadn't shown up. Her heart ached. It was hard to stay hopeful. With glazed eyes, she watched Ben's feet walk away from her, tracking him to Larry's body, where he started tugging at something, which made the body jerk around. She looked away quickly. Her traitorous body shocked her with a loud growl from her stomach. When was the last time she'd had food? Or water? Now that she was thinking about water, she realized her mouth was so dry it felt like it was filled with sand.

"What are you doing?" Chester said to Ben.

"Taking off his coat."

Ben turned back to Trish with a quilted jacket. She wanted to protest. The thought of the garment touching her was disgusting. But she was cold. Unbelievably cold. Ben draped it over her shoulders. The collar was damp against her neck. Damp with blood. She cringed. The coat was warm, though. Her shivers subsided. She was so grateful, she wanted to sob. She wanted to lie down and go to sleep. She needed to fight, but one warm, smelly coat and her resolve crumbled.

"Ain't that sweet," Chester said. "Now tie her feet."

Ben shot his dad a dirty look, but Chester didn't seem to notice. Trish wondered whether he was still drinking. It didn't matter. He was an asshole whether he drank or not. Ben went to the tent and returned with a piece of rope.

"Sorry," he whispered as he pulled her legs out straight and tied her ankles together.

Trish's heart sunk. It didn't have much farther to go to hit rock bottom.

"Get a shovel, Ben," the uncle said as he stacked branches for firewood.

Trish's stomach growled again. She reached up with her bound wrists and scooted first one shoulder and then the other of the jacket farther around her. She stared at her fingers. They were red with Larry's blood. She wiped them on her jeans.

"Why?" Ben asked.

The uncle straightened up. "We can't have a

body lying around the campsite. It will attract predators. You need to bury it. We'll set her up while you're gone, then leave when you get back."

Trish looked up at Ben. His expression was one of sheer horror. She was sure hers matched his.

"What?" Ben said.

"You heard me. Try to dig down as far as you can. Then cover it with dirt and rocks. And be sure it's out of sight of any trails."

"But how do I get him there?"

Chester snorted. "Quit sniveling. We've got horses, don't we?"

Ben glanced at Trish. His mouth was in an O, and his eyes told her that he wished they'd run away. But it was too late now. He trudged toward the horses. Five minutes later, he was riding out on Goldie, leading a skittish second horse with Larry's body tied across its back.

And Trish was left alone with Chester and the uncle. Completely alone.

CHAPTER THIRTY-SIX: SHOCK

SOUTHWEST OF BRUCE MOUNTAIN, CLOUD PEAK WILDERNESS AREA, WYOMING
SEPTEMBER 21, 1976, MIDNIGHT

Patrick

Patrick's guts rumbled as he dismounted. He hated slowing them down, but he couldn't wait any longer. They were running out of trees and cover for what he had to do. He checked his pocket. He still had the last few scraps of toilet paper he'd stuffed in there that morning. The scream from earlier still echoed in his mind. Had it been his daughter? At first he'd been convinced it was a girl, but it could have been a mountain lion. It had left both him and Perry a little rattled. A lot rattled. If it was Trish—well, he just couldn't think about what would elicit a scream like that from her.

A knifelike cramp drove him to prop his hands on his knees. Sweat popped along his hairline and down his back even though he was racked with chills. At least it had stopped snowing. He looped Reno's reins around a rock.

"You're sure you don't need to go, too?" he asked Perry.

"I'm good." Perry had taken his break earlier when they'd given the horses a drink of water at a creek. "I'm thirsty, though."

"Sorry about that. I had to pour the water out. It made me sick. We'll boil water when we stop for the night. Back in a second. Don't move."

"Yes, sir." Perry looked worried.

Patrick knew he was a big, tough guy in his son's eyes, but sadly, even big, tough guys could succumb to protozoa. He hobbled to the nearest cover, a little tree. Sparse might have been an even better way to describe it. His stomach popped and gurgled. Thank goodness he hadn't had anything to eat recently except the MREs. He checked around him for critters and drew his revolver out. He put the gun on the ground beside his boots. Dropping trousers made a man vulnerable.

Things didn't go well and took more time than

he liked. After, he took a moment to rest. His balance was off, and he had rested his head in his hands while the cold air dried his sweat. He had no water, and he was going to get really dehydrated in a hurry. He reholstered his gun, then hauled himself up. His legs were shaking so badly it was hard to walk, but he made it a few steps before he fell back against a narrow tree trunk. Sweat oozed out of him again. The tree bent. *Get it together, man.* He took off the extra flannel shirt and tied it around his waist.

An out-of-place sound came to him on the wind from past a stand of bushes. He strained to hear it, but it was competing with the noises from his midsection. Cupping a hand around his ear, he pointed it in the direction the sound had come from. He heard the noise again clearly. Metal hitting rock and dirt. Horseshoes? Then grunting. A voice. *Trish.* It had to be someone who was up here with her. It was just too improbable that anyone else would be all the way up here at midnight in mid-September. Or ever.

He waved a hand until Perry made eye contact with him, then pressed a finger to his lips. He walked back to his son, forgetting the intestinal distress.

As softly as he could whisper, he said, "It's time to hide."

"Where?" Perry whispered back.

Patrick scoured the area and found a gap behind a pile of rock. Perry rode Duke to it, and Patrick checked to be sure they were hidden. Perry's hat was visible, but just barely. Patrick left Reno where he was. The big horse was black as pitch, melting into the nightscape. He had his head down and eyes closed. Unless he got spooked, no one was going to see him, either.

He tiptoed closer to the sounds in a slow fox-walk, past where he'd been earlier, then closer, closer. He patted his holster. The gun was secure and reachable. Each step he placed so as not to roll a stone or break a twig. Every breath was modulated and quiet. Every step was timed so that his senses, especially his peripheral vision, could keep up with him. The sound of metal on rock grew louder. He crept to a stand of scrubby trees and peered through the branches. A young man—tall, dark hair, in jeans and a plaid flannel jacket with elbow patches—was digging. Futilely digging. The ground here was mostly rock. But he was giving it everything he had. Two horses waited on the opposite end of the clearing, their ears pricked toward Patrick.

It wasn't the kid or the horses that caught his attention, though. It was the dead body near his feet. A dead body with light hair.

For a split second, his heart stopped. *Trish. No!* He stepped around the tree to get a better angle. His relief nearly dropped him to his knees when he saw the body was longer and thicker than Trish, with short hair. A man. But who was it?

No sooner than he'd exhaled, a small figure barreled past him and into the clearing.

Perry. *Perry!*

"No," he wanted to shout. But he didn't, not wanting to alert the gravedigger. So he ran, but not fast enough.

Perry leapt onto the much taller man's back. The man hollered. Perry wrapped his legs around him and hung on with one arm, his other fist pounding and flailing. Perry got in one, two, three, four, five licks while his opponent bucked and swatted at him. Then the young man seemed to get his bearings. He ducked his shoulder and rolled Perry onto the rocky ground under his heavier body. Patrick heard Perry's "oomph." The horses had enough. They bolted.

Patrick drew his gun. Still, Perry didn't let go. The gravedigger kept rolling. Patrick couldn't land a shot or blow without the risk of hitting Perry. On the second rotation, Perry lost his grip, and the young man shucked him away. Perry landed on his back, between the empty grave and the dead body.

The gravedigger grabbed the shovel and turned on him.

Patrick had no choice. He lifted his revolver and cracked him on the back of the head with the grip.

CHAPTER THIRTY-SEVEN: SEPARATE

Southwest of Bruce Mountain, Cloud Peak Wilderness Area, Wyoming
September 21, 1976, 12:30 a.m.

Patrick

Patrick kneeled beside the gravedigging kid, weak as a newborn kitten. He tied the boy's hands together and put a gag in his mouth. Perry had brought Duke and Reno to join them. The horses didn't like the dead body, the grave, or the unconscious young man, but after a few antsy minutes, they settled down.

Although, to call him a young man was stretching it. He was as tall as a man, but still lanky like a colt, with a baby-smooth face. A kid, around Trish's age. And that set Patrick to wondering again if Trish was up here on a lark with Brandon or some of her friends. He couldn't rule it out anymore, even if it made no sense. She wouldn't steal their vehicle and leave him and Perry stranded. He and Susanne had raised a good girl. And what kind of kid's prank resulted in burying a dead body in the wilderness?

Unless . . . unless she wasn't in her right mind. The silver trailer. The speed dealers. *Shit.* Had Brandon come back with drugs? He didn't think she was that stupid, but then again, how many times had he consoled parents in the ER who swore their kids would never do whatever it was they had irrefutably done? He needed to pull his head out of the sand. Quit being an ostrich. She was secretive. Moody. Rebellious. Seeing an older boy he knew little about.

So, sure, she could have done drugs. People do stupid, out-of-character things on drugs all the time. Maybe even become convinced they have to bury a friend who dies in an accident.

Maybe.

But whether she came up here of her own free will or not, with kids or adults, she was in danger. This was no place for a pack of teenagers to gallivant off to, especially if they were high. He had to get her down off this mountain. And that meant, no matter how bad he felt, he had to get moving again. With their extra passenger.

He tied Reno to a tree. "I need your help, bud," he said to Perry.

Perry, who knew he'd messed up, was eager to make amends. "No problem, Dad."

"We've got to get him on Duke, over the saddlebags."

"Where am I going to ride?"

"In front of him."

Perry looked dubious. "Okay."

"Let's put him on this rock first. You take his legs."

Patrick hoisted the kid's shoulders up and onto a table-topped rock nearly three feet high and twice that long. Perry followed with his feet. Then Patrick climbed up onto the rock with the kid. The world spun, and he crouched to rest for a moment.

"Now what?" Perry asked.

Patrick wiped sweat out of his eyes. "Line Duke up."

Perry brought Duke over and positioned him next to the rock.

"Stay on the other side. I'll lift him on. You make sure he doesn't fall off on your side."

"Okay."

"Then we'll tie him on together." Patrick had

already scavenged all the rope they had out of the saddlebags. "Ready?"

"Ready."

Patrick waited for a wave of nausea to pass. *Mind over matter.* He slid his arms under the kid's armpits. He counted to three, then stood, legs quaking from the effort and illness. The boy's body was longer than his. He stepped toward the horse and lowered the kid until his knees rested on the rock. Then he laid him over the saddlebags as gently as he could. Duke hopped forward with a snort.

Shuffling sideways to keep up with the horse, Patrick held the kid on by his hips. "Stop your horse," Patrick shouted.

"Whoa, boy," Perry said.

Duke huffed and stilled. He seemed a little embarrassed to have lost his cool.

Patrick nodded. "Good. Let's get him tied on."

Patrick snaked the rope through D rings and around the cumbersome, heavy body. It took five minutes of shifting, lifting, turning, and tying before they had him secured. By then, Patrick was sweating like a sumo in a steam room, despite the temperature.

Perry had moved to Duke's head. "Are you okay, Dad?"

Patrick bent over, leaning on his legs. "Good enough."

He shook his head to clear his thoughts. The world tilted and his vision clouded for a moment. After his equilibrium returned, he said to Perry, "We've got to find a place to hide him. And you. You can't leave him. You understand? You absolutely, positively, cannot come barreling in like you did before. I have to be able to trust you. You could get one of us killed."

"But I didn't. I counted coup."

Patrick rued the day he had taught Perry about the Plains Indian tradition of touching enemies without harming them during battle. It was a demonstration of great skill as a warrior. Or great foolhardiness in a child. "You were lucky."

Perry's face crumpled.

"Brave, though. And fierce. I thought you had him for a second."

His son ducked his head, hiding a smile. *It isn't the size of the dog in the fight, it's the size of the fight in the dog,* Patrick had always told Perry. He'd bought the kids boxing gloves when Perry was four. Seven-year-old Trish had dominated their first fight, but Perry fought like a wolverine, and she'd resorted to shoving him into a wall to win. Suffice it to say there'd been a lot of blood. And shouting by Susanne, who had thrown away the boxing gloves.

“Will you promise me you’ll stay put and keep an eye on this guy?”

“Yes, sir.” Perry’s face looked sincere, and his voice sounded contrite.

Patrick wasn’t convinced, but what choice did he have?

He gave Perry a leg up into the saddle in front of his passenger, then mounted Reno. They walked the horses up the trail, Duke first this time, moving very slowly under his heavy, wobbly load. The wind blew like a gale behind them, pushing them up and across the mountain. Pellets of snow swirled across the ground, but none fell from the sky. Patrick was on the lookout for an alcove or standing rock that would provide good cover, but so far, he hadn’t seen anything that would work. When they neared the top of the boulder field on the last switchback, Patrick looked over his shoulder. A flicker of orange caught his attention. He stopped. Was that a flame he saw through the trees?

Ahead of him, Perry had stopped, too. He must have seen the fire, because he said, “That’s their camp!”

“It may be.”

“Trish’s there. It was her we heard.”

The memory of the scream, the fear that it was his daughter—Patrick had to get to that fire.

“We need to find you and this guy a hiding

place. Fast."

They turned at a brisker pace to continue up the trail. A cluster of rocks leaning together to create a sheltered space caught his eye. He stopped Reno and hopped off.

Suddenly, Reno shot forward. Patrick felt more than heard a WHOOSH of air. The animal's rump tucked under. Way under. The horse whinnied frantically, twisted, stumbled, righted himself, and then reared. His front hooves were like a combination punch to the sky. Patrick scrambled to avoid them. Reno screamed in terror, fury, and what sounded like pain.

Then he saw the reason for his horse's distress. A mountain lion had dug its claws in Reno's neck, right in front of where Patrick had been sitting. Reno. *Perry.* But it was Susanne's face that he saw. She'd been right. This trip had been a horrible idea.

Patrick launched to his feet as he grabbed his sheath knife from his hip scabbard. Working on a surge of pure adrenaline, he dove at the now-snarling cat. Its eyes were rolled back in its head, and it struggled to hang on to its frenzied prey. As Patrick lifted the knife over his shoulder, his mind flashed an image of Perry on the back of the gravedigging kid, swinging wildly—the courage of a lion. Then he drove the blade into what he hoped was a soft spot below the back of the lion's skull.

The animal yowled and let go of Reno at the same time that Patrick's momentum drove him on top of the cat. He twisted the knife, holding the handle now with both hands. The weight of the lion and the torque on the handle snapped the blade off. It stayed lodged in the back of the cougar's neck.

No longer tethered to the cat, Patrick crumpled to the ground, landing awkwardly on his ankle. The muscular lion tottered a few steps before collapsing at Patrick's feet. A spurt of joy raced through him. Everything would be all right. His chest heaved, his heart raced, his insides raged, yet he had saved his horse and son from a lion attack. And the scream wasn't Trish being raped or murdered. It was this animal. And then he looked more closely at it. This beautiful, tawny creature who'd done nothing more than pick the wrong meal at the wrong time.

"Are you okay, Perry?" he shouted.

"I'm good."

He stole a glance at Perry and Duke. Duke was panting and standing with his legs wider than usual, but he was stationary, and Perry and the kid were still on his back. *Good.*

But before Patrick could utter another word, Reno took off, bucking wildly. In his panic, he threw himself into the edge of the boulder field. Patrick heard a sickening crack, and Reno bellowed. Patrick knew that sound. Bone breaking. Reno thrashed even more wildly, bawling and squealing with every step.

"No," Patrick shouted. "Stop, Reno. Whoa."

He pushed himself up and his ankle buckled. *No. Mind over matter.* Limping, he struggled against the wind toward his horse. He worried for a moment about the noise he and Reno had made, but the wind was whipping sound up and away from the camp. He turned all his attention on his horse.

Holding his hand out palm down, he murmured. "Hush, boy. Shhh, you're okay."

Reno flailed and kicked, but otherwise he stilled. From five feet away, Patrick could see what his ears had told him. Reno's lower right rear leg was definitely broken. The line looked ominous, like the bone might have broken the skin, too. Patrick had to stop him before he completely destroyed his leg. But those lethal hooves—how was he going to keep Reno calm? First, he had to calm himself. Breathing deeply, he allowed himself a second of intense sympathy for his friend. Of sadness. Then he was down to business, years of emergency medicine training kicking in. He disassociated his own feelings and concentrated only on solutions.

He took another step forward. Reno pawed with his left front hoof, his horseshoe like an anvil on the stone. Patrick had seen him strike another gelding with that hoof before, lifting his upper leg parallel to the ground and fully extending the rest of it, ending with a wicked downward swipe. He stepped in closer. Reno's nostrils flared. The whites of his eyes flashed in the dark. The coppery scent of blood mixed with sweat and fear. Patrick leaned down slowly, scooped the thick mecate rein into his hand, then straightened at the same nonthreatening speed. He pulled on the rein now. With a snap of his wrist, he tried to wrest the animal's attention away from his pain and fear. At the same time, he carefully removed the spare flannel shirt from around his waist.

Reno threw his head skyward, but he quit pawing. He stood on three legs—his right rear resting on the ground with no weight on it—blowing hard, and locked eyes with Patrick.

"Hey now, boy. Let me help you out." Patrick poured confidence and compassion into his voice. Horses respond to human emotion, even more than some people do. He didn't know how, but they did, and he needed the big guy to trust him. Three feet away now, he moved slowly closer, hand out with the flannel shirt balled up in it.

Reno huffed. His eyes were wide and unblinking, fixed on the shirt.

Patrick was close enough for the horse to crush him now. If Reno pulled back on a rein, the bit could gouge the roof of his mouth. He stroked

Reno's neck, then fashioned the mecate into a lead rope. Then he began rubbing the flannel shirt on Reno's neck in slow, circular motions. Reno's muscles twitched and hardened. Patrick gave him time to get used to it. When he relaxed, Patrick slid the shirt around his face and over his eyes. Reno snorted. Patrick tucked the shirt into the browband and cheek straps of the headstall, then tied the sleeves under his chin. He rubbed him some more, all the while murmuring comforting nonsense to him.

Softly, he called to his son. "Perry, come hold Reno, please."

"What about Duke?"

"Bring him with you. It will help Reno."

Perry did as he was told, the first time, with no arguing. Patrick was thankful for small miracles. And even though Perry lacked Trish's easy way and fearlessness with horses, he had enormous empathy. He stood almost underneath the head of the giant horse, holding his lead in the same hand that held Duke's. He stroked Reno's lathery neck.

"That looks like it hurts, Reno. But my dad is a doctor. You've got to trust him. He's going to help you."

Patrick felt a flicker of emotion, and he pushed it back down. Now he just had to figure out how to help his big buddy enough that he could leave him safely with Perry and get back to his primary mission—finding his daughter. He'd worry about getting everyone down to safety later. Reno wasn't likely to make this easy, either. Patrick didn't have a nose twitch, so he'd have to work on the back leg with nothing to distract Reno or keep him from lashing out in pain.

Patrick leaned over and looked under Reno's belly. His worst fears were confirmed. Bone jutted through the skin. Blood ran down the leg, almost the same color in the dark as the black hair.

"Shit." His medical kit—with antibiotics and painkillers—was in the stolen truck, back in Woodchuck Pass.

"Will he be okay, Dad?"

"I don't know, son. It's a compound fracture."

"What's that?"

"A bad break where the bone sticks out of the skin."

"Poor Reno." Perry sounded close to tears. "Can you fix it?"

"Not here. At least not completely. I can splint it so he can walk out with it." *I hope.* Reno walking out was a long shot. Patrick fought back a wave of despair. *Focus.*

Still limping, Patrick found a stubby tree and hacked it down with the trail ax he kept in the saddlebags. Good green wood. Nice and hard. He eyeballed the horse, then cut the wood until it looked to be the right length. Abdominal cramps gripped him again, and he paused, holding his breath, then forced himself past the pain. He took off another shirt, then put his coat back on over his last layer, a T-shirt. He soothed Reno and gently wrapped the shirt around his leg. The horse lifted it and threatened to kick. That would be very bad, for Reno and him.

He petted Reno's side as he spoke to his son. "I have another idea. I need you to lift his left front hoof and hold it up." Patrick said a word of silent thanks to Joe Crumpton for handing off veterinary call a few days before. Because of it, Patrick had met Mildred and had occasion to learn this trick.

"Why?"

"So that he'll hold still. He won't be able to move if we have two legs up."

"Oooh." Perry tied Reno to one of the big rocks, then pressed the chestnut on the inside of the horse's leg. The horse didn't respond immediately. Perry did it again, then grasped the feathery hair on the back of the leg near the hoof. He pulled for several seconds. Finally, Reno lifted his hoof, and Perry caught it and held it off the ground in both hands. The leg weighed nearly as much as he did, but he didn't say a word about it.

"Good, Perry. Now, let's try this again, Reno."

Patrick wrapped the shirt quickly, careful not to jar the broken bone, ripped skin, and torn muscle any more than he had to. Then he taped it to hold it up, above and below the break, as well as at the top and bottom of the shirt. Reno swayed, but he remained in place. Patrick wiped sweat from his brow. The easy part was over. Now he had to get the splint on. He needed the hoof to just barely touch the ground. The splint wouldn't bear Reno's weight, but it would have to stand up to considerable counterforce.

Reno already had his back leg cocked at the correct angle. Patrick positioned the section of green tree trunk against the outside of the leg. Reno quivered and groaned. Perry hiccupped, and Patrick knew he was crying. Luckily, the bone had snapped forward. If it had been sticking out to the side, there was no way Patrick could have splinted him without painkillers and sedation.

"I'm so sorry, boy. This has to be done."

Patrick pulled the stick away and stuck strips of tape to it at the top and bottom. Then, with one hand, he held the stick in place. With the other, he wrapped the top piece of tape as fast as he could, just enough to secure the stick. Reno made a hideous high-pitched yawp and shifted his weight forward onto Perry.

Perry squeaked. "He's heavy, Dad."

"Smack him on the shoulder with your fist, but don't let go of that hoof."

He heard the small fist make impact. Reno straightened back up. The horse's coat was slick with sweat.

"Good job, son."

Patrick wasn't sure how much longer Perry could hold up Reno's hoof. He secured the tape on the lower half of the stick. It looked right to him, so moving rapidly, he added more and more and more tape. Reno was either delirious or the support of the splint was giving him relief, because he relaxed some as Patrick worked. When he was done, Reno looked like he was wearing a cast, and the roll of tape was empty. The last thing Patrick did was unsaddle him carefully and remove his bridle, replacing it with a halter and lead, but leaving the blindfold in place.

"That should do it, Perry. You can put his hoof down."

Perry did, and he came around to where Patrick was standing. Patrick turned to his son and put his hand on the boy's face. It was as wet as Reno's coat.

"Reno can't move yet, son. I hate to do it, but I have to leave you out here. I'm trusting you with these animals."

"And the bad guy."

"And the bad guy."

Again, Patrick wondered if this kid was a friend of Trish's. If he'd find his daughter in a tent with another teenage boy, high, and God knew what else. Or was she a captive of one or more men?

He pushed his thoughts aside. "If I get to Trish and someone has her, this kid might be important, which makes you watching him very important."

"Why?"

"Well, for starters, it's one less person for me to fight. But also, they might trade for him."

"Trade Trish?"

"Maybe."

"Oh." The clouds had passed, and the whites of Perry's eyes shone in the starlight.

"You can't lose him. We can't lose him."

The boy's shoulders straightened, and he rose two inches in height. "I won't lose him." He glanced at the lion. "At least the cougar won't get us."

Patrick followed his gaze. It looked like a male, although he hadn't examined it closely. He was counting on the solitary nature of the animals to mean there were no others around. "Now, here's the hardest part."

Perry swallowed.

Patrick retrieved extra ammo, the flashlight, and the rope from Reno's saddlebags. He patted his revolver and pocketknife. How he wished he hadn't lost the sheath knife to the lion fight. "Do you know how to find your way back down? In case you have to go alone?" He'd said roughly the same thing to him at Woodchuck Pass, but everything was amplified out here in the wilderness. And there was no road.

Perry's voice was anguished. "Dad, don't say that."

"You're nearly a man, Perry. Just answer my question."

"Yes, sir." Perry's voice cracked. He swiped at his eyes.

"Duke will know the way, too, so trust him. I want you to hold the horses from in here." Patrick motioned to the little shelter between the rocks that had originally caught his attention and got him off Reno. With Perry still up here in this cold and altitude, hypothermia was a real fear. "Put Reno's blanket over you, and the saddle outside the opening to block the wind. There's a jacket and another shirt in the saddlebags if you want them. And you've got the bow and arrows. Keep the bow out with an arrow, okay?"

"Okay."

He ruffled his son's hair. Perry didn't duck away. Patrick's voice grew thick. "See you when I've got your sister back."

And he struck out into the darkness, leaving one child alone to go find the other, God help him.

CHAPTER THIRTY-EIGHT: PRAY

SOUTHWEST OF BRUCE MOUNTAIN, CLOUD PEAK WILDERNESS AREA, WYOMING
SEPTEMBER 21, 1976, 12:35 A.M.

Trish

Ben had been gone a long time. Too long, Trish thought. Of course, she didn't know how far he had to go or how long it took to dig a grave. But any length of time alone with Chester and the uncle was too long. The wind howled. Snowflakes melted in midair as they fell toward the fire. She shrunk away from the firelight, wishing they couldn't see her. Not that they were looking at her. Chester was muttering to himself and swigging from his bottle. The uncle was sitting on a rock, sharpening a knife.

She traded off putting each of her hands in her jeans pockets to warm them. She pulled the left hand out of one and stuffed the right hand in the other. The rock was still there. She clutched it. It made her feel safer. She didn't know how she was going to use it. She just hoped that when the time came, her fighting spirit returned. Right now, she was just numb.

Numb and sad. Her head slumped forward under the weight of her emotions. She hadn't been nice to her dad on this trip. She'd been hard on her mom last time she saw her, and had teased the shrimp too much. She'd give anything to be home with the three of them now. Or anywhere. Even at the camp on Walker Prairie. She knew she needed help from someone, and since her dad hadn't shown up and she hadn't been able to convince Ben to run off, that left nobody. Except God, but she couldn't remember what the rules were for praying. Despite her years of Sunday school and Vacation Bible School, she hadn't prayed much before. Was she just supposed to talk to him like he was sitting beside her? It seemed like there was another way to do it. The memory came slowly in her cold, sluggish brain.

Chanting with fifteen other elementary school kids. A Sunday school teacher in front of the class, over-enunciating the words, bright red lipstick on her teeth.

Our Father, who art in heaven, hallowed be thy name. Thy kingdom come, Thy will be done, on earth as it is in heaven.

She paused for a moment. *God, I really hope it's not your will that these guys murder me or do awful things to me. I want to go home. I promise to hug my parents, and I'll try to be nicer, to everybody.*

Give us this day our daily bread. And forgive us our trespasses, as we forgive those who trespass against us.

She'd never really been sure what that trespass thing meant, but she understood she was supposed to forgive other people. *Also, God, I don't think I'm supposed to forgive these guys for kidnapping me.*

And lead us not into temptation, but deliver us from evil, for Thine is the kingdom and the power, and the glory forever.

There, that was the part that fit. *Deliver us from evil.* To her, that sounded like it meant "Get me out of this mess. Get me away from this evil." She vaguely recalled her teacher talking about it, and her interpretation had been different than Trish's was now, but Trish didn't care.

Deliver me from these evil men, God. Please. If

you do, I promise to start going to church even when Mom doesn't make me.

"Amen." Too late, she realized she'd said it aloud.

Chester grunted. "What are you doing, girl?"

She shrank further into the darkness. The snowflakes were falling faster now, some making it all the way to the fire, where they sizzled. The ones that landed on her cheeks made cold wet spots. She brushed some away with the back of one hand.

"I said what are you doing over there?"

"Praying."

He snorted out a few laughs that sounded more like he was hawking loogies. "You think he's going to help you now? Only thing'll help you is if you're nice to me, and if you are, I'll give you a swig of my drink. That'll make you feel a lot better."

The uncle glared at Chester behind his back. Trish clenched her fists. *No, no, no.* The uncle had killed his cousin Larry for acting like that. Before Chester could take it any further, though, the scream of an animal cut through the sound of the wind.

"That sounded like a horse," the uncle said.

"Ben?" Chester lumbered to his feet. "Ben?"

"I'll go find him. You're too drunk. But stay away from the girl. You hear me?"

Chester saluted him. "You may be older, but you're my half brother, not my daddy."

The uncle's grayish-black hair looked almost white with snow now. "With our mother dead, I'm not feeling much family loyalty."

"We're in this together. As a family. Paying that quack doctor back for killing Mama." Chester sipped again.

The bottle must have been empty, because he threw it into the fire. The glass shattered. A piece flew out and hit Trish on the cheek. It stung. But she didn't raise her hand to her face. She was riveted by Chester's words. *What was that about?* Trish knew they were using her, somehow, as repayment on a debt, but it sounded like they thought her dad had killed their mom. That was impossible. Her dad saved people's lives, when they could be saved. He would never kill anyone. She wasn't supposed to know it, but he even volunteered once a month in Fort Washakie clinic at the Wind River Indian Reservation. Her mom didn't like it. She worried that it was a dangerous place and that someday something bad would happen to him there.

"As long as you don't get me in trouble, we're together. I'm not going back to prison because you're a dumbass." The uncle mounted one of the horses, shaking his head.

He rode out of camp without a backward

glance. For a moment, Trish worried about what Chester might do to her with the uncle gone. But then a thought dawned. A horse. It could mean help was on the way. Maybe the praying thing had worked. Trish started over at the beginning. *Our Father, who art in heaven . . .*

CHAPTER THIRTY-NINE: ATTACK

Southwest of Bruce Mountain, Cloud Peak Wilderness Area, Wyoming
September 21, 1976, 1:15 a.m.

Patrick

From behind a cluster of pines with thick branches down their trunks, Patrick peered into the campsite while he recovered from the hike. The effort had been slowgoing. It was all he could do to stay upright, between his nausea, cramps, light-headedness, and blurry vision. He'd vomited a few yards back, the last of anything left in his stomach. From the sounds in the camp, it didn't seem like anyone had heard him. Thank God for the wind.

At the fire, a large, bearded man was gesticulating and talking. Patrick drew in a quick breath. He recognized him. The asshole who'd given him a hard time about the campsite at Walker Prairie. But what relation did the kid have to this guy? When it hit him, he felt stupid. *Of course.* He hadn't recognized the kid at first, but now he did. He was the quiet one who had kept his head down during the confrontation. But there'd been three of them on Walker Prairie. Where was the third? *Maybe he was the man the kid was burying*, he hoped. That would improve Patrick's odds to one-on-one, although his "one" was stricken with giardia. But he couldn't make assumptions. He'd have to make sure the third one wasn't there.

The big man started pacing, and Patrick's heart stopped. There was another figure sitting by the fire. It looked like Trish. Light hair, small, feminine frame. It definitely wasn't the third man, nor was there any sign of him yet. It was all starting to fit together, even if it still made no sense. These guys had been near their camp on Walker Prairie. He didn't know why they would have taken his daughter, but they had known she was there, and they were hostile. Very hostile. Another realization struck him. The big man had been one of the two elk chasers. The second one wasn't the kid, though. That must have been the third man. He scanned the camp again, worrying about where he was.

The big guy stood, unsteady on his feet, and weaved over to the girl. Unsteady . . . sick? Drunk? Patrick catalogued the possibilities with growing optimism. The big guy flopped down and lurched onto her. From the way she awkwardly and unsuccessfully tried to get away from him, Patrick thought she was bound, hand and foot. He couldn't hear the words the big guy was saying, but a familiar feminine voice shouted.

"No! Don't touch me. He'll kill you. You know he will."

There was no doubt now that it was his daughter in the clearing, or that the man was assaulting her. Rage pulsed through him, breaking through his resolve to stay calm and cool and to figure out where the third man was. His anger overcame his weakness and dizziness, and he literally saw red. Patrick barreled into the camp, straight at them, revolver drawn.

"Dad," Trish screamed.

No, he thought, wishing she hadn't spoken. Surprise was no longer on his side. He got one shot off, wild and wide, trying to scare the big guy.

The man pulled Trish in front of him in a headlock. "You're not going to risk shooting your pretty daughter, are you, Doctor Flint?" His voice was slurry. His cheek bulged with chewing tobacco.

Definitely drunk. Patrick locked eyes with Trish, willing her to be brave, trying to tell her that he loved her. "Let her go."

In response, the big man drew a knife from a scabbard at his waist. "Why should I let her go? Or even let her live? You had the chansh to let my mama live, and you didn't take it."

Patrick frowned. "Your mama?"

"I'm Cheshter Jones. My mother came to you for help. You killed her."

All the air rushed out of Patrick, and for a moment, he deflated like a tire with a nail in it. "Bethany Jones. You're her son."

"Isn't that what I just said?"

Oh, sweet Jesus. They'd taken Trish because of him. For revenge. It was his fault his daughter was here with a knife at her neck. Susanne's face filled his mind. *I'm sorry, baby. So sorry.* He had to fix this. Had to get Trish away from this lunatic. Cramps tore through his belly. *Mind over matter, dammit. Mind over matter.*

He spoke, looking for a way to get a shot off at the same time. "She had sepsis, Mr. Jones. Blood poisoning. By the time she got to me, she was past saving. I'm sorry she died, but I didn't kill her."

"Bullshit." Chester spit a stream of tobacco juice that landed on Trish's feet. She didn't flinch. "I dropped her off myshelf. She was fine. She was going to be fine. Until you pumped her full of poison."

"Those were antibiotics, not poison. They were her only chance. It was just too late."

Chester roared, his voice clearing a little. "You're lying. You killed her. Now you've ruined things again. You weren't supposed to see me. You were supposed to pay a ransom. This changes everything. Everything."

There was nothing Patrick could say. Slowly, he started working his way around them, trying to get a better angle for a shot. Chester hauled Trish's body around, too, keeping her between them. The whole time, she held her neck rigid and arched away from the blade, but she never broke eye contact with Patrick.

Chester put his head and tobacco-stained beard against Trish's face. He seemed to relax again. "The way I shee it, you're going to throw your gun over there"—he gestured away from the fire with his head—"and lie down on the ground with your hands behind your head. Then you're going to get to see how Bethany Jones's sons collect their debts, with your little blondie here. Or I shlit her throat now, and she bleeds to death while we fight it out."

Trish's voice was high and loud but strong. Steady. "No, Daddy. Don't do it. Fight, fight, fight."

Her voice repeating his words back to him nearly brought tears to his eyes. But Patrick didn't see a choice. He couldn't run for help, leaving Trish with this monster. Besides, there was no help, not for many miles. And he couldn't take the chance that Chester would really draw that knife through her soft, vulnerable neck. He'd comply, lull Chester into submission, then find another way to get Trish away from him.

"It will be okay, Trish. Trust me."

"No," she moaned.

He tossed his gun, then lowered himself to the ground. He laced his fingers behind his head.

"You don't got mush fight in you, do you, *Daddy*?" Chester's voice was mocking.

He shoved Trish aside and started hefting himself up from his knees. Patrick turned to watch. Chester stumbled and went down. The man was really plastered. While he was down, Trish jerked her arms up over her head. She brought her bound hands down hard, smashing them into Chester's temple. Patrick didn't expect her blow to do much, but Chester made a "HUH" sound and keeled onto his side. Patrick was on his feet and running toward his .357 Magnum before Chester hit the ground. Trish crawled away from Chester on her elbows and knees. But the blow didn't knock Chester out. Before Patrick got to his gun, Chester shook his head and growled. Blood gushed from the side of his head, down his face and into his mouth.

He grinned, showing red demon teeth. "Let's see who gets to her first." He stood and dove toward Trish.

Patrick jumped between them. Acting on pure instinct, he whipped his pocketknife from his jeans. He flicked it open and held it straight out in front of him, pointed at the base of Chester's throat. Patrick hated that he knew from anatomy class where the soft spot was. Chester's momentum drove his body weight into the knife and Patrick. He gurgled, and the two men went down together, with Chester on top, limp. Blood spurted around the entrance wound onto Patrick's face. He tried to pull the knife loose, but it was lodged in Chester's spine. Chester gurgled and his neck twitched. Patrick released the knife, his eyes fixing on the word SAWBONES as his hand fell away. He drew on his last reserves of strength and rolled the bigger man off of him. Chester still twitched, but Patrick knew he would bleed out in a matter of minutes.

"You did it, Daddy. Untie me. We have to get out of here. The uncle's coming back."

Patrick barely registered her words. He rose to his knees, feeling an immense sadness. He saved lives, he didn't take them. Then he slumped over beside Chester, clutching his guts.

CHAPTER FORTY: DEFEND

Southwest of Bruce Mountain, Cloud Peak Wilderness Area, Wyoming September 21, 1976, 1:30 a.m.

Susanne

Susanne let out a jittery breath as she rode up the narrow switchback trail. "I feel as nervous as a long-tailed cat in a room full of rocking chairs."

Ronnie turned back to her. "Courage is when something scares you and you do it anyway."

The unexpected compliment brought a lump to Susanne's throat, even if it didn't quell her fears. The snow was stinging her eyes. The wind made her feel unsteady, and her horse was jumpy. Patrick had always told her that whatever she felt, her horse felt, too. She hadn't believed it, thought it was just Cindy that was flighty. She was beginning to think there was something to what he'd said now, but it didn't help things. One wrong step by this animal, and it would all be over. They'd tumble together down the impossibly steep mountainside and be smashed in the rocks.

All her nerves fled in an instant when the crack of a gunshot rent the quiet.

"It's them," she shouted. "It's got to be them."

Ronnie turned to Susanne. "It came from over there." She pointed. "You ready?"

Susanne would have to trust Ronnie on the direction. Close noises sounded far away, and far away noises sounded close. All sounds seemed to come from everywhere and nowhere at once, to her ears.

"I'm ready."

Ronnie clucked to her horse, and it picked its way faster along the trail. Susanne's did, too, stumbling occasionally, but for once, Susanne didn't notice. She patted the gun in the holster she'd remembered to use this time. *Long-pull trigger, ten to fifteen feet. Long-pull trigger, ten to fifteen feet,* she chanted silently. At the next switchback,

Ronnie went off-trail instead of turning back and uphill.

"It looks like we're not the first ones to take this route," she said.

Susanne couldn't see a thing. But she said, "Uh-huh."

The horses slowed for the rougher terrain. A few hundred yards off the trail, Ronnie's horse shied hard to the right. Susanne's followed, and she clung to the saddle horn. Her legs flopped up and back against the animal's sides.

"What is it?" she asked, panting.

"I'm not sure." Ronnie reined her horse back to within ten feet of a mound on the earth. The horse refused to go any closer. "Oh my God. It's a dead guy."

"Do you think that was the shot we heard?"

Ronnie shook her head. She pointed at a heap of dirt and rocks beside a shallow hole. "Looks like someone was trying to bury him." She got the horse a few steps closer. "His throat was cut."

"Oh God. The people that took Trish are murderers." Susanne shuddered, her central nervous system on fire. Her daughter. Her husband and son. Up here somewhere, with one man already dead.

"Unless the good guys won this round."

Susanne tried to imagine her husband, daughter, or son putting a knife through someone's throat. It didn't seem possible.

Ronnie said, "Keep your gun handy, and stay behind me."

Susanne straightened in the saddle. Hell yes, she'd keep her gun handy and ride a horse into the darkness behind Ronnie. Her family needed their help. She only wished they could ride faster. After a few minutes, Ronnie held up a hand, then pointed through the trees. The two of them stopped. Susanne saw an orange glow. With her poor night vision, she couldn't see anything else, though.

She whispered, "What do you see?"

Ronnie's voice was harsh and urgent. "Trish upright, and two guys on the ground."

"The shot."

"Maybe. I'm going in. You stay here."

Susanne didn't want to stay here alone. She wanted to go with Ronnie, grab her daughter, and run all the way back down to Sheridan. But she said, "Okay."

Ronnie walked her horse to the edge of the clearing and dismounted. Susanne lost sight of her on the other side of the animal. She heard a loud THWACK, and then a thump. The horse sprang forward. Ronnie's body lay crumpled on the ground, with a man standing over her that Susanne had seen once before, and in her mind nearly every moment since then, wearing her husband's plaid flannel shirt.

Billy Kemecke.

Her own horse decided he'd had enough and bucked once, bolting after Ronnie's horse before his feet landed. Susanne crashed to the ground, hands first. Pain shot up her fingers and wrist. The landing knocked the wind out of her, but she rolled to face Kemecke.

She tried to speak, but all that came out was, "Guh. Guh."

He grinned and started walking toward her. "Mrs. Flint, fancy meeting you again."

Susanne drew a gasping breath, then refound her voice. "What are you doing here?"

"Repaying a debt I owed to your husband for killing my mother."

What kind of nonsense was he spouting? But clearly he had kidnapped Trish, and now had knocked Ronnie out. Susanne didn't have time to yak with him about what he meant. By her reckoning, he was fifteen feet away and closing. She pushed herself to her feet as she yanked the revolver out of its holster and pointed the gun at Kemecke. A shooting pain in her fingertips surprised her, but she ignored it. She pulled the trigger hard and long, over and over, flinching and yelling a war cry that she hadn't known she had in her at every shot. Pull.

Boom. Pull. Boom. Pull. Boom. She didn't count, just kept pulling until when she pulled she got a click. She did it again. Another click. Smoke curled from the barrel of the gun. Beyond it, she saw the writhing body of Billy Kemecke. She looked at her hands. Her fingers were bloody, and her nails were broken to the quick. It took her a moment to realize it was from her fall, not some spontaneous reaction to shooting Kemecke. She dropped the gun and got to her feet.

"Trish," she screamed. "Trish!"

"Mom, is that you?"

Susanne ran past Kemecke and into the campsite to her daughter. Trish was tied up, hands and feet.

"Oh, my sweet girl. My poor brave girl." Susanne knelt and kissed her face, then unhooked the belt restraint around Trish's wrists. She drew her into her arms and hugged her hard. "Are you okay?"

"I'm fine. But, Dad." Trish started to sob.

Susanne drew back, but left her hands on Trish's shoulders. "What about your dad?"

Trish couldn't speak. She just pointed.

Susanne looked. Patrick was lying motionless on the ground.

CHAPTER FORTY-ONE: SYNCHRONIZE

Buffalo, Wyoming
September 23, 1976, 11:00 a.m.

Patrick

Patrick heard noises in his hospital room. He rolled his head a little on his pillow to test how he felt, keeping his eyes closed. Better, although a headache was new and unwelcome. He knew he didn't make the world's best patient. Doctors rarely did. But after a day on IV fluids and antibiotics, he was coming around.

"You're alive." Susanne squeezed his hand.

He fluttered his eyes open. "Barely. Where are the kids?"

"Down in the cafeteria. Probably signing autographs."

Laughing hurt his guts, but smiling felt okay, so he did.

"You've been talking in your sleep," she said.

"Did I say anything smart?"

"Every time your lips move." She smiled at him. "Which is a lot."

"Ha ha." He readjusted on the bed. His body ached, but the cramps had ebbed.

Wes appeared in the doorway. He walked up to the bed and patted Patrick's shoulder. "Doc, good to see you awake. And I hear your survival is all thanks to the beautiful Mrs. Doc."

"What?" Patrick asked.

Susanne shook her head. "Only partially. You were there, too, Wes."

Wes cocked his head, his words an echo of Patrick's. "What?"

Patrick didn't like remembering the knife plunging into Chester's throat. But he was damn glad he'd had it. "I got Trish away from her kidnappers with the pocketknife you gave me." He left out the gory details.

"You're kidding."

"Nope. Sawbones to the rescue."

"You might fit in around here someday after all, Doc." Wes beamed. "Speaking of the Joneses, did the coroner ever reach you? He wanted to finalize some things in Bethany Jones's report."

"Nope."

Susanne pounded a fist on a knee. "Spit in a well bucket. Did Trish not tell you he called?"

"Still a nope."

Wes held up his hands in front of his chest. "He said it's just a formality. His findings are that you didn't do anything wrong."

A weight lifted from Patrick's chest. He believed in himself, but anytime he lost a patient, he second-guessed his every decision and action. Even more so when the family came after him and his so aggressively. "Good to hear. Very good."

"Well, I'm off shift. I'll leave you two to canoodle. Or whatever you were doing."

Patrick snorted. "Too weak to canoodle."

"Soon." Susanne smiled.

They waved as Wes left.

Patrick sighed. "Honestly, I don't remember anything after Chester."

Susanne inspected her nails. They were short. Broken-looking. "You missed me shooting Billy Kemecke."

"Did you just say Billy Kemecke? The fugitive who killed a game warden and a deputy?"

"I did."

"How and where?"

"At the campsite. When you were passed out by the fire."

His jaw hung slack. "I'm completely lost. Billy Kemecke was there? And so were you, shooting fugitives? Tell me everything."

Susanne filled him in quickly, starting with all she'd been through after he left. He was horrified about Kemecke and the wreck, and that he hadn't been with her. Chagrined that she'd come to Hunter Corral looking for them, then up into the mountains with Ronnie because of her premonition. Dumbstruck that she had ridden in the dead of night on a strange horse into the wilderness and saved his life by shooting Kemecke.

"I went with my gut," she said.

"So an old dog learned a new trick?"

She dipped her chin and looked up at him. "Who are you calling old? Or a dog?"

"It's an expression, mostly because I don't know what to say. You're amazing."

She nodded. "Thank you. I amazed myself." Then she frowned. "Kemecke said you killed his mother."

"I haven't had any patients named Kemecke."

"Kemecke is Chester's older half brother. Bethany was his mother, too."

He groaned. "Now it makes sense."

"Except for the part where they believe you

killed their mother. The dead guy on the mountain—who Kemecke killed, according to Trish—was their cousin."

"And the kid?"

"Ben Jones. Chester's son."

Patrick massaged his temples. All this new information was making his head hurt worse. "But how did Kemecke get from our place to the mountains to meet up with Chester and the rest of them?"

"In our station wagon. Which was found up in Woodchuck Pass, hidden by Woodchuck Creek."

Patrick shook his head. "That still doesn't explain how he knew where to find them."

"Ronnie had that answer for me. There's another Kemecke sibling in Buffalo. And she doesn't like you much, either."

He put a hand on his chest, looking mock offended. "Everybody likes me."

Susanne laughed. "Not Brandon Lewis's mom. The one you got fired? When her brother Billy Kemecke left our place, he went to see her, and that's where he learned you guys were up on Walker Prairie. Because Trish had left a message about it with her for Brandon. Honestly, Kemecke was trying to find you, not his brother."

"I guess he got doubly lucky."

"And us doubly unlucky."

"Tell me about it." Patrick yawned. The protozoa were still doing a number on him. "Go on. What else?"

She told him about the search team arriving and the group that had gone after Perry and the horses.

"Did they get Reno off the mountain?"

She stroked his hair off his forehead. "They did, supporting him from behind with ropes. Perry insisted on staying with him, too."

A one-ton horse with a compound fracture and fly-by-night splint, on three legs? It had to have been hellishly slow. Dangerous, too. "And no one got crushed?"

"Nope. I think it took them six hours."

"Wow. It only took us one or two to ride up there."

Susanne smiled. "Perry said Reno was a trooper."

"Where is Reno now?"

"They hauled him straight to Joe Crumpton's veterinary hospital."

Susanne kept talking, and Patrick closed his eyes and listened. She told him Reno would be lame, but since Crumpton owed him one—*hell, he owed him more than one*—he promised to doctor Reno like he would a Kentucky Derby winner. Luckily, the horse had only broken his splint bone, which was less severe than a cannon fracture. Reno hadn't shown any sign of infection or joint sepsis yet, either, which was another of Patrick's fears. With luck and good care, Reno would live. And then Patrick would make sure he had the best of feed and pasture mates for the rest of his life. It was the least he could do after the ride Reno had given him to find Trish.

"How did I get down?" he asked.

"A horse-drawn stretcher. It was quite an event. Trish, Ronnie, and I rode down beside you. An ambulance was waiting for you at Woodchuck Pass."

Chester had been pronounced dead at the scene, Susanne told him, but Kemecke would live to face death-penalty charges. Ben Jones was no worse for his knock on the head. He'd likely finish his youth in juvenile detention. Trish had tried to plead his case, how he hadn't wanted to kidnap her, that his violent family had forced him to go along with them, but Patrick knew that would be for the law to decide. As for Ronnie, the sheriff had blistered her hide about riding up into the mountains with Susanne, but in the end, she'd kept her job.

Susanne kissed his forehead. "And that's about it, except that Perry has renewed his demand to play football. He said he tackled one of the bad guys and took him down."

"Not that successfully." Patrick pretended to

grumble through his smile. "But the kid was incredible."

Susanne shrugged. "So he's told everyone. I know I was against it before, but I think we should let him play."

"Over my dead body." But Patrick knew he would cave. "And Trish?"

"She seems good. Better than good. Dare I say *nice*?"

"You're probably going too far."

"She wants to go to church this weekend. She said she promised God she would if she got away."

Despite the pain, Patrick laughed. "I seem to recall the Lewis family goes to our church."

Susanne laughed, too. "And there's that."

"A little awkward, given his family ties."

"It may have a dampening effect on the relationship."

Patrick wouldn't mind that at all. "Imagine those Christmas dinners, with an in-law who kidnapped our daughter, tied you up, and tried to kill us." He scooted up in his bed.

"Hopefully Kemecke will be out of the picture for good, soon." Susanne cranked him to a seated position.

He cleared his throat. "I need to say something to you."

"I have something to say to you, too."

"Ladies first."

She took a deep breath and blew it out. Her eyes were moist. "I'm really, really sorry I didn't go to the mountains with you guys. And not just because I was held hostage and had a wreck and had to ride up into the mountains to save you." They smiled at each other. "But because I missed you. Wherever you are, that's where I want to be. Even on an elk hunt. In Wyoming."

Patrick's throat closed. After he was able to swallow down a lump, he said, "And I shouldn't have tried to make you do things you didn't want to. I want to do things you'll enjoy, too."

"Thank you." She kissed his lips softly, then stood up. "I'll go tell the kids you're awake."

"Wait, I didn't get to say my piece yet."

"I thought that was it."

"Nope." He took her hand. "You need to know that you are okay with me just like you are. You don't ever have to ride another horse or go hunting, or even love Wyoming. I love *you*. And I'm also so proud of you. Coming after us like that? You saved us. You faced your fears, and you saved us."

Susanne wiped a tear. "Patrick Flint, that may be the nicest thing you've ever said to me."

He grinned. "I guess nearly dying makes a guy romantic."

She adopted an officious expression and formal

voice. "You didn't nearly die, you know. It was just a glorified case of diarrhea."

"Hey now! You sound like me." But he laughed. "Seriously. I owe you one. I shouldn't have left you. How can I make it up to you?"

Her expression was reflective. "I want out of our house. I feel . . . differently about it after being held hostage there by a killer who kidnapped our daughter."

Patrick steeled himself. "Back to Texas?"

"Eventually. But I'd be willing to compromise for now with a house near a creek. With a couple of acres and a mountain view."

His face lit up. "Really?"

"Really." She kissed him again, a little longer and a little less gently.

"Canoodling is starting to sound better and better," he said.

From the doorway came the sounds of gagging and fake retching.

"Gross," Perry said.

"Like, get a room," Trish added.

Patrick threw his voice to sound like hers. "Like, get a life."

"Like, I already have one, and it's pretty awesome." She tossed her hair, but the snotty expression she'd been wearing lately was gone.

He nodded. Something they could agree on. It

was a good life they had. He patted the bed beside him. "I'm busting out of this joint today. We've got these elk tags, and we didn't get our elk. Who's up for a little hunt this weekend?"

He girded himself for the anticipated response, smiling ear to ear when he got three groans and an eye-roll.

***

Next up: There's more **Patrick Flint** and family in *Snake Oil*. Get yours at https://www.amazon.com/gp/product/B083TZBCQS. When Patrick Flint goes after a murderer on the Wind River Reservation, he puts everything —and everyone — he cares about on the line.

Or you can continue adventuring in the *What Doesn't Kill You* mystery world:

Want to stay in **Wyoming**? Rock on with Maggie in ***Live Wire* on Amazon** (free in Kindle Unlimited) at
https://www.amazon.com/gp/product/B07L5RYGHZ.
Prefer the **beginning** of it all? Start with Katie in *Saving Grace* on **Amazon** (free to Kindle Unlimited subscribers), here: https://www.amazon.com/Saving-Grace-Doesnt-Romantic-Mystery-ebook/dp/B009FZPMFO.

Or **get the complete WDKY series** here: on Amazon.

***

And don't forget to snag the **free** *What Doesn't Kill You* **ebook starter library** by joining Pamela's mailing list at https://www.subscribepage.com/PFHSuperstars. It includes an epilogue to *Switchback* called *Spark*!

For my dad, who gave me all my best traits and a few of my others. You have always been my hero, Papasan—totally book worthy!—and I love you. And for Eric, without whom there would be no books, for so many reasons.

ACKNOWLEDGMENTS

When I got the call from my father that he had metastatic prostate cancer spread into his bones in nine locations, I was with a houseful of retreat guests in Wyoming while my parents (who normally summer in Wyoming) were in Texas. The guests were so kind and comforting to me, as was Eric, but there was only one place I wanted to be, and that was home. Not home where I grew up, because I lived in twelve places by the time I was twelve, and many thereafter. No, home is truly where the heart is. And that meant home for Eric and me would be with my parents.

I was in the middle of writing two novels at the time: *Blue Streak*, the first Laura mystery in the What Doesn't Kill You series, and *Polarity*, a series spin-off contemporary romance based on my love story with Eric. I put them both down. I needed to write, but not those books. They could wait. I needed to write through my emotions—because that's what writers do—with books spelling out the ending we were seeking for my dad's story. Allegorically and biographically, while fictionally.

So that is what I did, and Dr. Patrick Flint (aka Dr. Peter Fagan—my pops—in real life) and family were hatched, using actual stories from our lives in late 1970s Buffalo, Wyoming as the depth and backdrop to a new series of mysteries, starting with *Switchback* and moving on to *Snake Oil, Sawbones, Scapegoat, Snaggle Tooth,* and *Stag Party*. I hope the real life versions of Patrick, Susanne, and Perry will forgive me for taking liberties in creating their fictional alter egos. I took care to make Trish the most annoying character since she's based on me, to soften the blow for the others. I am so hopeful that my loyal readers will enjoy them, too, even though in some ways the novels are a departure from my usual stories. But in many ways they are the same. Character-driven, edge-of-your-seat mysteries steeped in setting/culture, with a strong nod to the everyday magic around us, and filled with complex, authentic characters (including some AWESOME females).

I had a wonderful time writing these books, and

it kept me going when it was tempting to fold in on myself and let stress eat me alive. For more stories behind the actual stories, visit my blog on my website: http://pamelafaganhutchins.com. And let me know if you liked the novels.

Thanks to my dad for advice on all things medical, wilderness, hunting, 1970s, and animal. I hope you had fun using your medical knowledge for murder!

Thanks to my mom for printing the manuscript (over and over, in its entirety) as she and dad followed along daily on the progress.

Thanks to my husband, Eric, for brainstorming with and encouraging me and beta reading the *Patrick Flint* stories despite his busy work, travel, and workout schedule. And for moving in to my parents's barn apartment with me so I could be closer to them during this time.

Thanks to our five offspring. I love you guys more than anything, and each time I write a parent/child (birth, adopted, foster, or step), I channel you. I am so touched by how supportive you have been with Poppy, Gigi, Eric, and me.

To each and every blessed reader, I appreciate you more than I can say. It is the readers who move mountains for me, and for other authors, and I humbly ask for the honor of your honest reviews and recommendations.

Thanks mucho to Bobbye and Rhonda for putting up with my eccentric and ever-changing needs. Extra thanks to Bobbye for the fantastic *Patrick Flint* covers.

Patrick Flint editing credits go to Rhonda Erb and Whitney Cox. The proofreaders who enthusiastically devote their time—gratis—to help us rid my books of flaws blow me away. My gratitude goes to Anita, Caren, Karen, Kelly, Misty, Ginger, Lanier, Tara, and Pat.

SkipJack Publishing now includes fantastic books by a cherry-picked bushel basket of mystery/thriller/suspense writers. If you write in this genre, visit http://SkipJackPublishing.com for submission guidelines. To check out our other authors and snag a bargain at the same time, download *Murder, They Wrote: Four SkipJack Mysteries*.

BOOKS BY THE AUTHOR

Fiction from SkipJack Publishing

The *What Doesn't Kill You* Series

Act One (WDKY Ensemble Prequel Novella): Exclusive to Subscribers

Saving Grace (Katie #1)

Leaving Annalise (Katie #2)

Finding Harmony (Katie #3)

Heaven to Betsy (Emily #1)

Earth to Emily (Emily #2)

Hell to Pay (Emily #3)

Going for Kona (Michele #1)

Fighting for Anna (Michele #2)

Searching for Dime Box (Michele #3)

Buckle Bunny (Maggie Prequel Novella)

Shock Jock (Maggie Prequel Short Story)

Live Wire (Maggie #1)

Sick Puppy (Maggie #2)

Dead Pile (Maggie #3)

The Ava Butler Trilogy*: A Sexy Spin-off From *What Doesn't Kill You

Bombshell (Ava #1)

Stunner (Ava #2)

Knockout (Ava #3)

The Patrick Flint Series

Switchback (Patrick Flint #1)

Snake Oil (Patrick Flint #2)

Sawbones (Patrick Flint #3)

Scapegoat (Patrick Flint #4)

Snaggle Tooth (Patrick Flint #5)

Stag Party (Patrick Flint #6)

Spark (Patrick Flint 1.5): Exclusive to subscribers

The What Doesn't Kill You Box Sets Series (50% off individual title retail)

The Complete Katie Connell Trilogy

The Complete Emily Bernal Trilogy

The Complete Michele Lopez Hanson Trilogy

The Complete Maggie Killian Trilogy

The Complete Ava Butler Trilogy

The Patrick Flint Box Set Series

The Patrick Flint Series Books #1-3

Juvenile Fiction

Poppy Needs a Puppy (Poppy & Petey #1)

Nonfiction from SkipJack Publishing

The Clark Kent Chronicles

Hot Flashes and Half Ironmans

How to Screw Up Your Kids

How to Screw Up Your Marriage

Puppalicious and Beyond

What Kind of Loser Indie Publishes,

and How Can I Be One, Too?

Audio, e-book, and paperback versions of most titles available.

ABOUT THE AUTHOR

Pamela Fagan Hutchins is a *USA Today* best selling author. She writes award-winning romantic mystery/thriller/suspense from way up in the frozen north of Snowheresville, Wyoming, where she lives in an off-the-grid cabin on the face of the Bighorn Mountains. She is passionate about hiking/snow shoeing/cross country skiing with her hunky husband and pack of rescue dogs (and occasional rescue cat) and riding their gigantic horses.

If you'd like Pamela to speak to your book club, women's club, class, or writers group by streaming video or in person, shoot her an email. She's very likely to say yes.

You can connect with Pamela via her website
(http://pamelafaganhutchins.com)
or email (pamela@pamelafaganhutchins.com).

PRAISE FOR PAMELA FAGAN HUTCHINS

2018 USA Today Best Seller
2017 Silver Falchion Award, Best Mystery
2016 USA Best Book Award, Cross-Genre Fiction
2015 USA Best Book Award, Cross-Genre Fiction
2014 Amazon Breakthrough Novel Award
Quarter-finalist, Romance

The Patrick Flint Mysteries

"Best book I've read in a long time!" — Kiersten Marquet, author of *Reluctant Promises*

"*Switchback* transports the reader deep into the mountains of Wyoming for a thriller that has it all--wild animals, criminals, and one family willing to do whatever is necessary to protect its own. Pamela Fagan Hutchins writes with the authority of a woman who knows this world. She weaves the story with both nail-biting suspense and a healthy dose of humor. You won't want to miss *Switchback*." --- Danielle Girard, *Wall Street Journal*-bestselling author of White Out.

"*Switchback* by Pamela Fagan Hutchins has as many twists and turns as a high-country trail. Every parent's nightmare is the loss or injury of a child, and this powerful novel taps into that primal fear." -- Reavis Z. Wortham, two time winner of The Spur and author of *Hawke's Prey*

"*Switchback* starts at a gallop and had me holding on with both hands until the riveting finish. This book is highly atmospheric and nearly crackling with suspense. Highly recommend!" -- Libby Kirsch, Emmy awardwinning reporter and author of the *Janet Black Mystery Series*

"A Bob Ross painting with Alfred Hitchcock hidden among the trees."

"Edge-of-your seat nail biter."

"Unexpected twists!"

"Wow! Wow! Highly entertaining!"

"A very exciting book (um... actually a nail-biter), soooo beautifully descriptive, with an underlying story of human connection and family. It's full of action. I was so scared and so mad and so relieved... sometimes all at once!"

"Well drawn characters, great scenery, and a kept-me-on-the-edge-of-my-seat story!"

"Absolutely unputdownable wonder of a story."

"Must read!"

"Gripping story. Looking for book two!"

"Intense!"

"Amazing and well-written read."

"Read it in one fell swoop. I could not put it down."

What Doesn't Kill You: Katie Connell Romantic Mysteries

"An exciting tale . . . twisting investigative and legal subplots . . . a character seeking redemption . . . an exhilarating mystery with a touch of voodoo." — *Midwest Book Review Bookwatch*

"A lively romantic mystery." — *Kirkus Reviews*

"A riveting drama . . . exciting read, highly recommended." — *Small Press Bookwatch*

"Katie is the first character I have absolutely fallen in love with since Stephanie Plum!" — *Stephanie Swindell, Bookstore Owner*

"Engaging storyline . . . taut suspense." — *MBR Bookwatch*

What Doesn't Kill You: Emily Bernal Romantic Mysteries

"Fair warning: clear your calendar before you pick it up because you won't be able to put it down." — *Ken Oder, author of* Old Wounds to the Heart

"Full of heart, humor, vivid characters, and suspense. Hutchins has done it again!" — *Gay Yellen, author of* The Body Business

"Hutchins is a master of tension." — *R.L. Nolen, author of* Deadly Thyme

"Intriguing mystery . . . captivating romance." —

Patricia Flaherty Pagan, author of Trail Ways Pilgrims

“Everything about it shines: the plot, the characters and the writing. Readers are in for a real treat with this story.” — *Marcy McKay, author of* Pennies from Burger Heaven

What Doesn't Kill You: Michele Lopez Hanson Romantic Mysteries

“Immediately hooked." — *Terry Sykes-Bradshaw, author of* Sibling Revelry

"Spellbinding." — *Jo Bryan, Dry Creek Book Club*

"Fast-paced mystery." — *Deb Krenzer, Book Reviewer*

"Can't put it down." — *Cathy Bader, Reader*

What Doesn't Kill You: Ava Butler Romantic Mysteries

"Just when I think I couldn't love another Pamela Fagan Hutchins novel more, along comes Ava." — *Marcy McKay, author of* Stars Among the Dead

"Ava personifies bombshell in every sense of word. — *Tara Scheyer, Grammy-nominated musician, Long-Distance Sisters Book Club*

“Entertaining, complex, and thought-provoking.” — *Ginger Copeland, power reader*

What Doesn't Kill You: Maggie Killian Romantic Mysteries

"Maggie's gonna break your heart–one way or another." *Tara Scheyer, Grammy-nominated musician, Long-Distance Sisters Book Club*

"Pamela Fagan Hutchins nails that Wyoming scenery and captures the atmosphere of the people there." — *Ken Oder, author of* Old Wounds to the Heart

"I thought I had it all figured out a time or two, but she kept me wondering right to the end." — *Ginger Copeland, power reader*

OTHER BOOKS FROM SKIPJACK PUBLISHING

Murder, They Wrote: Four SkipJack Mysteries, by Ken Oder, R.L. Nolen, Marcy McKay, and Gay Yellen

The Closing, by Ken Oder

Old Wounds to the Heart, by Ken Oder

The Judas Murders, by Ken Oder

The Princess of Sugar Valley, by Ken Oder

Keeping the Promise, by Ken Oder

Pennies from Burger Heaven, by Marcy McKay

Stars Among the Dead, by Marcy McKay

The Moon Rises at Dawn, by Marcy McKay

Bones and Lies Between Us, by Marcy McKay

When Life Feels Like a House Fire, by Marcy McKay

Deadly Thyme, by R. L. Nolen

The Dry, by Rebecca Nolen

Tides of Possibility, edited by K.J. Russell

Tides of Impossibility, edited by K.J. Russell and C.

Stuart Hardwick

My Dream of Freedom: From Holocaust to My Beloved America,

by Helen Colin

FOREWORD

Switchback is a work of fiction. Period. Any resemblance to actual persons, places, things, or events is just a lucky coincidence. And I reserve the right to forego accuracy in favor of a good story, any time I get the chance.

Made in the USA
Columbia, SC
29 October 2021

48048608R00257